FLEA FLICKER

Books by David Chill

Post Pattern

Fade Route

Bubble Screen

Safety Valve

Corner Blitz

Nickel Package

Double Pass

Tampa Two

Flea Flicker

Swim Move

Curse Of The Afflicted

FLEA FLICKER

A Novel By

DAVID CHILL

ISBN: 978-0-9904167-9-1

This book is a work of fiction. Names characters, places and events are products of the author's imagination and are used fictitiously. Any resemblance to actual events, locations or persons living or deceased, is purely coincidental. We assume no responsibility for errors, inaccuracies, omissions, or any inconsistency herein.

For Joanne Baker

One

A wayward drunk can cause a lot of harm, but he normally inflicts most of it upon himself. This was true in the case of Tyler Briggs, although being accused of cold-blooded murder meant there was obviously some collateral damage.

Tyler Briggs was an unemployed former football coach with a nasty drinking problem. And a womanizing problem. So, when an upstanding citizen like this fails to arrive home one night, it's normally not a cause for alarm, except perhaps for the man's long-suffering wife. The police might pacify her by checking the drunk tanks, the local ERs, and then the county morgue. If none of these prove fruitful, the cops will just shrug and say she has to wait 24 hours before filing a missing persons report. Some wives rail at the narrow-minded rules. Some just shrug and go along. And then there are the ones, be they peeved or petrified, that get the innate sense that something is very wrong. That's when they talk to someone like me.

I normally don't make house calls, but this was an exception. Hannah Briggs worked in the City Attorney's office with my wife, Gail. When her husband Tyler had moved to Los Angeles to take over the Chargers' head coaching job last year, he reached out and asked if I knew where a beautiful attorney might find gainful employment here. He figured I might know something about this, and he was right. My wife was an attorney, and she was also beautiful. I personally didn't think Hannah was in Gail's league, but I admittedly looked at the world through a different lens.

Tyler and Hannah Briggs lived in a spacious five-bedroom house along the Silver Strand in Marina del Rey. A century ago this area was mostly wetlands, not far from the Pacific Ocean, largely uninhabitable and mostly populated by an occasional duck hunter and his prey. That changed dramatically in the 1930s with the discovery of crude oil beneath the terrain, and for decades it featured an ungodly skyline of oil wells. Once the black gold was pumped from the ground, though, the oil men left and the real estate people swooped in. What they inherited was an ugly mess, but any property close to the ocean had value. Lots of value. After the cleanup, Marina del Rey was born, home to everyone from yacht owners to flight attendants. And within the Marina was the Silver Strand, a narrow strip of gorgeous homes, and to a certain extent, gorgeous people.

Today was overcast, and there was even some fog rolling in. It was typical of L.A. weather in December, a phenomenon that happened like clockwork. I waited a minute before ringing the doorbell, taking time to step back and admire the home and admire the neighborhood. The house was the type of elegant structure you might see featured in architectural magazines, owned by people who earned or inherited fortunes. In the case of Tyler Briggs, it was actually a combination of the two. Born into a coaching family, his father had been an NFL head coach for years and had raked in the money. Even before the NFL coaching boom had begun generously paying head coaches upwards of $10 million a year, they were still very well-compensated.

Other young men in Tyler's situation had drifted into becoming trust fund babies, enjoying the fruits of their fathers' labor. But Sid Briggs was old school, and he wasn't keen on his offspring becoming an idle layabout. He pushed Tyler into playing football, but he wasn't able to go far; his talent earned him a college scholarship, and a seat on the Miami Hurricanes bench for four years. Tyler did take an interest in coaching though, and soon found himself rising quickly through the ranks. Too quickly perhaps.

The front door opened and a tall blonde with platinum hair and high cheekbones opened the door. She was attractive, but her face was taut, her comely looks impacted by a harsh weariness. Her brown eyes sagged, and her pink mouth was drawn. But she was still quite fetching. Some women look good no matter what storm they might be weathering.

"Mr. Burnside," she managed, her voice lightly brushed with a melodic southern twang.

"That's me."

She opened the door and motioned me inside. She was wearing a pink sweater and faded blue jeans, slashed appropriately at the knees. Her legs were like long sticks, seemingly going on forever until they nestled into a new pair of pink and white Nikes.

The Briggs's home was impressive. The foyer opened up into an expansive, sunken living room. A pair of blue velvet couches faced each other, and an assortment of toys, games and stuffed animals were sprinkled haphazardly across the floor. A working fireplace crackled in the corner. I stepped over a colorful little toy piano and found a seat on one of the couches. Hannah Briggs sat down on the other side of the couch after discreetly scooping up a few errant Cheerios in her hand and dumping them onto the corner of a walnut end table.

"Thank you for coming on a Saturday," she started. "I didn't know who to call. Then I thought of Gail. And you."

I shrugged. "It's okay, this is what I do for a living. I only take weekends off when there's no work."

She looked around the room and sighed. "I apologize for the mess. With a toddler, our home is in a constant state of chaos."

I waved a dismissive hand. "No worries. I have a little one at home, too."

"How old?" she asked.

"He'll be five in a couple of weeks. Born on New Year's Day. We're planning on taking him to the Rose Parade in Pasadena. Maybe to the Rose Bowl game, too. If I can score a few tickets, that is."

"Yes," she said absently. "I've been to the Orange Bowl game a few times. That's where we're from. South Florida. Although it seems like a lifetime ago."

"You've only been in L.A. for a couple of years."

"A tough couple of years," she sighed. "You know about Tyler's situation. The Chargers brought him out here and then fired him after one season. He's had it rough."

In some ways that was true. Tyler Briggs had been the boy wonder of football coaching, and as such, he had been cursed with achieving success at a too-early age. When he took over the New York Jets five years ago, he became, at age 29, the youngest head coach in the history of the NFL. Following three years of progressively worsening results, the Jets fired him. The Chargers, thinking he might regain the magic he once had, quickly brought Tyler in upon moving to L.A. from San Diego, then just as quickly fired him when the team had a spectacularly awful season. No one hired him this year, and rumors were rampant that no one would, at least not anytime soon. In shooting up the coaching ranks quickly, he had alienated more than a few people with his attitude. Arrogance probably helped propel his career, as team owners often equated that with confidence. My experience had been the two were not always connected.

"So Gail told me a little about your situation," I started. "Tyler didn't come home last night. Ever happen before?"

"No, never," she said, shaking her head briskly. "I mean, Ty would go out drinking plenty of times. Too many. But I'm used to that. I just go to sleep and he's always next to me when I wake up."

"Except for this morning."

"Yes," she said, her face becoming even more drawn. "I went to the police, but they couldn't help much. He wasn't in the system, at least I know that. They said I'd need to wait a day before I could file a missing persons report. I knew that, but, well, it doesn't hurt to ask."

"And that's what led you to me," I mused. The police would look the name up in the system, but beyond that, they were much too busy to do any investigation. The reality was that people who didn't come home one night often came home the next day, and often with a lame excuse, a sheepish expression, and the enduring scent of alcohol and infidelity oozing out of them. But my 13 years with the LAPD also taught me something else. If they didn't come home the next day, the chances that they'd never come home increased exponentially.

"You have a unique background," she said. "You're a private investigator who's been active in the football world. Not too many people like that around here."

"I'm indeed unique," I agreed, not bothering to stray further down that path. Potential clients don't like to know their new hire had once been kicked off the police force and endured more public humiliation than any decent person deserved. The fact that I hadn't broken any laws was immaterial. My reputation as a disgraced former cop would overshadow and stain the fact that I was a darned good investigator.

"I need you to find Tyler. Bring him home. Wherever he wound up. I'm hoping he just realized he drank a little too much and slept in his car."

"Always a possibility," I acknowledged. "I'll need a few things. Recent photo, type of car he drives, license plate number, bars he frequents. Whatever might be relevant. Names of people who might know something about this.

What he was wearing last time you saw him. Anything would help. No detail too small at this stage. And I need to tell you my rate is a thousand dollars a day. I'll prorate it by the hour so it doesn't pile up too quickly."

Hannah looked down at the gray-and-blue speckled berber carpet. "All right. Money's obviously not an object for us. You know, Tyler often frequents some of the bars along Venice and Washington. He likes a place called the Alibi Room. He took me there once, they serve this bizarre plate of Korean tacos. There's a few other places. Babe's, the Harborside Grill, The Mar Vista."

"Those are very different types of bars," I mused. "I don't see a pattern."

"Are you familiar with alcoholics, Mr. Burnside?"

"Somewhat," I said, recalling that my past careers as a police officer and football coach both had more than their share of heavy drinkers.

"Well then you know they are not always particular about where they drink. In Tyler's case, he hasn't been particular about where he eats these days, either. Sometimes he ends up at one of those greasy spoons like Tito's Tacos, Johnnie's Pastrami, or that awful Tom's Burgers. Sometimes it's a donut shop, depending on what time of the night it is and how many drinks he's had."

I took this in. All of those greasy spoons were well-known; all had been local landmarks for many decades. But a few were familiar simply because these were the places I frequented as a teenager growing up in Culver City. They were also the places I stopped going to when I became an adult with an occasional interest in eating healthy. The things that tasted great at age 17 no longer tasted so special.

"Let's step back a little," I said. "Did Tyler always have a problem with alcohol?"

Hannah frowned for a moment. "Drinking's been part of his life since high school. That's where we met. Sophomore year. He was the quarterback, the captain of the football team, the big man on campus everyone looked up to. I was this nerdy, awkward girl no one noticed."

I looked at her. "That's a stretch."

She shook her head. "I was always tall, and I had a weight problem. The summer before my sophomore year, I lost the weight and suddenly became popular. Funny how that works."

"High school kids aren't known for their depth of character," I commented.

"Yes, that's for sure. I let my hair grow, too, and well, the ugly duckling turned into a swan. People noticed. Tyler noticed."

"You've been together ever since?"

"Pretty much," she replied. "He got a football scholarship to Miami. I got a financial aid package and cobbled it together with student loans. I actually turned down a scholarship offer to Duke to be with him."

"Duke's a great school."

"Yeah. But love makes you do strange things. I figured if I let Tyler go, I'd never get him back."

I thought back to that old chestnut. If you love someone, set them free. If they return to you, they're yours. If they don't, they never were. It's an easy bromide to recite, a tough one to follow. After Gail and I had been together for a year, she was accepted into law school at Berkeley, and was even offered a fellowship. She was torn about going, upset about the three years we'd be apart, but I convinced her she shouldn't pass up the opportunity. I wasn't actively trying to set her free or provide a test for us; I just wanted her to take advantage of something good. If I held her back by not being supportive, she might have resented me for it. Maybe not overtly, but I knew there would be disappointment. I also figured our bond was strong enough to survive three years of separation.

"Okay," I said. "So, how did Miami work out for you guys?"

"Better for me than for Tyler," she admitted. "I made the dean's list every year, he couldn't get past third string on the football team. Miami recruited lots of good quarterbacks. By his senior year he was ready to quit the sport. He was also drinking a lot, but you know, it was college. Everybody was drinking. Then his dad suggested coaching, not surprising since his dad's been a coach since like, forever. Tyler gave it a shot. Took to it well. The following year they gave him a graduate assistant's role, and he moved up to QB coach the next year. Then he got really lucky."

"How so?"

"Miami's offensive coordinator got a job in the NFL. Larry Tenant. He got hired as an OC with Jacksonville, and he brought Tyler along as his QB coach. I don't think they even interviewed anyone else. I swear, that profession is so insular, it's almost inbred. After a couple of years, Larry moved up to head coach at Jacksonville and he promoted Tyler to take over his job. He's now the offensive coordinator. Ty was all of 26 years old. That was a blessing and a curse."

"I can imagine. Pretty hard for someone that young to command respect from players who might be five or ten years older. Guys who had to work like a dog for everything they got."

"Yes. And that's when the drinking started getting out of hand."

I thought back to my own days as a former football coach at USC. I was only in the coaching ranks for three years, but the pressure to win was enormous. Most coaches are driven to succeed, but at some point they need something to take the edge off. The smart ones find a physical outlet, be it lifting weights, running, something that can create positive energy when blowing off steam. The others usually turned to alcohol. Drinking was an easy lure. You didn't have to do much beyond open a bottle or a can. And it could take the edge off quickly.

"He seek out any help?"

"The usual. AA. But he couldn't stick with it. And by that point, I had my own career to think about. I was a straight-A student throughout school, and here I am, sitting in a big house in Jacksonville, with not much to do. When he became the Jets' head coach and we moved to New York, I applied to law school. Tyler did his thing, I did mine. It worked out fine. For a while."

"Then the Chargers made him their head coach last year," I said. "He just kept hitting the jackpot."

Hannah Briggs drew in a breath and thought twice about what she was about to say. She smoothed her blonde hair back, and at that moment an adorable toddler with the same light blonde hair as her mother skipped into the room. She wore pink and light blue as well. She was followed by a heavy-set nanny who smiled apologetically.

"*Madison. Ven aqui!*"

"It's all right, Tia," said Hannah, and scooped the little girl in her arms.

"I want Da Da," the little girl said with a small pout.

"We're working on that, hon," Hannah replied, rocking the girl in her arms as she turned back to me."You may recall I had a job offer lined up with the U.S. Attorney's office in New York. Southern district. It was a big deal."

"And you had to pass because of Tyler's job offer here."

"And because I was suddenly expecting. The funny thing was, if we didn't have Madison, I might have just stayed in New York," she said a little wistfully.

I nodded. This was not unusual, either. Women sometimes put off their own career ambitions in deference to their husbands. They get paid back with a big house, stylish clothes, and a lot of empty nights. Then, just as the woman's questioning if it's worth it, a baby comes along. Sometimes it's a blessing, in that they turn their attention to the child. Sometimes they resent both the husband and the child. As they say, kids change everything.

"Okay. Anyone on the Charger staff that Tyler stayed close to? Or really anybody who might know something?"

"Not many. Oh, there's Anthony Riddleman, he's been friends with Tyler since Miami. He's actually still with the

Chargers, coaches the quarterbacks. Most of the coaches fanned out around the country, got jobs with other teams. Funny how they can just up and move, and keep doing what they're doing. I've moved three times in six years, and I'm just over it."

I understood. Coaches were like soldiers of fortune, always moving around, their loyalty intense to the team employing them, and then becoming equally intense with the next team that hires them. It was a life which required adapting quickly while still maintaining ties within the coaching fraternity. Getting fired was an occupational hazard, and not always the coach's fault. But if he handled it well, there would normally be another gig around the corner. One door closes, another opens.

"All right. I'm not sure how long this case will take. Could be an hour or two, could be a couple of days. It's hard to guess," I told her, thinking if I didn't find her husband today, I might be looking for weeks or months.

"The important thing is you find him."

I watched Madison climb across Hannah's lap onto the couch, reaching for a little stuffed blue octopus. I didn't want to ask this in front of her daughter, but sensed I wouldn't have an opportunity to ask again. "And might there be anyone who was on any not-so-so friendly terms with Tyler?"

Hannah Briggs drew in a breath. She looked down at her daughter playing with the toy, oblivious to what we were discussing. She turned her big brown eyes back to me. "Yes. In fact, there might be a few of them."

*

Having moved from San Diego recently, the L.A. Chargers were a team in an unusual transition. They had moved to L.A. without a home, and as they waited for their new stadium to be finished in Inglewood, they were playing their home games at a soccer arena in the South Bay. Soon they'd be sharing a sparkling new stadium with the L.A. Rams, but for now they were splitting time with the L.A. Galaxy, a pro soccer team. If the world is becoming a shared economy, the Chargers were the NFL's version of this.

The Chargers were also in the process of building a state-of-the-art practice complex in Costa Mesa, a nice bedroom community Angelenos sometimes refer to as "behind the orange curtain." It wouldn't be ready until next year, so their short-term answer for a practice facility was dubious at best: a shuttered junior high school in El Segundo, just south of the terminals at LAX. While conversations would occasionally be interrupted by jets taking off and landing, additional hazards were being spewed into the air from both a nearby oil refinery and the Hyperion sewage treatment plant a few miles away. A pungent odor hung over the community, and the small town of El Segundo was sometimes coined El Stinko, and with good reason.

The junior high campus consisted of half a dozen dilapidated buildings that the team quickly transformed into locker rooms, whirlpools and makeshift offices. But the main feature was a large soccer field that the team tore up and replaced with artificial turf. Goal posts were installed, yard lines painted, and while its appearance suggested it barely fit the needs of a mediocre high school team, this was where L.A.'s newest pro football franchise was calling home for the time being.

Befitting the rumpled conditions was a weary-looking security guard who asked if I had prior approval for watching practice. I crossed my fingers and told him I had, and I also dropped a few names, including Anthony Riddleman, the current QB coach. The guard, not surprisingly, couldn't find my name on a lengthy sheet of paper, but finally gave me a wave, and let me wander onto the grounds. When the season is almost over, and the team has lost more games than it's won, tight security is not a high priority.

For the most part, a visitor to a football practice is treated to long periods of monotony. Watching players stretching, doing agility drills and just sitting on their helmets chatting took up over an hour. Scrimmages in full pads were usually reserved for a couple of days each week, and Saturdays were mostly walkthroughs, going over certain situations. But as decrepit as the surroundings were, the practice itself finally became energetic and lively when the head coach walked onto the field. The team was in the midst of going through their reps, and there was a lot of shouting of assignments, and an occasional burst of encouragement whenever a coach noticed someone making a good play. While everyone was in shorts today, the offense still wore its traditional white jerseys, and the defense wore blue. The quarterbacks normally wore red, so even a highly engaged defender would know not to clobber the most important guy on the field.

There was a smattering of visitors on the sidelines, and I recognized a couple of them. One was a former colleague, a USC assistant coach who had taken a job at a Texas school after our head coach, Johnny Cleary, departed SC for the Chicago Bears. There were a few others who looked like coaches, most likely networking and seeing if they could land a new gig. But there was one man who stood out; he was short and lean, but he had a presence about him that gave him a large aura. He was a well-known sports agent, and I took pains to hide from his view. But some people have a radar-like sense when it comes to spotting people, and it took Cliff Roper all of about 30 seconds to notice me.

"Well, get a load of this, will you," he crowed, as he walked over and looked me up and down. "Thinking of getting back into coaching? About time. That two-bit job as a private dick doesn't come close to paying what coaches make, now does it, Burnside?"

"Nope," I said warily. "But I normally don't have 16 hour days to put in, either."

"Yeah, yeah, you're a real family man now. Wife and kid. Or is it kids now? Slip another one past the goalie?"

"You have a sweet way of putting things. But no, we just have one."

"Yeah, yeah," he said. "Hey, that boy of yours in school yet?"

"Preschool," I said. "He'll start kindergarten in the fall."

"You get him into a private school?" he peered at me, and as if reading my mind, he started curling his lip. "Don't tell me you're one of those parents who think there's a moral obligation to use public schools?"

"We're weighing our options," I said evenly, wondering how the conversation started veering off in this direction.

"Geez, Louise. Thinking of sending your kid to L.A. Unified? That'll toughen him up, I'll bet. Turn him into a gritty football player in a hurry. That hot wife of yours okay with him growing up quick?"

I shook my head. If there was one person in the world who knew how to get under my skin, it was Cliff Roper. Wildly successful as an agent, he had no boundaries when it came to social skills or polite pretense. He was, in an odd way, one of the sharpest people I'd ever met, yet also one of the most perplexing.

"You send Honey to public school?" I asked, thinking of Cliff Roper's beautiful daughter, Honey Roper, possibly the only thing in the world that kept him sane.

"Nope," he declared. "Bishop Gorman. Best school in Las Vegas."

"I didn't know you were Catholic."

"They don't discriminate," he said.

"Make a large donation, did you?"

"Hey, you listen. They let Honey in because she's terrific. And she started on their varsity basketball team. And yeah, maybe I was generous. Geez, what world do you think we live in?"

"The type of world where someone like you would position himself to make friends with their best football players," I countered, knowing Bishop Gorman High School consistently had one of the top prep football teams on the West Coast, and was something of a pipeline to USC. It was also a pipeline into Roper's agency, which regularly signed some of the premier football talent in the country before they entered the NFL draft.

"Hey, hey, hey" he said, wagging a finger in my face. "Making some contacts was just icing on the cake. You'd think I'd pimp my only daughter out just to earn a few bucks? What kind of a father do you think I am?"

I shrugged and raised my palms skyward. In actuality, I really didn't know the answer. I did know that Cliff had once gone by the name Hal Delano and had been brought up on manslaughter charges, although three separate trials resulted in three separate hung juries. The prosecution debated bringing him up on separate charges of jury tampering, but they finally concluded they'd have even less luck making that stick. Cliff Roper was a piece of work, and he often operated in a way that kept everyone guessing.

"And here I was," he said, "about to offer you a big payday."

"You were, were you?" I started, not entirely sure of how to separate fact from fiction.

"I was thinking about it. You've got the perfect background for an assignment."

"Is any of it legal?" I asked.

Roper pointed a finger at me again. "Watch it with the wise cracks. And yeah, what I need from you is perfectly legit."

“Go on,” I said.

“I’ve got this client. Or potential client I should say. Patrick O’Malley. He’s finishing up his junior year at SC. Plays quarterback. You might have heard of him.”

Indeed I had. I knew Patrick for years, just like I knew most of the upperclassmen on USC’s football team, having coached there for a number of years. I worked with the defensive backs, and while I didn’t have regular interaction with Patrick, my guys went up against him every day in practice. He was a gifted quarterback, and a true surprise. Patrick had secured one of the last scholarships we had that year, the coaches debating tirelessly over whether he had enough experience to play college football. He was mostly a skateboarder and a surfer and a snowboarder, a kid whose high school coach discovered him one day playing catch on the soccer field. What stood out was his ability to throw a football 70 yards in the air.

“Sure,” I said. “Why the interest? Patrick’s just a junior. He’s only started one season. He’s as raw as they come. He didn’t even play high school football his first two years.”

“You think I don’t know that? I know all about Patrick. He’s got a rare gift. Trouble is he doesn’t know it. He’s more interested in going out for the winter Olympics. Thinks he can medal in the halfpipe. What a freaking waste.”

“It’s all about competition,” I said, echoing something my longtime friend Johnny Cleary liked to say.

“No, it’s all about money,” Roper answered. “Look, here’s the deal. Patrick got involved in some rough stuff.

He lives with a bunch of guys in some animal house near campus. There was a, well, how do I put this, an incident last week. Him and his housemates roughed someone up. It's okay, the guy was a burglar. But the thief is making some serious allegations. Beating, torture, imprisoned against his will, real ugly crap. If charges get filed, Patrick's career is toast. The NFL won't touch him. And SC will kick him out of school, too. They don't mess around anymore."

"And you want me to find out if it's true."

"I want you to fix the freaking thing is what I want!" Roper hissed, the volume of his voice falling in the same way the intensity was ratcheting up. "Do you know how many tens of millions of bucks this kid stands to make? Sheesh, what do I have to do to get through to you?"

I shook my head. The memory of past headaches while working for Cliff Roper were returning to me in full force. "I don't do cover ups," I finally managed.

"You don't have to cover anything up. Just investigate. Make things whole if you can. You used to coach at SC, I figure maybe you still have some influence. I'll pay your ridiculous daily rate. But I'll pass you another twenty grand if Patrick goes pro next month and signs with me. Call it a bonus."

I looked up at the sky. The thought of a lucrative assignment was attractive. I had made great money as a football coach, but a private eye's income was a step down and then some. The thought of working for Cliff Roper again, however, made me blanche. My job was full of tradeoffs, and I surmised that was why they called it work.

"Here's what I can do," I said. "I'll look into it. I'll see what actually happened. And if it's nothing serious, I'll see how I can help. But if it the allegations are true, there may not be much I can fix. And there's only so many things I'll do for money."

Roper shook his head. "People like you confound me."

"Imagine what people like you do to me."

"Hey, hey, hey. I'm not going to warn you again."

"I'm really scared. Look. I've got a little extra time, I can squeeze this in and take the case. I charge fifteen hundred a day," I said, adding some money in for combat pay. "We'll see what comes up. I know Patrick, and he's a good kid. Some of the guys he lives with, well, I don't know about them. You want I should swing by your office on Monday?"

"No," he said, "I want to move on this. What are you doing tomorrow?"

"Spending time with my family," I said involuntarily, suddenly thinking I also needed to spend time looking for Tyler Briggs.

"Good, you'll be free after noon. I'll send a car around for you at 12:30pm."

"Car? To go where?'

"To go where. To the Charger game! They're playing the Raiders. Do I really have to lay everything out for you? Sheesh. Good help really is hard to find," he said, and turned and began walking to the other side of the practice field before I could respond. I watched him go for a long moment, and then I turned to see if I could find a familiar face, hopefully one that wouldn't leave me shaking my head in disgust. He finally materialized, seemingly out of thin air, but unlike Cliff Roper, this guy seemed genuinely happy to see me.

"Coach B," exclaimed a clean-cut young man wearing a light blue golf shirt and carrying a clipboard. He had short blond hair, a freckled face, and was bursting with the unabashed enthusiasm that only a person under the age of 25 could muster.

"Derek," I said, and gave him a bear hug. "Good to see our analytics guy found a job after college."

"It's worked out great for me," he gushed. "What brings you here? I heard you became a detective, that's so cool. You're not looking to get back into coaching, are you?"

"Nope. Just here on some business," I said. "How're the Chargers treating you?"

"Good, real good. I love it here. Didn't think I'd find something as good as SC, but this job may be even better."

Derek Altman started out as one of our USC team managers, carrying water bottles, fixing equipment, shagging punts, doing just about anything we asked of him. He was majoring in math, and we had him keep the statistics for a while, but he also showed remarkable acuity in breaking down game film and understanding opposing players' tendencies. He quickly gleaned when a play would be a run or a pass by the manner in which certain offensive linemen dropped into their stance. He understood a running back might wiggle his fingers when he knew the ball was about to be handed off to him. The little tendencies, or tells, could often be the difference between winning or losing a close game. Some guys just had the gift of insight, and Derek was one of them.

"Glad to hear it," I said, motioning for us to walk down the sidelines to a more private spot a few yards away. "Mind if I ask you a couple of questions?"

"Okay," he said, looking at me curiously.

"You're not in any trouble," I smiled. "But I wanted to ask you about Coach Briggs."

The smile disappeared from his face. "Oh. Yeah. That didn't work out very well."

"What happened? He was only here one season."

"That was more than enough," Derek said, shaking his head. "It started off okay. We were 4-2 after our first six games. Then we dropped a couple of close ones and things just went off the rails. Coach Briggs started losing control of the team, players weren't respecting him. Once we started losing and got out of playoff contention, guys started playing to pad their stats. Make themselves look good for negotiating their next contract."

"The team went on a bad losing streak," I recalled.

"Bad doesn't fully describe it. We lost our last 10 games. It was tough. The drinking made it worse."

I frowned. "Tell me about that."

"It was kind of an open secret. Coach Briggs would keep a case of beer in his office fridge all the time. Made me restock it. Got to the point where I was going to the store every other afternoon. A few times he even started putting it away before practice. He hid the drinking for a while, but you know how it goes. Drunks get sloppy. Our final game, I swear he had a few before opening kickoff. I think by then the owner caught on and pulled the plug on him.

Too bad. He was a nice guy. And smart. He was a great play caller when he was sober. But he had his demons. Couldn't keep 'em at bay."

"Anyone stay in touch with him after he got fired?"

"Yeah, Anthony Riddleman probably did. He was Briggs's QB with the Jets, known Tyler for years. Tyler was the one who hired him here."

"Any way I could get to speak with Anthony?"

Derek shook his head. "Probably not. The team's going straight to the hotel after this. I can let them know, maybe ask to call. Anthony's a good guy, he'll probably follow up. I think he's still close to Tyler. Anthony was one of the few guys on the staff they kept on after they let Tyler go."

"They kept you on," I reminded him.

"Yeah," he said a little shyly. "I don't get paid a lot, so I can fly under the radar. But maybe someone noticed my hard work. It's like Johnny Cleary once told the team at SC. Character is what you do when you think no one's watching. Turns out someone was watching me here. They not only kept me on, but gave me a promotion. I'm starting to work on things like salary cap space, trying to calculate who's worth how much. It's interesting. Putting my math skills to work. I might have a shot to be a general manager one day. That'll be a ways off, though."

"Great," I smiled. "I always love to hear someone doing what they're good at."

"Never dreamed it would work out like this. When I started at SC, I thought I'd end up going to work for Facebook or something. This is a thousand times better."

"I'll say."

"So, is something going on with Coach Briggs? I know he took a year off of football. Everything okay with him?"

"I don't know," I said, lowering my voice to a whisper. "This is confidential. I'm trying to find him; he didn't make it home last night. Any thoughts where I might hunt him down?"

Derek Altman looked down at the turf. "There's lots of bars in L.A. It'll take some doing, but I wouldn't be surprised if he's hanging out at one of them."

Two

My first stop after leaving the Chargers' energetic practice field was at a dive bar at Sepulveda and National called Babe's. Years ago, this bar was called The Date Room, and I'm sure it was called something else before that. It was not a place many people would take their dates to. It was dark and dingy in the middle of the afternoon, the type of hole-in-the-wall a drinker was left with if the nicer taverns suggested the person take their business elsewhere.

I was familiar with Babe's only because of a few stakeout assignments near the end of my tenure with the LAPD. If the brass wanted to crack down on drunk drivers, we would be situated outside bars like Babe's after midnight. Invariably, some poor soul would stumble outside, fumble with their keys, fall into their car and attempt to navigate home.

It rarely took more than a few blocks to confirm the weaving-across-traffic and slow reaction times that were indications of a seriously inebriated driver. Pulling them over with the flashing lights was easy. Getting them to hand me the keys and climb out of their vehicle was quite another matter entirely. A few would turn belligerent, but most would just have that crestfallen look on their faces, knowing what was in front of them: a night in the drunk tank, a litany of court appearances, attorney fees, and in some cases, suspended drivers licenses. That's when the shameless begging and pleading began. Getting pulled over for driving under the influence was a major hassle, which made it surprising that I encountered more repeat offenders than one might imagine.

I entered Babe's and noticed it hadn't changed much in 20 years. There were some uneven tables with a few people already going through pitchers of Budweiser, even though it was the middle of the afternoon. The bar itself was unremarkable, a long slab of wood with a few cheap stools, most of which were unoccupied. A number of flat-screen TVs were mounted on the walls, and all were tuned to a pro football game. Even though this was Saturday, we were in that narrow period where the college football regular season had ended but bowl games had not yet begun, and the NFL was able to schedule a couple of their games today. The Colts were playing the Browns, but the few patrons in the bar did not seem to being paying any attention.

The bartender was a solidly built middle-aged man with a crew cut, and a three-day stubble on his face. He wore a black apron across the top of his jeans, and a dirty white t-shirt that said "Black and Gold Brigade." There was a Pittsburgh Steelers helmet on the sleeve. He was busy washing glasses, or what passed for washing them, dunking a pair in soapy water and then dunking them again in what might once have been clean water. He shook them a few times as he pulled them out, errant drops of water spilling on the floor. I waited a minute before he looked up at me.

"Get you a beer?" he asked.

I looked down at the wet glasses lining the bar. "No thanks," I said and reached into my pocket. I pulled out a photo that Hannah had given me and placed it on the bar. "Ever seen this guy before?"

He took a long look and shook his head. "Can't recall. Any reason I would?"

"I'm a private investigator. He's gone missing. Trying to find him."

"Maybe he don't want to be found," the man said with a laugh.

I sighed and reached into my wallet and pulled out a twenty. When you drag a $20 bill through a trailer park, you never know what type of gems you can unearth. "Maybe this can help."

He looked up at me curiously. "Look, I was just joking. I'm not trying to hustle you," he said, wiping his hands on the apron. "I don't recall the guy is all. But I only work weekends."

"Anyone around here who might know?" I asked, scooping up the bill, and shoving it in my pocket.

He drew a breath and yelled across the room. "Hey, Darlene!"

A slender, curly haired waitress in her mid 40s looked up from wiping down a table. "Whaddya want?"

"Come here. This detective guy wants to talk to you," he said, motioning to me. "There might be something in it for you."

"Like what?" she asked, walking over to the bar and giving me the once over.

I ignored her question, picked up the photo of Tyler

and handed it to her. "Look familiar?"

She gave it a good five-second review, including moving it back and forth a few inches. "Yeah. I know him. He was in here a few weeks ago. You're a detective or something?"

"Yeah, something. Has he been in here since?" I asked.

"No, and I doubt he'll be back. Said he was some kind of football coach. Got into it with one of the regulars. Tomas. The fellas had to separate them."

I frowned. "What happened?"

"Ah, nothing out of the ordinary. You can talk to Tomas. Maybe even arrest him, I'm sure he's done something wrong."

"Haven't we all."

She looked down the bar. "Hey, Tomas! What'd you say to that Charger coach a few weeks ago? The thing that got him all ticked off. I mean, besides telling him his team stunk."

A short, squat young man with a wispy beard looked up unevenly. The bar area immediately in front of him was littered with empty shot glasses. A half-full schooner of beer sat nearby.

"You mean that Briggs jerk?" he asked, in a voice that was just a little too loud.

"Yeah."

Tomas shook his head and didn't bother to get up, which was reasonable, seeing as he probably would not have made it more than three feet. But as he began to speak, he managed to become a good bit more coherent, as if the memory of a bad incident was tattooed on the front part of his brain. It's interesting the things that drunks quickly recall, because I got the distinct feeling it might take Tomas a couple of tries to pronounce his own name correctly.

"Stupid bastard. He coached the Chargers last year. Eh, I wasn't sure it was him at first, he was wearing this green Miami Hurricanes cap. What a dork. Yeah, I told him the Chargers sucked – which they *did* – I ended up losing a bundle betting big on them against the Broncos last year. I took 7 points and the Chargers were down by only 3 at the end of the game. It all looked good. Then Briggs calls a trick play at the end of regulation. Some kind of flea flicker play, or something. Anyway, the Chargers fumbled, and the other team picked it up and scored on the last play. Broncos won by 10, and I lost my wager. What a dope."

I took this in. Of all the opportunities to lose money in the world, betting on sports was probably the surest and most complete way. A dropped pass, an ill-timed fumble, a missed field goal, all could easily determine who won and who lost a wager. My friend Captain Juan Saavedra from the LAPD once told me of a bookmaker he had arrested, and in the course of their discussion, Juan happened to ask how many clients came out ahead at the end of a season. The answer surprised him. Zero. Gamblers might win some games, get on a hot streak, but over the course of a season, they all ended up in the red. The bookie himself made the comment he would never bet on anything that could talk.

"So, what happened, Tomas?" I asked. "You let Briggs know what you thought of him?"

"Sure I did. I got my rights. I told him the Chargers should have stayed in San Diego and he should have stayed wherever the hell he came from."

"Uh-huh. Sounds like he didn't appreciate it."

"Nope. And the dirty little prick told me where to go. After a little back-and-forth, I says, let's you and me walk into the parking lot out back and settle it. You know, man-to-man and all."

"Oh, yeah?" I asked, eyebrows raised. "Who won?"

"We never made it that far. He sucker-punched me," Tomas hissed. "Like a little girl."

"What happened next?" I asked, not bothering to point out that little girls rarely sucker-punch anyone.

Tomas threw his arms forward as if he were a fighter loosening up. "I was about to clean his clock. But Craig, he's the regular bartender, he jumped in and broke it up. Grabbed me so I couldn't bash his teeth out."

"Craig suggest you take the fight outside?" I asked.

"Yeah. But then Briggs disappeared. Ran right out the door, jumped into his Mercedes, and took off. I still got a bump over my eye from that night," he said, rubbing the left side of his temple.

"He ever come back?"

"Nope."

"You go looking for him?"

Tomas drew his head back, ostentatiously accenting being offended. "Hey, I'm not that kind of guy. I've taken a few punches before. Didn't kill me."

I thought about this for a moment and decided to try another tack. "Ever wonder why a guy like that would come in here?" I asked. "Nothing personal. But this is just a neighborhood bar."

He thought for a moment, and the haze of alcohol seemed to return. "Nope, never thought about that," he muttered.

I turned to Darlene. "He mention anything to you about why he was here?"

She shook her head. "He said something weird about trying to find a donut shop nearby. He probably meant Primo's on Sawtelle, but he was already three sheets to the wind. Besides, they close early. He came in drunk, left drunker. He was putting it away pretty good. Must have had three beers in 10 minutes. Looked like he was trying to drink a problem away."

"That always works," I said dryly, taking out a couple of business cards. I laid them down on the bar. "If you think of anything else, let me know, would you?"

"What's the interest?" she asked.

"He's gone missing. I'm trying to find him."

"People like that," she said absently, "they may not be worth finding. You could be wasting your time."

"I'm getting paid for it."

Darlene's eyes opened a little wider. "Oh, I get it. Hey, I heard there was something in it for me."

I gave a little laugh and reached into my pocket. Out came the $20 and I slapped it on the bar. "Maybe you and Tomas can split it. Hey, it's almost Christmas. Consider it a bonus."

Both of them smiled. Burnside, the local Santa Claus. As I walked outside, the cool, damp air softly brushed my face. It felt good. It felt better to be out of that bar.

*

It was a twenty-minute drive to the Alibi Room, a straight shot that normally took one-half the time. I made the mistake of going onto Venice Boulevard, an artery that used to allow for clear sailing, but now was a hurdle due to what locals sneeringly referred to as a “road diet.” The street was cut from three lanes to two for drivers on both sides of the street, so that a curbside bike lane could be added. This was intended to encourage motorists to shed their cars and begin pedaling. From what I could tell however, few people changed their habits. But it did cause traffic to slow dramatically, and red-faced motorists would curse at the inconvenience, sometimes silently, sometimes not-so-silently.

The Alibi Room was a bar that was in stark contrast to Babe’s. It had polished oak paneling, indirect lighting, and a hundred different bottles of beer on a shelf near the ceiling. The clientele was more upscale, there were a few couples sitting and talking quietly, and a nicely dressed bartender with a trimmed beard walked over. He smiled at me as I sat down. He wore a dark blue shirt with the name Gene sewed above the breast pocket.

“Afternoon,” he said pleasantly. “What can I get you?”

“Nothing just yet,” I said, looking around admiringly at the collection of beer bottles. “You carry all of those?”

“Most,” he laughed. “We specialize in craft beer. Among other things. You have a favorite?”

"I have a preference for amber beer, I guess. Sierra Nevada, Blue Moon, that kind of thing. Feels a bit early to start."

"It's always five o'clock somewhere," said a rotund guy sitting two barstools away. "At least that's my philosophy."

I smiled and turned back to Gene, the bartender. "Okay. What do you recommend?"

"We have something called Beach House. Medium body, clean, earthy taste, some citrus notes. It's a good ale."

"I'll give it a try," I said. The days of going into a bar and simply ordering a draft were fading, although the crowd at Babe's would probably demur.

Gene returned with a pint of ruddy-colored liquid with a small, creamy head. I took a sip and then another. "Good recommendation," I said. "Say, you mind if I ask you a couple of questions?"

"What's that?" he asked, taking a glance down the bar to make sure no customers were going untended. All were either deep in conversation, deep in thought, or deep in craft beer. He turned back to me. I laid the photo on the bar.

"This guy look familiar?" I asked.

Gene took a glance down and immediately recognized him. "Sure. Tyler Briggs. Used to coach the Chargers. Comes in here quite a bit. Almost a regular."

"You see him recently?"

"Last night. He didn't stay long, though. Had a drink, met someone and left."

"Who was the someone?" I asked, watching him closely.

Like all good bartenders, Gene hesitated. I didn't think this was the kind of place where a discreetly placed twenty-dollar bill would loosen lips. Instead, I reached into my pocket and pulled out my fake badge and flashed it quickly.

"I'm doing an investigation." I said, not exactly lying. "It's important."

Gene pondered this for a moment. "It was a woman. Can't say as I know who, but she's been in here a few times. Well-dressed, short, blonde, nice figure."

"Does she typically come here alone?" I asked.

"Arrives alone, leaves with someone," he shrugged. "I try not to judge. That's why a lot of people go to bars. That's what keeps us in business."

"I've seen her around," piped up the rotund guy. "I think she probably works in the area."

"What makes you say that?" I asked.

"Seen her at a few community events. Meetings and such."

"When was the last time you saw her at one of those?" I asked.

"A few weeks ago, maybe. About that nonsense on Venice Boulevard. Traffic easing, I think they call it. Whole neighborhood's ticked. The mayor even came by and made a speech about how it decreased traffic deaths and only added one minute to the commute. What a bunch of bull. They averaged traffic for 24 hours, that way the numbers are low. Liars and their statistics."

"Uh-huh. You by chance know the woman's name?"

"Nope. Never even talked to her."

"Maybe seen what kind of car she drives?"

"Sorry," he said with a shrug. "Didn't spend much time focusing on her. Good-looking lady, but you know. This is L.A. and all. Nothing special."

I turned back to Gene the Bartender. "It would really help if you could tell me anything more. Tyler Briggs never made it home last night," I said. "May simply be sleeping it off someplace. But he's never done that before."

Gene shook his head. "Sorry. Like to help, but you know ... "

"Any other places Tyler mention that he liked to go to? Other bars maybe? Restaurants?"

"He'd sometimes laugh and say he'd be going to Tito's Tacos."

"Why's that funny?"

"We're known for tacos here. Pretty good. Short rib, tofu, kimchi. That's our specialty."

"Don't see that everywhere," I mused. "In fact I don't think I've seen that anywhere."

"That's how the owner of this place started out. Ran a taco truck, started experimenting with new fillings, it caught on. Made enough money on it so he could start his own place here."

"Only in L.A." I smiled. "The great experiment."

"Yup. Gotta be open to the new and different. Sometimes it works."

I took a long sip of Beach Head and tossed a twenty on the bar to pay for it. Tyler Briggs had been here last night, picked up a woman and never came home. But without anything else to go on, I was at a dead end. I handed both of the men my business card and asked them to call me if they thought of anything else. Or if the blonde woman stopped by again. Or if they came up with a new type of taco. They laughed the laugh of men who would probably never bother to call.

Three

I walked around the neighborhood near the Alibi Room and asked the few random people I met on the street if they recognized the photo of Tyler Briggs. Only one did, a Charger fan who suggested if Briggs were indeed missing to let him stay missing. I drove slowly around the area but saw nothing unusual. I also stopped at a small homeless encampment under the 405 Freeway. No one recognized Briggs, but I did get one offer to buy some heroin from a disheveled young man, and another offer for sexual favors at a discounted price. I declined both, and neither solicitation received a polite response.

It was well after 4:00 pm, and with the winter solstice just days away, it was already starting to get dark. After leaving a message for Anthony Riddleman, I decided to call it a day. I knew I wouldn't have much luck finding the mysterious blonde. In L.A. they're a dime a dozen, and frankly I didn't even know what she looked like. In a sprawling city like Los Angeles, if a person went underground, they could be inordinately difficult to find. The police could at least check hotels and airports, but not having that luxury, I concluded that my investigation would have to pick up tomorrow. I called Hannah Briggs, gave her an update, and told her I'd keep looking.

Our house was a few blocks off of Venice Boulevard., and the string of lights I had put up this week were already glowing along the exterior. I could see our

Christmas tree in the window, and there was bustling activity as I walked in the door. Gail and Marcus each had red and white Santa hats on, and they were laying out boxes of decorations. A few couples were chatting in the living room, and a couple of five-year-olds were playing with some ornaments on the floor. I had forgotten we had a tree trimming party scheduled for today.

"Daddy!" yelled Marcus. "You're late!"

"I know," I said, picking him up and giving him a hug. "Had some work that ran over."

Gail came over and gave me a kiss. "Did you find him?" she whispered in my ear.

I shook my head no, and Gail frowned. She put a finger to her lips, and turned back to our guests.

There were three couples actively engaged in stringing popcorn, removing decorations from boxes I had unearthed from our garage, and untangling cords of colored lights that would blink and flash in what was truly a random manner. We purchased some of these lights at a garage sale years ago, with various others being added as the years piled up. Gail inherited some from her parents, and some were leave-behinds from the home's previous owner, an elderly couple without children.

I walked over and said hello to our guests, the Parkers, Hartnetts, and Alperns, apologized for being late and noticed a few warm boxes of Julie's pizza on a table. They were all half-eaten, and I took this as a sign to dig in. I pulled a slice of mushroom pizza off and took a large bite. Gail had set a cooler of beer and sodas nearby, and I grabbed a Coke, deciding that one beer was sufficient for the time being, especially when we had guests with young children. I also didn't want an errant word to slip out about my current cases, or about much of anything else.

"Working on a Saturday?" asked Ben Alpern, smiling as he arranged some silver tinsel on one of the branches of the tree.

"Yes," I said, washing down another bite of pizza with a large swig of Coke. "My life has never been nine-to-five."

"Good and bad to that," he remarked. "Working for Boeing, my job was nine-to-five for a long while. Then smartphones got invented, and all of a sudden I'm on call all the time. This must be how doctors feel. I got a text from my boss the other night at 10:00 at night with a question. At least he didn't ask me to come into the office."

"Brave new world," I said.

Will Hartnett came over, reached into the cooler, and came out with a bottle of Blue Moon. "Good choice of beer. Do I credit you or Gail?"

"She bought the libations," I grinned, "but let's just say I had some input."

He popped it open and took a sip. "I got to watch it, this is my fourth one today. Lousy football game on TV this afternoon. Whenever I'm bored I have a beer or two."

"Who won?"

"Colts 9-7. It was that kind of game. Two bad teams playing in five degree weather. Real boring."

I took a sip of Coke. Whenever I got bored I took a look at Gail. That ended my boredom. Drinking large quantities of beer was just an excuse for some guys. A replacement for something else.

"So, where are you applying for kindergarten?" he asked.

I said we hadn't decided. After men dispensed with talk of work, sports, and beer, the conversation often segued to schools. Put L.A. parents together and it practically guaranteed that conversation.

"We're still talking about it," I said, not bothering to add it was mostly Gail doing the deciding, especially in terms of what schools to look at, how to assess them, and ways to get a leg up on the competition. For the most part I hung back, not quite recognizing why one school might be better for Marcus, or how a certain curriculum might impact his college prospects. I mostly thought about the cost, checked out security measures, and looked to see if the current student body had any bullies. Beyond that, my contribution would mostly be writing a check if we decided to pass on public schools, an option I wasn't giving up on just yet.

"Applications are due next month," Will said. "Can't delay too much. We're applying to Crossroads, Wildwood, and Westside Neighborhood School. Hope we don't end up at Wildwood. Jenny loved it, but the commute'll be murder."

I raised my eyebrows. "It's five minutes away."

"Have you driven down Venice Boulevard lately?" he asked, taking a pull of Blue Moon. "It's a traffic nightmare. Carmaggedon. Ever since they removed two traffic lanes, it's been killer trying to get through. It can take fifteen minutes to go three blocks."

"You complain about it?" Ben asked.

"I tried. Called my city councilman's office every day for two weeks. The jerk wouldn't talk to me. But I gave the people who answered his phone a piece of my mind."

"Who's the councilman?" I asked, a little embarrassed I hadn't bothered to keep up with my own district's rep.

"Colin Glasscock. Some name, huh? Ever since they implemented this last month, he's gone into hiding. No public appearances. Won't take calls. I tried contacting the mayor, but you could imagine how successful that was."

"Yeah," I said. "I can imagine."

"Think Gail has any pull?" he asked.

"Probably not," I said. "City Attorney's office just prosecutes criminals."

"That should include politicians," he said dryly. "Maybe Gail should run for office. Be nice to have someone with a brain running things."

I smiled and gave him a mini toast, tilting my can of Coke toward him. The last thing I would ever want was my wife entering politics. Not because of anything dangerous, but the high profile meant the end of any privacy. And as a private investigator, emphasis on the word private, that would be an enormous issue, not just for me, but for her as well. And Marcus.

"I remember when I coached at USC for three years. Seemed like half of L.A. knew who I was and knew everything about me."

"Ha," said Alpern, sitting down with us. "And the other half were UCLA people."

"You give up a lot when you become a public figure," I

said. "People who know nothing about what you do are suddenly giving you advice. Asking for favors, approaching you when you're with your family. It's not why I gave it up, but I don't miss all the publicity. And running for office? A lot of getting elected is about publicity."

"Be nice to know someone at City Hall though," Will continued. "That's how you get things done. Who you know is critical."

At that point, Gail called me over to open a cardboard box that had been glued a little too tightly. As I pried open the carton, which contained a variety of ornaments including red and green balls, snowmen, and a Santa laughing on a sleigh while smoking a cigar, Gail drew close to me.

"Are you planning out my career for me?" she asked, with the slight hint of a smile. Just a hint, mind you.

"Not exactly," I started. "Unless you're planning to run for office. Are you?"

"Well," she said, slipping her arm around my waist. "I'm not ruling it out entirely. Working in the City Attorney's office has allowed me to see a lot of things. How local government runs things. It's not always pretty. And the people in charge aren't necessarily the sharpest tools in the drawer. Know what I mean?"

I knew precisely what she meant, and having spent 13 years with the LAPD I could attest to the way bureaucracies might wreak havoc on a community. But I also saw the ugly side of being in charge of the system, the tough decisions for which no good answer is apparent.

And the public hue and cry, where innocent people are tried and convicted in the media. I knew all about that last part. I was one of its victims a decade ago.

"This is a discussion we should probably have at another time," I said, lowering my voice. "With more details as to what you'd be getting into. And how I can help you. Or possibly hurt you. The job I do isn't exactly pretty, and I have an unfortunate public persona which will stay with me forever. And will undoubtedly touch you."

"I know."

"Not to mention, Marcus," I said, and saw a spark light up in Gail's pretty gray eyes. Bringing children into a discussion like this would be necessary, but I also saw that I would need to tread carefully.

"I *know*," she repeated, with a tinge of annoyance in her voice. "Let's just get through tonight."

"Okay."

"On another topic, how is Hannah holding up?"

"Could be better," I said. "Finding Tyler may be like finding a needle in a haystack. L.A.'s a big place. I'm trying. Oh, yeah. I also ran into Cliff Roper today; he's got an assignment for me, too."

"Oh?" she said. "That's good and bad, I suppose."

"Yup. He pays well, but I'll earn every dime. I'm meeting with him tomorrow; for some reason he's invited me to the Charger game. Sorry I won't be around in 7the afternoon. But I might be able to speak with a few more people about Tyler there. We'll see where this leads."

Gail took this in. "Well, it's not all bad. We're going to

need some money if Marcus gets into private school this fall. It's not cheap, as you know."

I looked around the room and didn't respond. Arguing with an attorney is normally fruitless. And arguing with an attorney who is also your wife can be even worse. Winning such an argument is like being victorious in a war in the Middle East. Even if you win, you end up with more problems.

*

When I explained to Marcus that I'd be spending Sunday afternoon at the Charger game, his first response was to ask if he could go, too. The idea of exposing a young child to the uncouth mouth of Cliff Roper was a non-starter. I told Marcus I was still trying to rustle up a couple of Rose Bowl tickets, but didn't tell him the prices I was seeing were astronomical, nor that my USC connections were not as helpful as they once were. Regardless, the possibility of going to the Rose Bowl in a few weeks did little to brighten his disappointment. I finally suggested that I could record the Charger game on our DVR and we would watch it together later that night. He agreed, albeit with some hesitation, and then asked if I'd be on TV. I smiled and said I hoped not.

The car that Cliff Roper picked me up in the next day was actually a stretch limo made out of a converted black Cadillac Escalade. The back seat was outfitted with leopard trim, and there was an open bottle of Crystal Champagne jammed into a silver ice bucket. In addition to

Roper, there were two young men in the back seat, both in their late 20s, both looking like very fit athletes, or perhaps former athletes.

"Fellas," Roper crowed, as I climbed inside, "this is the guy I was telling you about. Burnside used to coach the secondary at USC. He's going to instruct you on everything you need to be a big-time college coach. He's going to be your *consigliere.*"

I gave Roper a sharp look. This wasn't part of any arrangement I had made, but Cliff Roper operates according to a rule book that is entirely his own, and one that changes on a dime. "Actually," I said, "I'm a former coach. Retired."

"Look, he's just weighing his options, this is the stuff you say to get teams interested. You can learn a lot from this guy. Now that Johnny Cleary moved up to coach in the NFL, Burnside's starting to get teams interested again," Roper said, eyeing me with the type of look that said I needed to play along in whatever rigged game in which he was engaged.

"I'm Devon. Good to meet you," one of the young men said, sticking out a hand. I shook it, and couldn't help noticing he had a grip of someone who most likely worked out continuously. The other one waved at me as he took a sip of bubbly out of an elongated flute glass.

"These guys are interviewing with UCLA tomorrow. Devon's a secondary coach just like you, and Alshawn coaches receivers. They're on their way. Straight out of Alabama, so they've got their pedigree."

"And you're representing them," I observed. One of the

things that surprised fans was that coaches had agents, just like players. They managed their careers, were on the lookout for job openings, and negotiated contracts. In the case of Cliff Roper, he was an agent who sometimes provided services that straddled the boundary between lawful and dubious.

“Of course I’m representing them. I want the best for these guys,” Roper said, offering me a glass of champagne, which I declined. “Help guide their careers. Figured you could give them some pointers. You being real smart and all.”

I continued to glare at Roper. Nothing should have surprised me about the workings of a super-agent, but Cliff Roper always managed to exceed all expectations. I took a glance out the window. Unlike yesterday, today was sunny and warm. December in L.A. was like that. You never knew what you were in for.

“Look,” Roper said to me, “we’ll get to our other issue later. First, give these guys a few pointers. You know the college game. Or you ought to. That Trojan team of yours went to a couple of Rose Bowls.”

“Sure,” I said, looking at the two eager young men. “What have you been doing recently?”

“We played together at Alabama. Came back around the same time and became graduate assistants,” Devon said. “Mostly grunt work at Bama, they were nice enough to give us a shot. But this year we moved up to position coaches. I was at Central Florida. Alshawn was at Southern Miss. We’re both looking to take another step up. UCLA has a new head coach and they want to bring in a new staff. Would be a great move for both of us. Cliff thinks so, too; he helped arrange the interviews."

"Ah," I said. "Okay. UCLA's a big-time program. Not like Alabama, but it's high profile. And L.A. is a different world," I told them. "Sounds like maybe you guys are used to being in smaller communities in the South?"

"Yeah, that's where we grew up. We played together at Tuscaloosa, we each spent a couple of years trying to make it in the league, but man, it's tough in the NFL. Make a mistake and you're gone. I don't want to go work in a mill, back in the same small town I grew up in. The coach at Alabama brought us back in as GAs. Good opportunity. Trying to make the most of it."

"Amen to that," Alshawn said as he drained the rest of his glass. "Looking to make it in big-time coaching. If we could get through Alabama, we can get through anything."

I didn't bother to tell them that the world of a college coach was very different from that of a player, or even a graduate assistant. Coaching was a full-tilt, non-stop, work-till-you-drop job that was for Type A personalities, guys who were driven to keep moving ahead regardless of the obstacles. It was not a world for everyone. It was not a world for me.

"I'll assume you guys know X's and O's," I said. "You've probably been immersed in it for most of your lives. And if you've been around college coaching at all, you've gotten a taste of that particular world. It's uber-competitive, and it gets more so the higher up you go. Pays well, but you'll earn it, trust me."

"The big bucks," chimed in Roper. "That's what these

guys are after."

I knew that was what Roper was after, his fifteen percent commission would come no matter how hard his clients worked. I turned back to them.

"We know L.A. is a different kind of place," Devon said. "But it's still football, right? Blocking and tackling, figuring out schemes, doing your job. That stuff never changes."

"Yes and no. Football is football, but L.A. is just different; the kids you're recruiting will be different. In small town America, especially in the South, football is everything. In some cases, football is the only thing. People build their lives around it. In L.A., it's just one other option. Lots of choices, lots of things to do. For football players, even the ones coming out of high school, they know they have lots of opportunities. In smaller communities, not so much. The attitudes are different here."

"Players are players," said Alshawn, pouring himself another glass. "If they want to make it to the big time, they got to put in the work. That's what we drill into them."

I groaned silently to myself. The level of talent in a place like L.A. was as good as anywhere. But when a kid knows he has other options, he doesn't always buy in to a program. The elite athletes often think they can coast along and make it to the next level, so college is a stepping stone. The next tier of athlete doesn't have that luxury. In a place like Alabama, they may not want to go back to a small town again. College football gives them a way out. In L.A., there are just too many choices. And that was what made coaching in L.A. a challenge. The world here was multidimensional, and you needed to communicate with players on different levels. Not everyone understood L.A. It helped if you grew up here and were already immersed in the culture. L.A. looked simple, but it's just not an easy place to figure out.

"All right," I said. "Best thing I can tell you about coaching in general is to prepare to move around a lot. Make lots of contacts, stay on good terms with everyone, especially your peers. Work hard, but keep a sense of humor and a sense of proportion. Make sure your head coach knows how hard you're working. It matters. You'll be dealing with lots of different personalities on the team -- and lots of different parents in L.A. Some have power beyond anything you've ever come up against. I kid you not. If your goal is to be a head coach, you'll probably have to change jobs every few years. It just comes with the territory. Not a bad thing, just keep learning from each job you get. Keep growing, understand you'll have setbacks, but stay positive. Motivate, inspire, be a role model for your kids. Keep the lines of communication open. Sounds easy, but you'd be surprised how quickly kids can shut down. Be honest with them. They'll know it right away if you're not."

The two of them nodded, taking this in. "This is great," Devon said. "Real helpful."

I'm not entirely sure how helpful my advice was, but when someone asks for my opinion, I normally give it to them. We chatted a little more. I told them why I left coaching, it's not a career for everyone, but it has a lot of good things, too. We arrived at the StubHub Center in Carson about ten minutes after the kickoff, but remarkably, we were whisked right into the stadium. There was no moving through a metal detector, which was the main reason I left my .357 at home. Cliff Roper high-fived one of the security guards who welcomed him, and I wondered if the high-five contained some paper currency.

The Stub Hub Center was a makeshift football stadium, a bizarre attempt to transform what originated as a 25,000-seat soccer arena into a place that could house an NFL game every other Sunday. It was cozy to some extent, but the type of cozy you might expect from a small college that didn't see a need to install a grandstand atop a single level of bleachers. The plan was for the Chargers to play here for a few years until their sparkling new palace was finished, and they could again play in an NFL-caliber home, replete with luxury suites and comfy chairs. For now though, they would be playing in a converted arena that reminded me of where San Jose State played its home games.

"That was a pretty quick entrance," I said to Roper as we climbed the steps toward our seats. "We didn't have to go through the security lines or walk through metal detectors."

"Damn right we didn't," he said. "I've got juice."

Indeed he did. Roper led us partway up the stairs and then ushered us into seats close to the fifty-yard line. It was not a corporate suite, but perfectly positioned, and the sight lines were great. If you had to watch an NFL match at a third-rate stadium, this was the way to go. We had some of the nicest seats in the house.

The game was scoreless when we arrived, and it was scoreless at halftime, a performance befitting two marginal teams who were out of playoff contention, and playing for what some might call pride. Roper handed Devon and Alshawn some sideline passes and told them to go on the field for a little while, something that gave us an opportunity to speak privately. As I was about to probe on my new assignment, we were briefly interrupted by a pair of distinguished-looking men wearing golf shirts and holding cocktails in their hands. They were both tanned and good-looking. One of them in fact, looked very familiar. His name was Eduardo Gonsalves, and he was the mayor of Los Angeles.

"Well, Cliff, glad you could make it today," the mayor smiled, shaking Roper's hand, and introducing his friend, who turned out to be the deputy mayor; his name was Neil Handler.

"Nice day to be outside, anyway," Handler remarked. "Glad the fog finally lifted."

"Yeah, and I wish the Chargers would lift the fog around their heads and provide us with some competition," Roper said. Then he pointed a finger in my direction. "Gentlemen, this is my friend, Coach Burnside. Used to play football at USC, you might have heard of him. He coached there, too."

"Of course I've heard of you," Mayor Gonsalves smiled. He was a swarthy man in his early fifties, with black hair graying at the temples, and marvelous skin that barely showed a blemish or a wrinkle.

"That's reassuring," I said, not entirely sure of whether he was telling the truth, but he sounded quite convincing.

"And I understand," Neil Handler said, "that your wife works for the city. She's a darned good prosecutor. Nice lady, too."

"Thank you," I smiled. "I'm impressed you know her."

"I make it my business to know everyone. In fact, I live in Mar Vista, too. We've got something in common."

"Funny I haven't seen you on my block."

"Ha ha," the Mayor broke in. "You'll be seeing much more of him next year, I guarantee you that. Neil's thinking of running for city council in your district. Give Colin Glasscock a run for his money, and I'll bet Neil unseats him. Lots of changes happening in our city. All good ones."

"These guys," Roper declared, "were instrumental in getting the Chargers and Rams back here to L.A. They're great leaders, they've made this city what it is."

The mayor smiled. "Got you to thank, too, Cliff."

Cliff Roper beamed and rubbed his thumb against the top of his fingertips. "Always happy to chip in to make the world a better place."

They laughed, waved, said how great it was to meet me, and moved on. I turned to Roper. "You travel in some pretty fast company."

Roper shook his head. "They're hacks. I donated a boatload of cash to the mayor's campaign last time, so we're on good terms."

"Didn't have you pegged as a Democrat," I said.

He looked at me with a pained expression. "Do I look

like an idiot? I also donated money to his opponent. Got to keep my bases covered. You never know when you'll need a favor. You ought to be taking notes."

"Ah," I said. "And did the mayor and his deputy know I'd be here today?"

Roper shook his head. "You're slow, but you're finally getting it. Politics is a show. Of course I told them. About you and that hot wife of yours. I hope you appreciate her. She'll help you more than you'll ever know."

"Uh-huh," I agreed.

"Look, enough with the small talk. Let me tell you about this assignment before those knuckleheads come back up from the field. You know I'm trying to sign Patrick O'Malley out of SC. You know because I told you yesterday. I'm hoping you remember."

"I remember. I also remember your wanting me to fix things. You remember what I said?"

"Yeah, yeah. Listen, here's the shot. No one cares about that burglar. Seriously. No one. Except maybe some do-gooder in the City Attorney's office. Maybe you can help with that. Trust me, no jury is going to side with a burglar who gets slapped around after he's caught."

I rubbed the bridge of my nose. In my years with the LAPD, I came across a few cases of a thief who got injured while on someone else's property and took legal action. As absurd as it might seem, there is no hard and fast law protecting homeowners from an opportunistic burglar. In one case, a group of teenagers hopped a fence to use someone's pool, and one fell as he was landing and tried to sue for damages. Fortunately, the jury sided with the homeowner, although he needed to spend thousands on legal fees defending himself. He tried to recover his money, but filing a suit against an unemployed teenager was a fruitless endeavor.

"Is the burglar pressing charges?" I peered at him.

"Let's just say I'm hearing things."

"And you want me to talk to the burglar."

"I want you to make this go away."

I shrugged. "Like I said, I'll look into it. And I appreciate your offer of a twenty thousand dollar bonus, but I think Patrick will make his own decision on whether or not to go pro."

"Look I have Patrick O'Malley's best interest at heart," Roper declared. "Believe me."

"How so? Because you'll collect a commission on negotiating an eight-figure contract?"

"Don't get smart with me. Patrick has a window of opportunity. This is the year half a dozen teams are looking for a quarterback in the draft. There are only a couple of studs who could become a franchise player. Elite QBs don't come along that often. Patrick's one of them. He's got the arm, he's got the vision, he's got the athleticism. And he's got the "it" factor. He's new and the NFL is excited about him. I don't want to see him mess things up."

I considered this. Patrick had spent his first two years as a backup QB, waiting patiently behind USC's highly recruited 5-star QB, who graduated last year. In practice, he was creating jaw-dropping moments, squeezing a pass into that little window where no margin of error existed.

Patrick could also do something called throwing a receiver open. This is when a receiver runs a route and is tightly covered. But because the quarterback throws the ball to a specific place where the defender can't reach – and only where the receiver can stretch to catch it – it becomes a pass that's impossible to defend. Not many QBs could do this, but even as a freshman, Patrick was doing it in practice on a regular basis.

"He's got a world of potential," I said. "But he's still raw."

"You think I don't know that?" Roper sneered. "The kid pays no attention to the game plan. I don't even think he cares about winning or losing. His whole goal is to see if he can outfox the defense. And he usually can and he usually wins. Sure he'll struggle. He'll also make a big pile of dough in the process."

"So will you."

"Yeah, yeah. What do you think, I run a charity?" he asked.

"Okay, look. I understand the situation. If there are charges filed, Patrick might lose his scholarship," I mused.

"Good chance."

"And the fact that my wife works in the City Attorney's office? I hope you don't think for twenty thousand dollars, I'd use that leverage."

"For twenty grand you should come off of that high horse of yours," he said, adding sarcastically, "but of course I wouldn't want you to do anything that makes you feel uncomfortable."

"No need to worry on that score," I said. "But let me ask

you something. You didn't know I'd be at the Chargers practice yesterday. Was our running into one another a coincidence?"

"Sure. Just like Tyler Briggs not coming home last night was a coincidence."

I stared at him. "How do you know that?"

"Because," he said quickly, pointing to the two young coaches making their way back up the steps, "I make it my business to know what's going on in L.A. And no, I'm not having you followed. But I put two and two together and figured you'd show up in El Segundo. And I made sure I did, too."

"You know anything about what happened to Briggs?"

Roper shook his head. "Who cares, he's not my client. He's washed up as a head coach. Needs to take a step back, be a coordinator, go back to coaching college. He has options, as long as he dries out. That's his biggest problem."

We turned our attention back to the field. Since both the Chargers and the Raiders were out of the playoffs, neither team put in any more effort in the 2nd half than they did in the 1st half. With six minutes left in the 4th quarter, Roper announced we were leaving, and we piled back into his Escalade. The trip back to the Westside was mostly filled with coaching gossip, who was likely going where, who was about to get fired. I began thinking about who I'd go talk to tonight in seeking out the missing Tyler Briggs. But as we neared my house, Roper's cell phone buzzed. He looked down at a text and shook his head.

"L.A. politics," he whistled. "I just lost a politician I had in my pocket."

"What's going on?" I asked.

"Your city council election just got easier for the deputy mayor. One less candidate."

"How so? Our guy retiring?"

"Oh, yeah," Roper sneered. "For good. The cops just found Colin Glasscock's body. Someone drilled him in the head a few times. Did it right in his own office. Looks like I'm going to give Neil Handler most favored nations status. He'll be getting a fat check sooner than we thought."

Four

The hastily written note on our front door was from Gail. She had dropped Marcus off with the Hartnetts, and had gone over to the Glasscock office near LAPD's Purdue division. I decided to drive over as well. I didn't know what I'd find there, but I was at least curious why Gail went. I hopped into my Pathfinder, and, on a late Sunday afternoon with the streets being gloriously empty, it took less than ten minutes to join her.

There was no mistaking the crime scene. Half a dozen black-and-white units were parked haphazardly in front of a gray stucco office building, the yellow tape stretched across the front to prevent looky-loos from wandering inside. I made eye contact with Gail, who was in mid-conversation with the City Attorney, and then I noticed another familiar face. He had bright lights shining down on him, a TV camera pointed his way, and a pretty on-air reporter peppering him with questions.

The reporter gazed intently at him, but it struck me that she was barely listening to a word he was saying; you could practically see the gears in her head spinning to come up with the next question. The silver-haired man was dressed in a well-tailored suit and tie, unusual for a Sunday, but this was an unusual situation. And Juan Saavedra was looking the part of the concerned leader, the distinguished LAPD captain putting the community at ease, and taking charge of the investigation.

I wandered over near the interview and listened in. Juan did a remarkable job of providing lengthy, articulate answers without really saying much. He was passionate about the LAPD using its full resources to bring this murderer to justice. He conveyed outrage while maintaining a cool exterior. He looked serious without being pedantic. It was an impressive performance, designed to paint himself in a favorable light, albeit under the guise of community concern. As he finished the interview, the lights dimmed, and a uniform went over and whispered in his ear. He responded with a few quick words, and pointed the officer toward the alley behind the office. Then he noticed me.

"Well, looky here," Juan said, taking a few steps toward me. "I didn't think this day could get any worse, but you never know."

"I always like to be where the action is."

"And you often get mired up in it," he mused.

"Aw, you're making me blush," I said. "But you sure have learned to handle the media well."

"I've had lots of practice. TV is actually easier than dealing with print. The TV guys just want a quick sound bite, something clear and concise, they want you to look good and sound good. The *L.A. Times* guys are the idiots. One time this cub reporter asked why an officer facing down a suspect with a pistol didn't just shoot the gun out of his hands."

"Just like in the movies," I smiled.

"Yeah. Some other *Times* reporter decided to get cute and asked me what was the dumbest question I'd ever been asked. I told him he just asked it."

"You looking to take a step up?" I inquired. "Head over to PAB and work with the suits?"

PAB was code for Parker Center, and stood for Police Administrative Building. It was where division cops looking to move up hoped to be. There were only so many opportunities for advancement in the field, and a captain in a Westside division was likely to languish there. Juan gave me a long look and changed the subject.

"So, what's your interest here? Hopefully you're just providing taxi service for Gail. I'd hate to think you're wrapped up in this somehow. But hell, I've seen it before."

"Probably not this time," I said.

Juan looked at me. "And just what are you working on these days?"

"Missing person. Former football coach, Tyler Briggs. Didn't make it home last night."

Juan looked at me curiously. "You check the drunk tank?"

"His wife did. Hannah Briggs. Came up with *nada*. You know about his drinking?"

Juan gave me another long look and then shook his head in disgust. "Yeah. Never understood oilers. Why some people can't have one or two drinks and stop. They say they like the feeling, but they lose all sense of responsibility. Some people call alcoholism a disease. I call it selfishness."

"That's a little rough, Juan."

Juan shook his head. "No it's not. You were on the job long enough. You saw the car accidents. Innocent people killed because someone decided to just have one or two or six more drinks. And half the time the drunk survives and the victims don't. I've talked to the victims' families and seen their faces. So no, I don't think I'm being too rough."

"But you apparently know about Briggs. Your guys must have picked him up before."

"Multiple times. And you know what? Each time Briggs got off, he got the charges dropped. Guy has some big-time connections. He needs them. He's got big-time problems."

"Uh-huh," I said. "And what happened here? A widely disliked politician gunned down in his own office?"

Juan looked at me. "You know something about him, do you?"

"Only scuttlebutt," I answered. "I don't follow local politics much, but looking into Tyler Briggs's disappearance opened my eyes about Glasscock. Lots of unhappy constituents in his district. Mostly related to traffic getting clogged up on Venice."

Juan gave a small smile. "In L.A., messing with traffic is a capital offense. Nothing pisses people off more than seeing their commute get longer."

It was a sad commentary, albeit an accurate one. Traffic in L.A. has long been a thorn in everyone's side. The beautiful weather, the opportunity to get a fresh start, the lure of Hollywood, all conflated to attract more and more people to L.A. every year. Some got disillusioned and went home, but a lot simply stayed and found a way to fit in. And with the mass influx of people, often from all corners of the world, the infrastructure became overwhelmed.

Traffic gridlock, soaring rents, and general overcrowding created an atmosphere that made a lot of long-time residents angry. As a cop, I saw lots of people's blood boil at how their lives had changed as L.A. changed. It was not the same city they grew up in, and they didn't like it one bit. Some people even put bumper stickers on their cars that read, 'Welcome To California. Now Go Home.'

"Kind of strange they'd remove traffic lanes from one of the biggest east-west arteries," I said.

"Yeah, their idea is to get people to bike. Brilliant, huh? People commuting thirty miles to work, moms with kids, gardeners with lawn mowers, sure, they'll be on board right away with that. But one unforeseen tragedy is occurring. More pedestrians are being hit by motorists. It's messy. I wish they'd change Venice back to the way it was."

"Think they'd listen to an LAPD captain?" I smiled.

"Politicians? They'd listen and then ask me for a donation. Nope. Besides, Mar Vista is technically in the Pacific Division. We've got our own problems here."

"I can tell," I said, looking around. "So, someone shoots a city councilman in his own office. Any chance of video footage nearby?"

Juan shook his head. "Uh-uh. Ever since Watergate, politicians have learned to keep their business discreet. They don't want cameras or microphones around unless they're getting on TV. They'd never install anything like that here. Can't blame them really. No sense hanging yourself."

"Spoken like a true public servant."

"I have a feeling this is an internal beef," Juan said. "Just between you, me, and the sidewalk."

"Internal, as in his own office?"

"City politics. There's some nasty stuff going on."

"Nasty enough to murder a city councilman," I mused. "Sounds like there's some money involved."

"For a politician, money trumps most everything, at least in some ways. Occasionally sex gets thrown in there, too."

I nodded. Most homicide investigations indeed have love or money at their root, sometimes both. The reason a distressed person could rise to commit the ultimate act was often a product of intense passion. Few things were as personal, or could generate more intense feeling than love. Except perhaps money.

"You think what was going on here was a money issue?" I asked.

Juan looked past me and paused. "You hear rumors. Some are true, some are nonsense. What I'd heard from PAB was that Glasscock was getting death threats. Not sure why, he didn't bother to include me in his conversations. But yeah, money's a possibility. I also want to talk with Gail about something."

"Oh?' I asked, eyebrows arching.

"Not quite what you think," he smiled. "But rumor has it Glasscock's had a few flings. Someone in the City Attorney's office might have been playing around. I want to get Gail's take."

I took this in and decided not to probe, I'd find out from Gail in due time. I pointed to the building. "You know when this actually took place?" I asked.

"Probably Friday night. Rigor mortis already passed, the body started getting flexible again, which means it had to be a couple of days. Last person to see him was a staff member leaving work at 5:00pm. Only reason we found out on a Sunday is the cleaning person came in this afternoon and discovered him."

"They don't clean on Friday nights?"

Juan shook his head no. "We ran the janitor through the wringer. Said he wanted to see his daughter's play on Friday evening, he figured no one was working over the weekend. Thought he'd just come in today and clean up and no one would know the difference on Monday morning."

"You have some thoughts on who did it?"

"Sure, Burnside," Juan said, rolling his eyes. "I'll have something on your desk first thing in the morning."

I smiled. "Hey, Juan, there's something else I'm working on. Mind if I stop by your office this week. Shouldn't take long. It's USC related."

"Oh, that's perfectly fine," he groaned. "I've got nothing better to do than help out our fine private investigators."

"It's all in the spirit of making the world a better place."

Juan glanced around at the scene and gave me a playful punch on the shoulder as he walked over to a group of uniforms. I looked around as well. The police weren't letting anyone into the building, and a few detectives were interviewing shocked bystanders. The ballistics crew would handle most things tonight, but the meat of the investigation would be done when the bulk of Glasscock's staff showed up tomorrow morning for work. I noticed Gail speaking to a young woman and walked over.

"Hi there," I said, giving Gail a peck on the cheek.

"Hi Sweetie," Gail said. "This is Emma Wick. She works for Colin. Or worked. I'm sorry."

"That's all right," Emma said, her eyes tear-stained as she shook hands with me. She was short and blonde and curvaceous, and she wore a black leather jacket over a bright red turtleneck sweater. I guessed she was approaching her late thirties. Then I stopped and realized I was a good bit older than her, and the definition of what was young sunk in hard. It did not make me feel good.

"Sorry for your loss," I managed.

"This is just tragic. We all loved him."

"I can imagine," I said. "What do you work at here?"

"Field operations," she said. "I organized town halls and community events for Colin. Background work mostly."

"Are you the only one who does this?"

"No, there are a couple of us. But we all do a little of everything. Colin liked people to be cross-trained. I pretty much did whatever he wanted me to do," she said with a sniffle.

"How did those community meetings go?" I asked. "I understand some people were upset with him. The traffic problem."

"Oh," she said with a wave of the hand. "People who don't want to accept progress. Don't like change, they just want to go on doing the same thing, not have their lives disrupted in the slightest. Whenever we suggested anything new, they just hated it. *Hated* it. Bunch of nimbys."

"Nimbys?"

"Not-in-my-back-yard types. They want change, but they want it done somewhere else. These people were difficult to deal with, they wouldn't even listen to Colin. At one event, they shouted him down and he was unable to speak. We finally just stopped doing those town halls."

"I'm sure that was frustrating," I said, looking at her closely. "You think one of the protestors had something to do with this?"

"I wouldn't put it past them. They're animals. Whoever did this had an agenda," she said. Just then, a number of employees from the coroner's office walked past, wearing dark windbreakers. Emma gasped, the wave of harsh reality seeming to swirl around her, and she buried her face in her hands. I turned to Gail. She patted Emma on the back, said something soothing in her ear, but Emma didn't seem to hear it. Gail took my hand and walked me a few feet away.

"Sweetie," she said slowly, "you're not working robbery-homicide, you know. There are detectives here for that."

I took a glance around. "I'm sure they're around here somewhere."

"I'm just saying that getting involved in a homicide investigation – no, make that an assassination – is beyond your role."

I shrugged. "Curiosity. It's in my blood. So, how come you're here?"

"I knew some people on his staff," she said. "I can't get

into anything more now."

I didn't press her. She asked who won the Charger game and I stopped and didn't have a good answer because I simply didn't know. In a lot of ways I didn't care. We made plans for dinner, the gist of which involved my stopping off at Versailles to pick up Cuban roast pork. And I was advised to make sure I got black beans and rice, since that was now one of Marcus's favorites.

On the way to the restaurant, I stopped off at a few more of Tyler Briggs's hangouts, various bars and greasy spoons, showed them his photo, but no one said they had seen him lately. I placed a call to Hannah Briggs but just got her voice mail and left a message that there was nothing new to report. I finally arrived home and we had a quiet dinner. Both Marcus and I forgot all about watching the Charger game we recorded, and instead had a marathon session of checkers. Marcus, not surprisingly, managed to win all the games, our night ending with him stretching out on the living room floor, leaving me to pick him up and carry him off to bed.

The next morning I went into the office, did some paperwork, looked up where Patrick O'Malley was living, and tried to find any and all tidbits about the career of Tyler Briggs. I took a mid-morning break and went over to Primo's donuts, another place Tyler Briggs had frequented, but all I left with was a warm bear claw, a cup of black coffee, and an uncertain feeling about this case. When someone has gone missing for more than 48 hours, it is not a good sign. I left a message with Juan Saavedra, but knew not to expect a call back any time soon. I was beginning to focus on where I should go for lunch when my phone rang. The number was local but I didn't recognize it. There was a more than 50-50 chance this would be another telemarketer, but I decided I didn't have the luxury of taking that risk. It was a good thing I picked up.

"Burnside."

"Hi there, Detective. It's Gene."

"Gene," I said, my mind combing through all the Genes I might have met in my life.

"From the Alibi Room."

"Sure," I said, hesitantly. "What can I do for you."

"You were looking for Coach Briggs."

"Still am. You know where he might be?"

"I do. As a matter of fact, I'm looking at him right now. And he doesn't look real good."

*

It took a while to reach the Alibi Room, and it was not a nice drive. The day had turned cloudy again and a few drops of rain had begun to fall. In L.A. that was reason enough for traffic to grind to a gnarly crawl. Cars inched along, with drivers undoubtedly cursing the car in front of them for not knowing how to drive in the rain. Or maybe for simply being out on the road in the first place.

A few years ago, someone hatched what they probably thought to be an ingenious plan to get Angelenos to better appreciate Mexican immigrants. They decided to organize a one-day-a-month boycott, whereby all Mexicans would stay home and not go to work. It was called "A Day Without A Mexican," and the goal was to slow the local economy down, helping Angelenos understand the impact that people of Mexican heritage had in L.A. They succeeded beyond their expectations, but not in quite the way they anticipated. Traffic was unusually light that day, people were very happy to see their drive time shortened, and some jokingly wondered if this could be expanded to three or four days a month. Not surprisingly, the boycott was quickly and permanently scuttled.

I walked into the Alibi Room and Tyler Briggs was sitting morosely at the bar, a pint of golden lager in front of him, his eyes staring intently into the glass, as if the secrets of the world lay buried inside. He picked up his beer and took a long, gulping swig. It was not the swig of someone thirsty, but more like the absent movement of someone who knew this was a means to an end. When he put the glass back down, half the beer was gone.

I said hello to Gene, then walked over to sit down on the barstool next to Tyler Briggs.

"That seat's taken," he said without looking up.

"Yeah," I responded. "By me."

This time he turned to look, ostensibly to give me the evil eye, but his glare softened as some form of recognition seemed to set in. "Do I know you?" he asked.

"You do. The name's Burnside. Ring a bell?"

"I think so. Pleasure to meet you again," he said, albeit without any sincerity.

"I'm sure it is," I said.

Tyler Briggs struggled to place me. He did not appear to

be a healthy man. His eyes were tired and his face was puffy. He looked as if he had been ill, his skin had a chalky coating to it, and his mouth drooped. I couldn't tell if he needed sleep, or had had too much of it.

"You used to coach," he finally managed. "At SC."

In his dismal mental state, I was almost surprised he could stitch even that much together. "That's right," I said. "Left SC when Johnny Cleary went to the Bears."

Briggs processed this slowly. "Yeah, it's coming back to me. I met you a couple of times on campus when I was with the Jets. USC's Pro Day. You had some good talent there."

"We did."

"You coaching somewhere now?" he asked, rubbing his face in a half-hearted attempt to energize himself.

"No, I left the profession."

"Me, too."

I didn't bother to clarify that he was fired. But to be fair, no matter how good or bad a coach might be, injuries, mistakes by key players, or sometimes the cruel winds of fate combine to end a coaching assignment. I knew one NFL coach who was fired because he failed to make the playoffs one year, even though his team had a winning record; he was replaced by the owner's son-in-law.

"So, I've moved back to my old career," I said. "Private investigator."

"Oh, yeah?" he said, perking up a little and managing a smile. "Big change from coaching."

"True. But I always seemed to get roped into something related to football. In fact, I'm on a couple of cases now that are football related. One of them includes you."

He peered at me. "Me? How's that?"

"Your wife hired me to find you. Hannah's been worried sick."

"Oh, man, I was meaning to call her last night. Shoot, I'm in trouble now," he groaned, then took another swig of beer. "Let me just get rid of this headache."

Now it was my turn to peer back at him. Something was not quite right here. "Do you know what day it is today?" I asked.

He looked at me. "Saturday. Why?"

I shook my head. "Not even close. It's Monday. You don't remember your weekend?"

Briggs tried to lean back, but we were on barstools and he came perilously close to falling over backwards. Grabbing the polished-brass edge of the bar, he lifted himself upright again, reached for the rest of his beer, and drained it quickly. He pointed to Gene for another. The bartender thought about this for a brief second before he refilled it, sliding it in under a clean white napkin. I looked at Gene.

"How many has he had?"

"This is number three," Gene answered.

"You keeping score?" Briggs asked the bartender before turning back to me. "Go on. Get lost. You did your job. You found me. I'll take it from here."

"I don't think so," I said. "I don't know how you got here, but you're in no condition to drive home. I'll take you. You can finish your beer if you think you need it."

"I need it," he said. "Believe me, I need it."

"You mind if I ask you what happened on Friday night?"

"Can you keep a secret?"

"Sure," I lied. At this point, my client was Hannah Briggs, she was paying my fee, and she was the one to whom I owed whatever information was worth sharing. And from what I could see, Tyler Briggs was little more than a walking grease fire, and keeping secrets from his concerned wife did not sound like a plan that would benefit either of them.

"Picked up some hot girl here," he said, taking another long pull from his glass. "We went to a motel, I banged her brains out and then fell asleep. It was a little weird. I had some wild dreams. Felt like I was banging her all night. Then I woke up and she was gone. And man oh man, did my head hurt. That's why I came here for a little pick-me-up. Figured I'd tweak the headache before going home."

"A motel," I said, starting to reconsider how much I would tell his wife. As much as people say they want to know about their spouse, the reality is they don't always want to know everything. I was also a little surprised that Tyler Briggs would share such intimate details, but never underestimate the lubricating power of alcohol.

"Yeah, that was weird, she said something about being separated from her husband, she didn't have a place. We went to some joint called the Snuggle Inn. From the outside it looked like they rented rooms by the hour, but it turned out to be decent. They even had HBO."

"That's great," I remarked absently. "Say, can I ask you something?"

"I guess."

"You have a beautiful wife at home."

"Thanks."

"I was actually complimenting her, not you," I said, starting to get a little annoyed. "Why'd you need to go off with someone else if you have a wife like that at home?"

"You married?" he asked.

"Yup."

"You ever stray?"

"Nope."

Tyler Briggs sighed, and I felt like doing the same. I had had my share of one-night stands, and there were a few nights where I drank more than I should have. But when I met Gail, everything changed. Maybe because I met her late in life, maybe because I became an older dad, whatever the ultimate reason, I appreciated what I had and didn't want to mess it up.

"I guess then maybe you wouldn't understand," he finally said.

"Things come easy to you, don't they?" I said, knowing the answer already. What I didn't understand was how those born into wealth could simply accept it as a given without looking around at the rest of the world. Without recognizing it, the shiny gift of being born on third base was an achievement accomplished by doing little more than winning the sperm lottery. There was a distinct lack of appreciation among some people when it came to where they had landed in life, as if it were all part of a master plan, one in which they were simply, and for all the right reasons, anointed as being special.

"Yeah, I suppose," he said. "Coaching, play calling, recruiting players. You know it's not all that different from picking up women. It's all about confidence. And it's about selling. I know how to sell."

"How are you going to sell your wife on the fact that you've been on a bender for three days?" I asked.

He laughed. "I'll come up with something. I always do."

"Okay. Why don't you finish your beer and get your story straight. I'll give you a ride."

Briggs downed the rest of his glass in one swallow and got up and walked out of the bar. I looked at him and looked over at Gene, and finally reached into my wallet and tossed a few bills on the bar. I had forgotten to inform Hannah Briggs that expenses were above and beyond my standard fee. Judging by her home on the Silver Strand, that shouldn't pose a problem, but you never knew. Some people were especially thrifty, and in that area, surprisingly, the rich were not all that different from the rest of us.

I hurried and led Tyler over to my Pathfinder, when all of a sudden he doubled over in what could have been pain. I thought for a moment he might get sick, and the idea of him regurgitating his liquid breakfast in my front seat was not a pleasant one. He finally stood back up, wobbled a little, and said he was just a little woozy. Happens all the time, he told me. Judging by the amount he was drinking before noon, I didn't doubt it.

"I'll tell you what. I'll drive you home in your car. That'll make life easier for you," I said, not bothering to add that it would make life far easier on me if he threw up in his own vehicle. "What're you driving?"

He looked around for a moment before pointing to a light blue Mercedes. He handed me the keys and we climbed in.

"You feeling okay?" I asked.

"I'm pretty hungry," he admitted. "Famished, actually. Can we stop for something to eat?"

It was almost lunchtime, so I said sure. "You got a favorite place nearby?"

"Oh, yeah," he responded. "I usually go there at night, but they open around ten in the morning. You ever been to Tito's?"

"Yes," I responded. "Know it well."

Tito's Tacos was an L.A. institution, not because the tacos were especially good, and not because it was especially authentic. Tito's was a place where kids growing up on the Westside often got their first taste of what used to pass for Mexican food in L.A. It had been around forever, located in the shadow of the 405 Freeway on Washington Place, a taco stand where you ordered at a window and picked up your food after an interminable wait. They served dishes that were more Mexican-American. Their signature item was a hard-shell taco filled with seasoned beef, lettuce, and a pile of shredded iridescent orange cheese of some sort. I once took an LAPD partner there; his heritage was Mexican, and he scoffed at the notion that this could be considered real Mexican food. It was like calling chop suey real Chinese food, he sniffed. Or like calling a barbecued chicken pizza real Italian food.

After our order was filled, we went over to a picnic table with our tacos and Cokes. At the table to our left were four teenagers tossing chips at each other. At the table to our right was a homeless person who was asleep on the bench. I watched Briggs pick up a taco, chomp it down in three bites, and then pick up another. I took one bite of mine and then put it down, the taste reminding me of a difficult childhood that did not improve upon reflection. Tito's was a jarring reminder of growing up, a sign that certain things deserved to be kept shrouded in the past. The food had not changed over the last three decades, but I certainly had. Tito's was old-school, and plenty of people still liked Tito's, but for me it was nostalgia, and in this case, nostalgia was overrated.

"What are your plans for next season?" I asked. "You trying to get back into coaching?"

Briggs chewed his second taco quicker and swallowed. "I don't know. Coaching is a rough business, I've been fired twice in two years. Tough to come back from that. I don't want to step down and coach college. Or be an assistant, watching someone else lead my life. Like I said, I'm a salesman. And I've still got a pile of money from coaching. Maybe I'll try the business world. I'm thinking of investing in commercial real estate. Means getting involved in politics. Donating to politicians. Or even becoming one myself. "

I took a sip of Coke and let both the bubbly soda and that bubbly comment sink in. My limited experience with politicians included an involvement in a gubernatorial campaign a few years ago, between Former Governor Rex

Palmer and the current one, Governor Justin Woo. Running for political office was not unlike running for class president in middle school. The most popular kid often wins, regardless of whether he or she is up to the job. I looked over at Tyler Briggs. At some point he was probably attractive and presentable. He might again be in the future. But today he was little more than a down-on-his-luck schlub, tossing down cheap tacos and beer before noon, and working through an enormous hangover after being unfaithful to his beautiful wife. Not the kind of stuff toward which an electorate gravitates.

"Tell me something. How did you come up with the idea of moving into politics?" I asked.

He looked down into his taco. "It's something I've kicked around over the years. Politicians are always looking for photo opps with coaches, I dealt with that when I was with the New York Jets. A little bit here in L.A. when I first started. Mayor Gonsalves was practically my best friend when the Chargers first arrived. Some of the city councilmen and county supervisors, too. Didn't seem like they were all that knowledgeable about public policy. It struck me their staff did most of the work, and they took in the big salaries and got all the fame. And whatever other goodies got dangled in front of them. Looked like they got a lot of perks. And it also looked like an easy job to me."

I watched him carefully as he dug into another taco. "By perks and goodies, do you mean bribes?"

"I wouldn't quite put it that way. But these guys live large. Lot of free meals, lot of boondoggles, private jets.

Investment opportunities just for directing resources toward a big donor. Lots of ways to do well without having to take an envelope stuffed with cash. That's passé."

"You've done some thinking on this," I commented.

"Haven't had much else to do this year. And look, it's not like I can go get a day job working for Google. You know, I tried to get something with a TV network, doing color commentary on NFL games, but no one would touch me. I feel like I've been blackballed. That means I've got to think out of the box. The more I talk to people about commercial real estate, the more they talk to me about needing to know how to grease the wheels of government. Meeting some of the people Hannah works with got me thinking more about it."

I picked up my taco and took another bite. The spicy beef and cheese seemed easier to swallow then Tyler Briggs's new career path, and it still didn't taste that great. I didn't know enough about politics to sense whether he would be any good at it, but lots of people have gotten elected with far fewer qualifications. I thought about Gail and her comments about maybe entering the political arena one day. She'd be good at it, I admitted, and I knew her well enough to know that she'd go into it for the right reasons. I looked at Tyler Briggs and did not get the same good feeling.

Briggs finished his last taco, crumpled his wrappers into a ball, and tossed them toward a garbage can. It missed by about six inches and landed on the ground. He looked over at me. "Ready to roll?"

I took a final sip of Coke and carried my trash to the

can, where I slammed dunked it in. I didn't bother to bend down and pick up Briggs's missed shot, and neither did he.

We cruised down Washington Boulevard, neither of us speaking. The rain had stopped, but the dark clouds still looked ominous. I turned left on Via Dolce and drove slowly for a few blocks into the Silver Strand. Off in the distance, I saw three black and white LAPD patrol cars parked in front of one of the lovely homes. The closer we got, the more I realized they were sitting in front of the Briggs's residence.

"That's your place, right?" I said.

Briggs, suddenly far more sober and alert than he had been over the past hour, stared intently at the scene. A couple of uniforms leaned against their cruisers talking amiably. That stopped when they saw our light blue Mercedes pull to a stop across the street. We got out and walked over to them. They met us halfway, and we stood in the street looking at each other.

"What's happened?" Briggs exclaimed. "What's wrong?"

"Take it easy, pal," one of them said. "Who are you?"

"I'm the guy who owns this house!" he said, practically shouting. "Is everything okay with my family?"

The two uniforms turned to look at each other. "I'll get Brown," one of them said, and walked into the house. Less than five seconds later, a burly, African-American man in his forties hustled outside. He was wearing a brown suit and he had a gold shield pinned to his belt. The big man looked familiar, and I was sure we had worked in the same division at one time, maybe Broadway, down by 77th Street. He approached us.

"One of you fellows Tyler Briggs?" he asked officiously.

"I am," Briggs said, starting to sound indignant. "Please tell me what's happened to my family."

"Your family's fine," he said evenly. "I wish I could the say the same for you."

"Huh?" he said.

"I'm Orlando Brown and I'm a detective for the City of Los Angeles. Turn around and put your hands on top of your head," he ordered.

"What the hell for?" Briggs said, his voice rising, his face wearing a picture of shock.

"You're under arrest for the murder of Colin Glasscock," he declared. "Now put those hands on top of your damn head. And don't say another word until I read you your rights."

Five

Hannah Briggs watched in stunned silence at the front door of her lovely home, as the police jammed her husband into a patrol car and drove off. The cruisers departed and I walked across the street to speak to her, although I didn't have any magic words to say, the verbal elixirs that might make her feel any better. There may have been worse things in life, but I could not imagine there would be many. Just like on Saturday, she still looked achingly pretty, an image that not even the searing edge of watching her husband be arrested and carted off to jail could remove. She didn't invite me inside, and I didn't bother to ask. I did, however, need to speak with her.

"I'm sorry," I began.

She blinked a few times. I thought she might tear up, but she didn't. "I can't even begin to comprehend any of this," she said.

I didn't bother to disagree. "You're not working this morning," I said, stating the obvious.

She shook her head, and the platinum blonde hair shook with it. "I just couldn't go in to work today. I knew I wouldn't be able to focus."

"What did Detective Brown say to you inside?"

"Detective Brown?"

"The African-American man. Big guy, wore a gold shield on his belt?"

"Oh. Yes. Just that he wanted to question Tyler about some things. The detective was vague. I told him I was with the City Attorney's office and I wanted to know what was going on. That didn't seem to faze him, I don't even know if he heard me. He was getting irritated that I didn't know where Ty was."

"Did you ever file a formal missing person's report?" I asked.

"Yes," she said. "I waited until Sunday morning, hoping beyond hope that Tyler would just stumble in. The police took the report, but it looks like you do your job better than they do theirs."

"Some of that involves being agile," I told her. "Plus, I can devote more time to cases."

"Where did you find him?"

I took a breath. "He was at the Alibi Room. On Washington," I said, choosing my words carefully.

"I know the place," she responded. "One of Tyler's haunts. Some name. Did Tyler say where he had been for three nights?"

"He wasn't in good shape," I said, soldiering through, as I told her some things but not others. Sometimes it helps if events unfold slowly in front of people, that way they can digest them easier. The shock of seeing her husband handcuffed and led away in a squad car was enough of a traumatic ordeal for now.

"He didn't look good," she agreed.

"You know, I'm not sure he even remembered everything. He had been drinking heavily, but it felt like there was something else involved. Is Tyler into anything stronger? Drugs?"

She shook her head. "No. Booze has always been his drug of choice, and it's mostly beer. He didn't tell you anything about what happened to him? I nearly fell over when that detective arrested him for murder. I've prosecuted a few homicides, but those were some really bad people. Hardened criminals. Nothing like Tyler. I'm just flabbergasted."

I considered this. When someone you love is accused of a heinous crime, the world changes, and it is a seismic shift. Things are no longer the way they were, and it was quite possible they might never be again. The reactions I saw were not unlike the stages of grief. Shock was the first thing that set in, followed by disbelief. Anger would come next. The question was who would Hannah Briggs be angry with. The LAPD made its share of mistakes, but initiating a homicide arrest was not something they took lightly. The cops arrested Tyler Briggs for a reason.

"Did the detective give you any idea of what evidence they had found?"

"No, but I'm going into the office this afternoon to try and find out."

"They won't let you near the case," I warned her. "You're the spouse. I can assure you, they'll be keeping you as far away from this as possible."

"I have to know," she said. "Look, I need you. You're good. You have to stay on this. I need to know what Tyler's involvement was in this. It's critical. I can't count on the police; they've already taken sides."

It was obvious they had, and it was obvious Hannah

Briggs needed outside help. The LAPD had landed on the decision Tyler had killed Colin Glasscock, the reasons for which had yet to be unveiled. The police had moved quickly, almost too quickly; it was inordinately likely they had uncovered highly incriminating evidence. They may have also felt Tyler Briggs was a flight risk.

"I can stay on this case," I said. "And I can probably find out some of what happened. Just to warn you, you may not be happy to learn more about it. That's just how these things go. But you're an attorney, so you obviously know you'll need counsel. Quickly. I'm sure you're aware the police are going to start grilling him the moment they get back to the station. They try to get an admission of guilt, and close the case fast. Raise their clearance rate and move on to something else. But you know that. You have to hire a good criminal lawyer and fast."

"I do know. And in a bizarre way, I'm fortunate. I've gotten to see quite a few criminal defense attorneys in court. Some are good, some aren't."

"Just like in any other profession," I pointed out. "And I'm sure Gail can provide a few more names if you need them."

She took a deep breath. "You know, when I saw Tyler's car and you two climbing out, my heart soared. I had been preparing for the worst. Then just seconds later, well, you know, everything fell apart. Everything changed in a heartbeat."

"It all came crashing down," I acknowledged. "Look, I have a few ideas of where I can begin investigating on my end. I won't get into details because they may or may not pan out. But I'll let you know how I'm progressing."

Hannah Briggs reached out and grabbed my arm, giving it a squeeze. I guess it was her way of expressing gratitude without saying anything, and it was possible she was not capable of saying anything more at the moment. I said goodbye and turned to walk back into the street when I realized I didn't have a car to take me anywhere, nor should I have been keeping Tyler's car keys. I did an about-face and sheepishly handed the Mercedes keys to Hannah, deciding it would be mildly inappropriate to ask to borrow their car, especially with no good way to bring it back.

After she closed the door, I pulled out my phone and tapped the Uber app. Shortly thereafter, a dark blue Acura pulled up. I climbed into the back seat. The driver, a young middle-Eastern man, well-dressed and smiling, greeted me with a big hello in a thick accent, and then reached over and turned the volume up on the stereo. It was fortunately a short ride back to my Pathfinder.

There was little to be gained by going back to the Alibi Room, but I went in nevertheless. I thanked Gene for calling me and passed him a fifty-dollar bill. He slipped it into his pocket and smiled. I asked him a few questions about Tyler Briggs, about the girl he picked up on Friday night, about whether the tacos on their bar menu were better than Tito's. But in the end, I didn't learn anything worth knowing. It was time to move on.

The Snuggle Inn was an oddly situated motel near the corner of Lincoln and Washington, two of the busiest thoroughfares on the Westside. There was a Costco across the street, along with a Starbucks and an In-N-Out Burger. There was a strip mall on the corner that had a check-cashing service, a nail salon, a 7-Eleven, and a bakery promoting Cronuts, an odd concoction that married the flakiness of a croissant with the sugary coating of a donut. It was the type of neighborhood that catered to locals. It was not where you'd expect a motel to be. But here it was.

I walked into the office and a thick-necked man in his late fifties looked up at me. He had medium-brown skin, an unshaven face, a crew cut, and thick forearms coming out of his short-sleeve shirt. He even looked a little sweaty, although that might well have been the raindrops that were still sprinkling intermittently outside.

"Hi there," I said.

"Can I help?" he asked, in an accent that made him sound as if he had just arrived from India. "Do you have reservation?"

"Nope, not looking for a room."

"Oh? What can I do for you then?"

I flashed my fake badge rather than hand him my business card. The LAPD might be here shortly, and I didn't think it would be wise to leave a trail of breadcrumbs implicating me in any way.

"I'm doing an investigation," I said and pulled out the photo of Tyler Briggs. "This guy look familiar?"

He gave a guffaw. "Oh, yes. Him I know. Checks in Friday for one night, no reservation, stays all weekend, and then just leaves this morning. I've got credit card, so we'll bill him for weekend. But it would have been kind if he had returned his room key. It is just common courtesy."

"Who did he check in with?" I asked.

He shrugged. "Some woman."

"What did she look like?"

"Blonde hair. Would not have guessed it to be wife. He was wearing wedding ring, not her. She seemed, how you say, uneasy? Maybe some couple that worked together, went for drink, decided to do more."

"You ever see the woman before last Friday?"

"Maybe yes. But you see, this is L.A. Lots of pretty blondes. You know."

"You rent rooms by the hour?" I asked.

He gave me a perturbed look, as if I had just insulted his sister. "We are not that kind of place. This isn't a ... how you say, no-tell motel. If you weren't police, I'd make you leave for that remark."

"Lucky me," I said, restraining myself from suggesting he go ahead and try to make me do anything.

"We run classy outfit here," he protested. "Get a lot of out-of-town guests."

"And some locals."

"Sure. Look, like I say, this is L.A. This a part of what we do. We don't judge our guests," he sniffed, and then announced with a small measure of pride, "we even get some celebrities in here."

I wasn't entirely surprised. The motel was next to Marina del Rey, and just down the road from Santa Monica. If a celebrity wanted an unlikely spot to go have a fling, this was it. No paparazzi, no security to speak of.

Just a room and a bed, an ice machine down the hall, and a 24-hour convenience store around the corner. One that sold liquor.

"Any celebrities I might know?" I asked.

"Sure. But I no say. I respect guests' privacy."

"Yeah, right," I said. "What else can you tell me about this couple that checked in on Friday? This is a criminal investigation and there's going to be more detectives coming by here, so maybe you should tell me what you know now."

The big man looked hard at me. "There's one thing that was funny," he said.

"What's that?"

"The man kept the *Do Not Disturb* sign up all weekend. The maid, she finally knocked yesterday afternoon, got no answer, so she opened the door. He was asleep by himself. Guess the blonde left, not sure why he wanted to spend the weekend sleeping, but people here are funny."

"Who was the maid?" I asked.

"Name's Teresa. She's doing up the rooms now. You can find her in the back. Say, what's your interest in all this? Guy do something wrong?"

I thought about this for a moment and shook my head. "We need to respect his privacy," I said, and walked out of the office, headed for the back of the motel. It was a cheap-looking place, but everything seemed neat and orderly and well-maintained. The exterior had been treated with a fresh coat of paint, the parking lot looked as if it had been blacktopped recently, and the trash bins were neat. Maybe this was a classy joint after all.

I found a young Hispanic woman wearing a light gray maid's uniform coming out of one of the rooms. She had the standard cleaning cart nearby, replete with sheets, blankets, Kleenex, and toiletries.

"Hello," I started.

"*Sí, señor*?"she answered.

"*Habla Inglés*?" I asked, depleting a large percentage of what little high school Spanish I still could recall.

"*Poquito*," she managed. "A little bit."

"All right," I responded. "You're Teresa?"

"*Sí, mi nombre es* Teresa Ortiz."

"Okay, Teresa. The man who left this morning. He was here all weekend. The one who left without checking out. Do you remember him?"

"*Sí, sí*," she said, nodding her head vigorously.

"What room number was he in?"

"Dieciocho."

I felt like I needed to pull up Google translate. "What is that in English?" I asked.

"I think ... eighteen?"

I flashed my fake badge. "Can you show me the room?"

Her eyes widened, and she paused for a moment. I wondered if she thought I was an immigration officer. It was common knowledge that Los Angeles had an above-average percentage of illegals, and their antennas were always out for the authorities.

"It's okay," I said, and held up my hand. "I'm not with ICE, and I'm not interested in you."

She still looked at me warily, rolled the matter over for a moment, and then led me down the hall. She opened the door to Room 18 with a swipe of her card, and we walked inside.

The room had been made up, and like most freshly cleaned hotel rooms, it looked immaculate. Cliff Roper's daughter, Honey, was working in management for the Disney hotels in Anaheim, and she once told me that hotel rooms were expected to look pristine to every guest. That it would appear as if no one had ever spent the night there before, that the bed should exude the feel of a brand-new, never-slept-in nook. The idea that hundreds of people had previously climbed into that very bed and performed an array of acts that went well beyond sleep was a fact to be disguised at all costs. And even this less-than-stately inn, situated in an unlikely section of an over-sexed city like L.A., had managed to achieve that lofty goal.

"Looks like you did a good job of cleaning," I observed, walking around the room a few times and not seeing anything out of the ordinary.

"*Gracias,*" she replied.

"Did the guest by any chance leave anything behind? Anything at all?"

A look of horror suddenly washed across her face. "*Sí.* They did."

"What?" I asked.

She licked her lips and led me back outside. We walked back down the hall and around a corner. She opened a door and pointed to a white, plastic garbage bag in the dumpster.

"*Aquí,*" she said.

"Would you mind removing it?" I sighed.

She hesitated, but then she put on a pair of gloves and pulled open the bag. Very carefully, she looked inside, moved her hand, and gently pulled an object out. It was a syringe.

"This was in the room?" I peered at her.

"*Sí.*"

"Okay. Here's what you need to do. Put that into a separate plastic bag, a small one. Make sure it's clean, and preferably new. Some other police officers may be here later. Give it to them. Okay?"

"*Sí.*"

"It's very important."

"*Sí.*"

I looked at her. "Did he leave anything else?"

She drew in a breath, thought for a long moment, and shook her head no.

*

When you're close to a Costco, you invariably stop in. It is like a magnet, grabbing your attention and tugging you toward the undersized parking lot, where you jockey for position to snare a vacant parking space. The fact that this was three in the afternoon on a Monday made no difference. Costco was always busy, and you simply gave thanks you didn't arrive on a Saturday afternoon, when it was *really* crowded.

I picked up a rotisserie chicken, along with over a hundred and eighty-five dollars worth of groceries I hadn't planned on buying. But when you walk into that high-roofed warehouse loaded with all sorts of apparent bargains, your mind stops functioning coherently. It was all I could do to not fill my cart to the point where it was overflowing. I purchased enough food to last quite a while, never stopping to wonder if all of it would fit into our refrigerator and cabinets. Sometimes you just have to wing it.

My arrival at home was met with the best part of every day, which is to say hearing Marcus yell "Daddy's here!" As he watched me lug a big carton of groceries into the kitchen, he caught my eye and asked the question he believed should prevail over all others.

"Did you get something for *me*?" he asked.

I smiled and said yes, tearing open an oversized container of colorful gummy bears. Seeing his wide eyes and bright smile was the unforeseen joy of being a dad, a prize I never anticipated. I simply fell into fatherhood, hapless and clueless, with no plan or idea for how to move forward. I read a few parenting books, but they really didn't give me much of a blueprint. I did not have a dad growing up, so most of my knowledge about fatherhood involved on-the-job training. Thankfully Gail came from a family of five, she was the oldest, and she had experience in the task of looking after kids. But a mom can only impart so much to a boy. A dad has a different role.

"How was your day?" I asked him as he carefully chewed a blue gummy. I bit into one also, and couldn't quite pinpoint the flavor. I read the package and the answer eventually became clear. Somewhere along the way, blue raspberry materialized in our society, odd in the sense that I never saw a raspberry that was any shade beside red or black.

"Okay," he said absently, and then he changed the subject. "Daddy, what am I getting for Christmas?"

I rolled my eyes and walked back into the kitchen. Our nanny was already unloading the groceries and putting them away as she gave me a smile and a hello. I tried to think of an answer for Marcus, and after letting it ping-pong around in my mind for a bit, I walked back into the living room to join him.

"Well?" he asked, looking up at me curiously.

"I guess you'll have to wait for Santa to come in a few days to find out," I said.

"Dillon Gelber says there's no such thing as Santa."

I looked at him. "Who's Dillon Gelber?"

"He's in my preschool class."

"Oh. Who do you think knows more – me or Dillon Gelber?" I asked, hoping he wouldn't get the right answer on that one.

"Well, you. But it doesn't make sense. Santa climbing down our chimney? He's too fat. And what about kids who live in houses without chimneys? And how does Santa get to everyone's house in one night? Everyone in the whole world?"

I looked down at the carpet. Questions like these were going to be inevitable with a bright, inquisitive child. "Marcus, Santa has a lot of helpers out there. It's not one Santa that makes it to everyone's house. There are a lot of Santas out there."

"Okay," he said after some processing, giving me a brief

respite of relief. I never imagined matching wits with a five-year-old could be this taxing.

"Good," I said.

"So, am I getting an Xbox for Christmas?" he asked.

I reached in and took another gummy bear. This one was green, and I couldn't quite figure out if the flavor of this one was apple, lime, or some odd multi-flavor combination someone dreamed up in a chemistry lab.

"We've talked about this, Marcus," I said, chewing carefully. "Mom and I think you're a little too young. We want your brain to develop more before you go get hooked on video games."

"But most of my friends have them," he pointed out.

"A lot of your friends have older siblings," I said, not reminding him that they also had parents who were more interested in appeasing their children, getting a built-in babysitter, and figuring they'd work out any issues caused by excess exposure to violence at some undetermined point later in life. L.A. was a burgeoning market for psychotherapists, and I sometimes wondered if one-half of L.A. was in treatment with the other half.

"So, because I don't have an older brother, I don't get to have an Xbox?"

"It's not that simple," I said. "Are you playing any of these video games at your friends' houses?"

"Um, yeah."

"Are they violent?"

"I don't know," he said, looking down.

"Marcus, when Mom and I feel you're old enough, we'll get you an Xbox. Until then, you'll have other toys to play with. And while I'm not thrilled to hear you've been playing these games at your friends' houses, I'm not going to do anything about it for now," I said, thinking a parent has only a limited amount of power over their child, even one who is five years old.

We spent some time playing Chinese checkers until Gail came home. She smiled at the bounty I procured at Costco, but mostly, I suspect, at the idea we wouldn't need to cook tonight. We split the rotisserie chicken, and I rubbed three potatoes with olive oil and speared them with a few pokes of a fork before putting them into the microwave. I threw a few large handfuls of cut lettuce into a bowl, splashed them with some Italian dressing, tossed the contents a few times, and *voila*, we had a fast and good dinner. As we cleaned up, Marcus wandered out of the room to play with Chewy, our Cocker Spaniel, who was more interested in scratching and ridding herself of the fleas she had somehow acquired. Once Marcus was out of earshot, I brought up the highlights of my day.

"So, I guess you heard about Tyler Briggs," I started.

"Yes," Gail said. "The police picked him up this afternoon."

"Actually, I picked him up. The police were just the ones who took him in for booking."

"Oh?" Gail looked at me. "How did that happen?"

"A sympathetic bartender followed up with me. Guess it sometimes helps to leave your business card. I also talked with Hannah. She wants me to stay on the case. She doesn't think Tyler did it."

"I understand," Gail said slowly. "She's the spouse."

"I also told her you'd pass along some suggestions on defense attorneys. I hope I didn't cross a line here."

Gail thought about this for a second. I loved watching her think, but I loved watching her, regardless. Her chestnut-brown hair, pulled back into a pony tail, her clear gray eyes, her bee-stung lips, they never failed to grab my attention.

"No, you didn't cross a line. She should know a few good ones, but I can provide some, too. I'm a firm believer that everyone should be represented well in court. Especially for a case involving a capital crime."

"Why do I sense some hesitation here?" I asked. "Am I wrong?"

Gail shook her head. "It's just some scuttlebutt I heard around the office. About this case. And I didn't hear it from the police, I heard it from a colleague. Someone knows a Glasscock staffer."

"What have you heard?"

"I've learned the police have some pretty concrete evidence."

'What's that?"

Gail smiled, and dried her hands on a towel. She put her arms around me and gave me a kiss. "You know, sweetie, there are some lines that I can't cross. Some things I'm not supposed to say in detail."

"I can keep a secret," I smiled, Burying my face in the nape of her neck. She started to wiggle but didn't withdraw from me.

"I've heard they found something near the scene. I don't know what. Just something that led them straight to

Tyler Briggs. There might be video too, but you know, it gets dark by 4:30 pm these days. I don't know how clear that would be. But there's something."

"I guess I should put my crackerjack investigating skills to work."

"I guess you should. The police have been wrong before. And I can't figure out the relationship between Tyler Briggs and Colin Glasscock."

"Neither is going to win any Mr. Popularity contests these days," I said. "Maybe that's it."

"I don't think so. Glasscock has been really unpopular since they instituted that road diet on Venice Boulevard. And Glasscock has also been rumored to be having an affair with someone."

"A politician cheating on his wife. Goodness, that never happens," I said. "Anyone you might suspect?"

"No, and I don't want to speculate. But do you remember the woman I introduced you to the other night, Emma Wick? Smart lady, I'm not sure that she'd be mixed up in Colin's private life, but I've learned not to rule anyone out. Still, she seems to know a lot and she can be chatty. Might be worth having another talk with her."

"Chatty? My favorite type of person to grill. You know, I didn't tell Hannah this, but her husband admitted to being with another woman himself this weekend, some one-night stand. Bizarre circumstances. He picked her up on a Friday night, slept through the weekend at a motel, and left on Monday morning, not realizing the weekend had slipped by."

"That doesn't sound good," Gail admitted. "If this is his

alibi, it's not a good one."

"So, what do *you* think?" I asked. "You've worked with Hannah. You've heard her talk about Tyler. She ever mention anything that might make you believe Tyler was capable of such an act?"

"Everyone's capable of murder," she said. "Put in the right situation."

"You know what I mean. In this particular instance."

"I'm not sure," she shook her head. "Just that her husband worked too much, and he had the maturity of a fifteen-year-old. Which I gather was his age when they met."

"Yeah, Florida. High school sweethearts. Went to college together."

"She's smart, I'll give her that. Good attorney. Maybe not the best taste in men."

"Uh-oh. Smart women, foolish choices?"

"Something along those lines."

"Hope that doesn't describe you," I said, continuing to smile and draw her closer.

"Not at all," she whispered in my ear, and hugged me tight. "Don't worry. You get into too many scuffles, but you've always been protective. I worry about you sometimes. But my choices regarding you? I have no regrets on that score, sweetie. In fact, I have none at all."

I admit that did make me feel a little better.

Six

The next morning remained cold, but at least the clouds were breaking up, the sun began to peek out, and there were patches of blue forming. It looked like it might be a nice day. I parked down the street from the Glasscock district offices and walked inside. The mood was quiet and somber, there was a minimum of activity, and it felt as if a dreary cloud was hanging over the office. Even the temperature in the office felt cool. I approached the receptionist and handed her my card. No sense flashing a fake ID to a city employee; they were the ones who would most likely insist on inspecting it assiduously, and asking the all-too-unnerving questions, which would be along the lines of why it looked blatantly illegitimate.

"Hi. I'd like to speak with Emma Wick, please."

The receptionist was a light-skinned African-American woman in her early thirties. She glanced at the card and then back up at me, before asking what this was regarding. I told her I was part of the homicide investigation, my tone brusque and demanding, the way an impatient LAPD detective would sound. She picked up the phone and pressed a button, talking quietly with the person on the other end. Even though I was just four feet away, I could barely hear a word she uttered. She replaced the receiver, got up, and told me to follow her.

We walked down a narrow hallway paved with soft blue carpeting, and she led me into a small office. Emma Wick was speaking rapidly into her phone, sitting behind a large oak-veneer desk that was scattered with black plastic letter trays, pencil cups overloaded with cheap pens, and a few dozen files sprawled in no particular order. She was still wearing the same black leather jacket, not surprising perhaps, since it was a little chilly in the office. A buxom woman, she was certainly attractive, although today her blonde hair was pinned up and she had on black framed glasses which served to make her look more professional. Under her jacket, she wore a red v-neck sweater that showed a hint of cleavage. I silently complimented myself on my keen observation skills. After a few seconds, I cleared my throat and she looked up before raising an index finger as she continued her conversation.

"Yes, we will be there. No, the work doesn't end. Yes, this was tragic, we're all in shock. Uh-huh. Sure."

She hung up the phone and gave me a curious look. "Aren't you Gail's husband? The private detective?"

"That's right," I said.

"You know, I've given my statement four times now. I'm not sure how much more I can help be."

"You never know. But I appreciate your taking a few minutes."

Emma Wick nodded her head rapidly, and pointed to a chair across from her. She shuffled a few papers on her desk, as if to let me know she had better things to do.

"I'm doing this as a favor to Gail," she told me. "I like her. She's nice."

"Yes, she is," I began. "So, I wonder if you can tell me a bit more about the councilman. I gather Colin was not real popular these days."

Emma Wick shook her head. "It depends upon on who you speak with. Colin was a visionary. He saw a world where people would get out of their cars. Take trains and buses. Bike locally. Walk more. He was very popular with people involved in our movement. He wanted an ideal world."

I let out a breath, not bothering to add that there were myriad definitions on what constituted an ideal world. People usually fell into two decidedly different camps, those who were perfectly happy keeping things the way they were, and those who wanted upheaval, so everything would change. In a different era, compromises could be forged, there would be some give and take, and each side got something they wanted. Those days were long gone. It was a zero-sum game now, a winner-take-all society. Making the slightest concessions was now tantamount to treasonous white-flag surrender.

"So, who might have had reason to take this type of action?" I asked.

She frowned. "I thought the police had a suspect in custody. That football coach. They were pretty confident they had their guy. They even found some evidence in the alley behind our office."

"What kind of evidence?"

"A baseball cap," she said. "Green. Had a big M on the front of it. I don't know a lot about sports, so I don't know what that was."

"It's the Miami Hurricanes, a college football team. Tyler Briggs played for them and coached there."

"I heard they had something else, too. Not sure exactly what that is. Just something I learned from our liaison at the Parker Center."

I nodded, interested. It made sense that a staffer at a city councilman's office had a mole within the LAPD brass. Sharing information was what made a bureaucracy hum, give a little to get a little. But it came at a price. Keeping secrets was becoming a lost art.

"There are some people who have doubts about this suspect," I said, thinking it might have just been myself and Hannah at this point. "We all want justice to prevail. Especially when it's a public figure like a city councilman. Any thoughts on who else might have been involved?"

She gave me an odd look. "Why?"

"There are some serious doubts about Tyler Briggs. What the motive could have been."

Emma Wick threw up her hands. "Who knows? There are a lot of people in the world who don't respect progress. Some people were angry about the traffic, some didn't want apartment buildings going up in their neighborhood. A few made threats. Colin even started carrying a handgun with him at times."

"Really?"

"Yes. Sad, isn't it?"

"Sure," I said."Do you know what type of gun?"

"No, sorry. I really don't know much about those sorts of things. I just know there are a lot of crazy people in this world. I don't know what Briggs's problem was."

"Whatever it was, murdering someone is a big jump," I pointed out.

"Yeah, I guess. I heard Briggs had some sort of an interest in politics. Maybe he wanted to move Colin out of his way. For Briggs's own selfish purposes."

"No guarantee Briggs would have won. Or that Colin's replacement, whoever he or she is, is going to think or act any differently."

"I don't know," she said. "There's a community meeting tomorrow night among some local homeowners. It's over at the Woodland School on Palms. These yahoos have been looking to cause trouble for a while now. They'd been talking about fielding a candidate to run against Colin next year."

"I heard the Deputy Mayor might be running for his seat," I mentioned.

"Neil Handler?" she exclaimed. "I just don't get that. He has no name recognition, there's no way he could have beaten Colin in this district. But I can't see Handler shooting Colin in his own office. Or having him shot. Whatever."

I looked at her carefully. "You think this might have been a planned hit?" I asked.

"No idea," she said, backtracking in a hurry. "I shouldn't have even brought it up."

"Don't even want to speculate? What if?"

"No," she said, turning back to some papers on her desk.

I rolled the idea of a planned hit around for a moment and let it go. There might be something to it, there might not be. But Emma Wick appeared to have shut down, and when someone shuts down, it takes a lot more effort than

I was ready to expend to get them to open up once more.

"Okay," I said, trying to move the conversation in another direction. "I've heard a few things. Was Colin involved with anyone? Romantically?"

"You mean besides his wife?" she sneered.

"Well, yes, now that you put it that way."

"Good heavens," she said, rolling her eyes. "Colin was a decent man, hard-working, loved the community, loved people. He was such a good public servant. The idea that you cops are dragging his good name through the mud makes me sick. Just sick."

I didn't bother to correct her that I was not a cop and that I was not dragging anyone's name through the mud, I was just exploring possibilities. Whoever shot Colin Glasscock had done this for a very specific reason, not that it was necessarily a good reason or a sane reason. Most people don't walk around with guns and they don't up and shoot a city councilman because traffic is making them late for work. And even if someone were unhinged enough to do so, the fact remained, traffic was not going to get any lighter because one disliked politician was now dead.

"Look, I apologize for having to put you through all of this. I'm sure it's painful. But were there any other incidents before this? Anything which might have led to what happened last weekend? I'm just exploring possibilities. Anything at all you can think of."

She shook her head and then froze. "Not here," she said suddenly. "But there was an incident at his home. It was a while ago. Six months, maybe. God, I hadn't even been thinking of that."

"What happened?"

"Someone tossed a rock through his front window. No note or anything attached to it. Just a large rock with the letter A painted on it in red. Happened in the middle of the night. Colin had video cameras set up, but you know those aren't always real good, especially when it's dark."

"Did he have any sense of who might have done it?" I asked.

"I'm sorry," she said. "Colin just shrugged it off, said it was the price of moving the world forward. He told us they also painted a red A on his front door with a circle around it. He said that's the Anarchist logo. In his opinion, it was at best, a prank, maybe from a neighborhood kid."

"Were there any threats?"

"There are always threats," she said with a dismissive wave of her hand. "Someone began sending Colin nasty notes at his home. He gave them to the LAPD, but I don't think they ever followed up on it or even took it seriously. They said the people who make threats are doing just that."

I agreed. The real threats come from the people who didn't tip their hand. Those who made threats simply wanted to create a climate of fear, but they rarely followed up with any action. And in today's internet-connected world, getting access to someone's home address was simple, especially if the person had any real estate. Property ownership was a matter of public record, and if you knew where to look, you could find out where almost anyone lived. Public figures were often able to disguise their home address by using a business office, but all it took was one indiscreet neighbor and everyone from TMZ to a shut-in living in their mother's basement could pinpoint where the person lived, and even know when they were home.

I thanked Emma Wick for her time, and she didn't bother to tell me I was welcome. I walked out into the bright, cold morning, and decided I needed a caffeine jolt. There was a Starbucks a few blocks away where I could also sit and plan my next move. There was always a Starbucks a few blocks away.

Deflecting the barista's recommendation of an ungodly concoction called a Blonde Roast, a curious amalgamation of under-roasted coffee beans I didn't even want to imagine, much less drink, I went instead, with a *grande* cup of the Christmas Blend. Aside from watching Marcus gleefully open his presents last year, I thought this was the single best reason to have Christmas. The Christmas Blend was dark and rich, with a nice bite. I joked with Gail that there was probably a third reason for Christmas lurking somewhere, but she failed to see the humor.

I placed my coffee order and looked down my nose at the nasty remnants lining the pastry shelf, unappetizing leftovers from the morning rush. Instead, I bought a pack of chocolate-covered graham crackers and ate them with my coffee as I sat in a corner working my iPad. I quickly found Colin Glasscock's address on Mar Vista Hill, a five-bedroom home located on a block called, of all things, Indianapolis Street.

I clicked through the internet for anything remotely

related to suspicious chatter about Colin Glasscock. I found a treasure trove of articles describing his vision, his goals, his election campaign from a few years ago, all standard, innocuous stuff. I discovered a few articles that focused on the unhappy residents of his district, but one could always find those stories associated with any politician these days. Facebook had a number of pages set up to both support and denigrate Glasscock, including the homeowner group Emma Wick talked about. That one discussed plans to unseat the councilman. It detailed a laundry list of scurrilous activities, the most salient being his odd dream of turning major thoroughfares into parks and eliminating L.A. car travel as we knew it. The ringleader was a man named Roy Woolley, who owned a coffee house along Venice Boulevard I had passed it by hundreds of times, but with an endless number of Starbucks available, I never saw the need to stop there.

After finishing the last drop of my Christmas Blend, I drove up to the address on Indianapolis Street. This was an odd name for a street in L.A., except I now recalled that in Santa Monica I once lived between Montana and Idaho streets, neither of which could claim much of a relationship with Southern California, except those were states where a surprising number of Angelenos fled to when they retired. Colin Glasscock's home was a modern, two-story glass-and-steel structure that looked like it had been remodeled recently. It was a big box of a residence, and the front yard offered a sweeping panoramic view of the L.A. basin. On a clear day this might have been a glorious vista, but there were still enough clouds in the distance to make today's view somewhat limited.

I decided not to bother Glasscock's family. Whatever the motivation for Colin Glasscock's demise, his family did not deserve yet one more visit from an investigator, especially while they were obviously still in mourning. There was no one out and about in this quiet, leafy neighborhood, so I walked down the street and began ringing doorbells. The first few I tried did not yield any results; either the people were at work, out shopping, or not answering the door. I wondered if I looked too much like a realtor, the type who would waste their time trying to convince them to put their house on the market. Finally, I hit pay dirt.

The first sound I heard after the standard ding-dong was the immediate high-pitched yapping of a small but persistent dog. When I was with the LAPD and responding to burglaries, most of which had been committed hours earlier and with the thief long gone, I often gave homeowners some advice. Video cameras were not always good at capturing images, and even if they did provide clarity, the thieves often disappeared quickly into the wind. Burglar alarms were fairly easy to disable if a robber knew what they were doing. The best deterrent to a break-in was a vocal dog, and the most vocal canines were often the smallest ones. Thieves liked to get in and out quickly and quietly, grab whatever cash and jewelry they could, and move on. Barking dogs drew the attention of any passersby, and they augmented this with the occasional habit of biting the intruder. Neighborhoods often got hit with a rash of burglaries at once, after which many people got dogs, and the robbers quickly pivoted to other areas. Dogs are often called man's best friend, but they are also known as a burglar's worst nightmare.

As I stood outside the pleasant-looking suburban home on Indianapolis, I heard a lengthy discussion between the homeowner and their dog, a discourse where the owner admonished their pet for not being a good listener. The lecture lasted a good twenty seconds before I finally heard the slow pitter-patter of footsteps and the door opened. A seventyish woman in a red robe peered out from the door, bent over, grabbing the collar of a very small white dog.

"Can I help you?" she asked, as she struggled with her pet.

I flashed my fake badge. "Don't mean to bother you, but I'm doing an investigation into what happened this past weekend. Councilman Glasscock. Wondering if I could speak with you."

"Oh," she managed, "I've already spoken with the police about that."

"It should only take a few minutes," I insisted. "It's important."

"Oh. All right. One moment," she said, and dragged her dog, which looked like a Lhasa Apso, a few feet away, where she attached a leash. The dog, still straining to get a closer look at me, didn't seem to notice the restraint. The woman walked back over to me, leash in hand.

"Any thoughts on what happened to Colin Glasscock? Anything at all?" I began, moving things along quicker than I otherwise might, because the pull of an anxious dog might make this a brief interview.

"Not really. We're all shocked. He was such a nice man."

"Did everyone in the neighborhood like him?" I asked.

"Oh. Well, I suppose not everyone. There are the usual malcontents that didn't like Colin's politics. Called him a liberal snowflake and accused him of wasting their precious tax dollars. But I guess that happens to all civic leaders."

"Ah, yes," I said, thinking about Gail and the public lumps she'd be taking if she ever decided to enter the roughhewn octagon of politics. "How about around here? Were there any serious problems with neighbors?"

"We always have problems with certain neighbors. You know. There's a few on every block."

"Oh?"

"Yes, well, the owners of the house on the other side of Colin's home. They filed a lawsuit against him a couple of years ago. When Colin was remodeling."

"Why?"

"Colin added a second story. The Bellow family said it blocked their view. Hurt their property value. They were really angry. There were a few screaming matches when the neighbors figured out what Colin was doing. The initial permits didn't say anything about an upper floor."

"I take it Colin won the lawsuit," I said, looking up at his two-story home.

The woman nodded in agreement. "Pretty obvious. They say you can't fight city hall. It's even tougher to fight a city councilman. Especially when they want approval for a personal project."

I paused for a moment. “Did this Bellow family stay in their house?”

“They did. Still there. Still ticked at Colin.”

“Ticked enough to take a violent step like what happened this weekend?” I asked, looking at her cautiously.

“I don’t know,” she said, pondering the thought. “You wouldn’t think. But hey, look, you mess with people’s property values, you never know what they might do.”

*

The Bellows were not at home, and neither were most of the residents of this idyllic bedroom community. I left a message with Juan Saavedra at the Purdue Division, but didn’t expect a call back. I wondered what other evidence they had that linked Tyler Briggs to the murder. I thought about eating lunch but it was only 10:30 am. Instead, I decided traffic had softened enough on the 10 Freeway to risk taking a drive down to USC. I hadn’t heard from Cliff Roper since Sunday, which only meant he’d be calling soon, chastising me for not working hard enough for him, demanding an update, if not a resolution to his problem. Time to begin working on my other case.

Hobart Street is tucked into the pocket that straddles the border between USC’s lovely new extended campus and a gritty, inner-city neighborhood. The residents of the two communities differ as much as one could imagine. The student body, who inhabit the bulk of the off-campus housing north of campus, often came from wealthy or at least comfortable backgrounds. The people who lived in the area north of Adams and east of Vermont made up the low end of the economic totem pole, were mostly people of color, and mostly people who had a limited supply of money. If they had more, they'd live somewhere else.

The house that Cliff Roper directed me to was a ramshackle place, a dilapidated Craftsman home, that might have been stately a hundred years ago, but had now fallen into disrepair. The front yard was mostly a patch of dirt. This was the type of property that an elderly person who didn't have sufficient means might live in, not wanting to move after many decades of staying in one place, but unable to fix it up. It was also the type of house a group of college students might fall into. Big, roomy, relatively affordable, and the landlord would likely shrug off any smashed windows or unhinged doors that might come with a group of post-pubescent animals living on their own for the first time. That the occupants of this house were football players made that outcome even more likely.

I knocked on the door and waited a long minute before hearing any signs of life inside. There were cars in the driveway, but that meant nothing; the students could have been in class, or in the library or out getting coffee. The door finally swung open, and a sleepy looking twenty-one-year-old opened the door. He was not a typical twenty-one-year-old though, something his 6'4" frame and 350 lb girth quickly communicated. He blinked a few times before recognition set in.

"Hey!" he said, and stifled a yawn. "I don't believe what

I'm seeing!"

"Me, neither," I smiled. "Incredibly, you seemed to have put on a few pounds."

"Coach Burnside," he shook his head. "Always with the jabs."

"Always," I agreed. "So, are you going to keep me standing on your doorstep Fili, or do I get an invite inside?"

"In," he said, moving his enormous body aside for me to pass by.

Fili Snuka was a Samoan kid I had helped recruit out of nearby Lomita, a blue-collar suburb in the nearby South Bay. Fili got injured on the first day of fall practice his freshman year, tore up his knee and sat out the season. That happened to be my last season in coaching, but I still followed his career. He rehabbed from the injury and went on to star for the next two years, playing defensive tackle. He always struck me as mean as a junkyard dog on the football field, but sweet as pie off of it.

"How's the knee holding up?" I asked.

"Good as new," he smiled. "No problems."

"You got lucky," I told him, tossing a crumpled can of Bud Light off of a gray vinyl couch and gingerly sitting down. "I got the same injury right after my senior year. They didn't have the procedures back then to fix it quickly. You were up and getting strong again within a month."

"I know. Life must have been tough way back in your day."

I gave Fili a playful punch on the shoulder. I don't think he felt it, but my knuckles started to tingle a bit.

"So, look," I said. "You know I have a new career now. Private investigator."

"Yeah," he laughed. "I heard. That's so cool."

"It has its moments."

"Okay. What are you investigating?"

"Well," I said slowly, looking across a living room filled with a hodge-podge of magazines, dirty sweatshirts, footballs, and four cases of Gatorade stacked up. A 60" flat screen was hung on the wall. "I'm actually looking into you guys. The incident."

"Oh," he replied, leaning back as his face grew serious. "Yeah. I guess about what happened here. That guy who broke in."

"Tell me about it."

"Not much to tell. Me and a couple of the guys came home from practice and we hear a weird noise in Patrick's room. So we go in there. We see some dude trying to crawl out the window, we grab him by the belt and yank him back in. We pin him down and see he's got a bag with a bunch of our stuff in it. Laptops, a Blu-Ray player, couple of rings. Guy had Patrick's ring from winning the state championship when he was in high school. We searched his pockets and he had some cash. We took that back, too."

"Was it yours?"

"Could have been," he shrugged.

I didn't like hearing that. Cash was something you could rarely pin on a burglary suspect. There was no good way to prove the money didn't belong to the burglar. The irony here was that removing the money from the burglar's pockets could be construed as a felony as well.

"And what happened next? I take it you didn't call 9-1-1."

"Nope. We have our own rules for thieves."

"Your own rules?" I asked, eyebrows raised.

"Kind of. Somebody takes something of ours, we take something of theirs. And then a little more, you know. Just to show them crime don't pay."

"Uh, where did you get this, Fili? Doesn't sound like any Samoan law I've ever heard of. Or anyone else's law, either."

"Rule of the house," he said. "We sort of made it up as we went."

I rolled my eyes. "Go on."

"That's pretty much it. We roughed him up a little and then threw him into the street."

"Roughed him up a little? How little?"

"Smacked him around. Hey, Coach B, you're not going to the police with this? You haven't turned into a rat, have you?"

I shook my head in disbelief. "No, Fili. I'm not going to the police. I'm still part of the Trojan family. You know the saying, you're a Bruin for four years and a Trojan for life. But that's not why. The cops wouldn't take my word over the word of five USC football players who have friends in high places. And I understand the police have talked to you."

"Yeah, that dope went to the cops. At first they laughed it off, a burglary suspect claiming assault. But then he went to a reporter. The media posted something, but it got buried quick. You're right about friends in high places. The police came by and took a report, though."

"And you told them ... ?"

"Pretty much what I told you. Except for the rule of the house."

"And when they asked how the guy got assaulted?"

Fili shrugged again. "We said he started fighting with us once we caught him. We were just defending ourselves, trying to get our stuff back. Hey why is this a big deal to you?"

"My client," I said, "is a high-profile agent. He thinks the NFL may get wind of this."

"Shit," Fili said.

His face started looking concerned, and he had every right to be nervous. The league has a different set of rules than the rest of the world. And there are no legal processes to go through, no opportunities for a well-connected SC alum to help fix things. The league is judge, jury, and executioner. If a player gets suspended, they can appeal the decision, but unfortunately, in the NFL, the people ruling on appeals are the same ones handing down the initial punishment. It's not fair, but the league never implied it was.

"The NFL is tired of players getting into trouble. They want the players to have a better image, that the teams aren't just employing a bunch of thugs."

"That's bad," he said. "I'm planning to go pro after the Rose Bowl. Trying to get things lined up."

I looked at him. "You're technically a redshirt sophomore. You've got two more years of eligibility. You can leave school now, but it's not always the best plan. Even if nothing comes of these allegations, you may have a tough road to go down. If you're not a high draft pick, pro teams aren't going to give you a long look."

Fili nodded. "Yeah. But my parents could use the money. Dad's been sick. Out of work for a while. My uncle's a paralegal, he's going to represent me."

"Why your uncle?" I asked.

"Don't know anyone else. But he says he knows all about contracts and stuff. Good to keep it in the family. He's got my best interests at heart."

I didn't want to tell Fili that family was the worst possible representation he could have, short of hiring a rapper to be his agent. There have been countless stories of kids being swindled by family members who come off as well-meaning, but had their own interests lurking beneath the surface. In too many cases, the player is seen as a cash machine for someone looking to take advantage of an unsuspecting kid, barely out of his teens. And while there are some well-meaning family members who sincerely want what's best for the kid, they're not professional sports agents. They often get swamped by the process, negotiating bad deals, or not prepping the player for what's in store when he's evaluated at the Combine, or especially the rigors of an NFL training camp.

"Okay. Look, you need to think this through. Not just about whether you should go pro, but everything. Does your uncle have a plan for you? Does he have an idea when you'll probably be drafted? How much money you should ask for up front, guaranteed money, signing bonuses. Not to mention where you might fit in best, and how to present yourself when teams interview you. All of that is bigger than you might imagine. If that's even what you should be doing now."

"I don't know. It seems as if you can make money, you might as well do it. Football careers are short."

"Yeah, I know," I said. "All too well. What about Patrick? Is he going pro?"

"Maybe. He's getting a lot of pressure from agents. They say this is the year for quarterbacks. Lots of teams are looking for good young talent right now. Patrick's one of the best. Maybe even the best player overall. If he waits a year, he might miss out on all the gold."

"You think he's ready? You play with him every day in practice."

"Not sure," Fili admitted. "There are times he can pull rabbits out of a hat. Make plays when nothing's there. He's got this gift, man. He can create stuff on the fly. Know what I mean?"

I knew, indeed. Patrick could quickly process the whole scene of constantly moving pieces and fit things together in an instant. He could find the one open receiver on a crowded field. And he had the physical gifts to scramble around until the precise moment he needed to release the ball. On top of that, he could usually put the ball in a receiver's hands without breaking their stride.

"I get the feeling there's a 'but' that's going to start your next sentence," I said.

"Uh-huh," he said. "But his head may not be in the game."

"Why not?"

"He doesn't love football. I mean, it's not like he hates it or anything. To him it's just something fun to do. There are times, though, when I think he'd rather be surfing or snowboarding or something else. That seems to be his passion. Too bad. Those sports don't pay much."

"What do you think Patrick's going to do?"

"Don't know. Patrick says he'll decide after the Rose Bowl. Talk it over with his family. But it's not like they have any more insight. His dad's a carpenter and his mom's an artist. They don't know a lot about the game. I think they're a little shocked at all the attention he's been getting. He was on the cover of *Sports Illustrated* last month. When you're a first-year starter, that's a huge deal. Heck, it's a huge deal for anyone."

"Is Patrick here now? Can I talk to him."

"Nah. He's probably in class. Or with his girlfriend. He spends a lot of his time with her."

"Okay," I said, and then I asked him the bulls-eye question. "What was Patrick's involvement in that incident here?"

Fili paused for a moment. "Like I told the cops. We were all here. Just protecting what's ours."

Seven

I checked my voice mail as I walked back to my Pathfinder. There was a brief message from Cliff Roper, who managed to be both demanding and condescending in the five seconds it took him to admonish me for not solving his problem, and for taking my sweet time about giving him an update. Since I didn't have anything to tell him, I didn't bother calling him back. Another call had come in from a number I didn't recognize, but the prefix told me it was from El Segundo. It turned out to be Anthony Riddleman of the Chargers, returning my call. I phoned him right back and he agreed to meet for lunch. When your team has missed the playoffs and lost more games than it's won, no one cares if you take an hour or two off in the middle of the day. Especially if it's on what is supposedly your day off.

In the NFL there are some basic scheduling rules. The team stays in a hotel on Saturday night, even if the Sunday game is at home. On Monday, the team comes in for meetings and players get treatment for injuries, which most of them have, especially by the tail end of the season. Tuesday is the day off, Wednesday and Thursday are for breaking down game film, and engaging in full scrimmages. Friday and Saturday are lighter practices. The only exception for this is that coaches normally don't take Tuesdays off. Big-time coaching is a 24-7 business, and it's not for everyone. I continued to feel good that I hadn't followed Johnny Cleary to Chicago to help him coach the Bears.

I met Anthony Riddleman at Paul Martin's, an elegant restaurant along Rosecrans in the South Bay. This was a redeveloped corridor of El Segundo that was far removed from where the Chargers' middle school practice field stood. A long strip of commercial real estate had been constructed a few years ago, with business parks and twenty-story office buildings cutting through a swath of what once was a sleepy venue. Before all the development, most people just used Rosecrans to navigate into the much nicer Manhattan Beach. Along Rosecrans, several cheap, run-down strip malls had now evolved into plush, upscale strip malls. The liquor stores, barbers and check cashing services were all gone, replaced by high-end bagel shops, trendy grocery stores, and an Old Navy.

The hostess led me to Anthony Riddleman's table, where he was already seated and working his iPhone. He motioned me to sit and I sat. After a few wordless minutes, he completed whatever important text he was composing and looked up.

"You must be Burnside," he said, reaching over and shaking my hand.

"I am, indeed. Thanks for meeting me."

"No problem. Hannah told me she had hired you this weekend when Tyler didn't make it home. Terrible thing. I couldn't have been more shocked when the police arrested him. Just stunning. Never in a million years could I have ever thought something like this would happen."

Anthony Riddleman was in his mid-thirties, slim, with

a receding blond hairline. He wore a blue golf shirt and shorts, even though it was barely 55 degrees outside. This was not uncommon for people who grew up in warm-weather climates. Even when the temperature plummeted, there was almost a sense of stubborn denial. Whether they were in Florida or California, their attire fit what the climate ought to be, not necessarily what it was.

"You've known Tyler since Miami," I started.

"Yeah, college. We were teammates, technically competing for the same job, but for backup QB. Miami was loaded a few years ago. Tyler and I were both good quarterbacks, but neither of us was a great QB. That's what it took to be a starter there. At least back in the day."

"You guys became friends."

"More like drinking buddies," he laughed. "I used to tell Ty we had the greatest gig in the world. Free tuition, full ride, get to play football with our friends every day during the fall, and we had the best seats in the house to watch big-time college games. But he didn't take sitting on the bench very well."

"And you did?" I asked a little suspiciously. At elite programs like Miami, the coaches liked to recruit players who lived to compete. Coaches want to create an atmosphere where everyone is pushed toward their limit, to give a full-throttle performance, knowing if they slack off there's a guy right behind them on the depth chart who is more than eager to move up.

"Look, I was a pretty good high school quarterback. Grew up in Boca. Great place, South Florida. I got offered by the U. Dream come true, right? But the first day of practice, I saw this other QB and knew I couldn't play at his level. Our starter, Chris Lacava, he could throw the ball farther than I could, and it got there a half-second faster."

"Tough to go through that. But you had to know, even back then, there's more to playing quarterback than just arm strength."

"Sure. But Chris had the whole package: big arm, accuracy, speed. Was a bright guy, too. I could have transferred to a smaller school and played, but hey, I had a good deal at Miami. And I made the most of it. I studied Chris hard, saw what it took to be great. Best way to become a future coach is to watch good players, break down a lot of film, carry the clipboard during games, and see how the coaches call what plays when."

"That what Tyler did, too?" I asked.

"Eventually. He was frustrated at first. Thought he should have gotten more of a shot at starting. Couldn't see the bigger picture, but he's a hyper-competitive guy. Likes to win at everything. He'd even beat his daughter at tiddlywinks. I had to remind him you're supposed to let your kids win when they're little."

I absently looked across the restaurant. What Anthony described was not uncommon with athletes. Coaches in youth leagues would channel their inner Vince Lombardi and teach kids that awful bromide, that winning isn't everything, it's the only thing. I once had a middle school coach tell me that losing was worse than death because you had to live with being a loser. There were clearly some very ignorant people involved in youth coaching, and it took years for me to unlearn some of their more grotesque lessons.

"And what happened with Tyler?" I asked. "I'm aware of the drinking, but you know the reality, coaching is a pressure cooker and a lot of coaches drink. And there are high-functioning alcoholics in many fields. Tyler was only with the Chargers for one season. Most coaches get at least a couple of years to prove themselves."

"Do you know much about science?" he asked. "Study it in college?"

I shook my head. I was much more interested in subjects like Psychology and English. My knowledge of real science was sorely limited, topping out when I was fifteen, getting the adolescent thrill of slipping a pack of Mentos into a two-liter bottle of Coke, stepping back, and watching it explode. For me, science didn't get any better than that.

"Not really," I admitted. "Why?"

"Pretty simple law of physics. For every action there's a reaction. It's like gravity. What goes up must come down. What goes up fast, comes down faster."

"You're talking about Tyler's career trajectory."

"Yup," he said. "The boy wonder of coaching football. He was 29 when he became the youngest coach in NFL history. Pretty sure he was the youngest coach to get fired, too."

"High risk, high reward. But most people only think about the thrill of victory, not picking up the pieces if you fail," I said, and then I thought of something. "How come that didn't happen to you? You're still there."

Riddleman smiled. "I pace myself. I know my limitations. I want to be a head coach one day, but I want to be ready for it. I also didn't have the opportunities Tyler had. Helped that his father was a coach and paved the way. But Tyler jumped at every opportunity, and he moved up the coaching ladder fast. Too fast. He wasn't ready to handle the intangibles. Like coaching NFL players who were actually older than he was. And they knew more about how to play their position. That's a tough one. Tyler struggled having to coach older players."

"Okay. You're a young coach. How do you do work effectively with grizzled veterans?" I asked.

"I don't try and be their superior, I let the guys know I'm there to help them. It's a little manipulative, but it works. Look, I'm two years older than our starting quarterback, so I'm not about to tell Ray Streams how to throw a football. But I can point out tendencies he has, like sometimes he locks onto a cornerback for a split second too long when he's backpedaling. Telegraphs where the play's going. I treat Ray as an equal, and he responds to it. Tyler had to act like the big boss. Didn't fly."

"I can imagine."

"Yeah. Tyler knows football inside and out. Great play-caller. Knows how to use guys, insert what player at what time, knows what buttons he has to press to get the most out of them. You know. Some guys need a pat on the head, others need a kick in the tail. He could practically figure out a guy by just looking at him."

"That's probably why he moved up fast," I observed.

"Big reason. But you know how a person's biggest strength can be their biggest weakness? Tyler's act was fake as hell. The guys figured out when Tyler was playing them and they shut down. After a while, the pats on the head were ignored as false flattery, and the kicks in the tail were answered with belligerence. I've been with him for a while. It took the guys on the Jets a couple of years to catch on. But once they did, the whole league knew about it. Guys talk. With the Chargers, things went off the rails in a hurry. Players can sense when a coach is snowing them, they are street-smart beyond anything you can imagine. Maybe they're not brain surgeons, but they can sniff out BS a mile away. It was okay when we won some games in the beginning. But you know losing breeds a nasty culture. And when we started losing last year, the team took a nose dive quick and never recovered."

At that point, a pretty, redheaded waitress came by and asked if we were ready to order. Riddleman immediately ordered a steak, baked potato, and two iced teas, both for himself. I asked the waitress what she recommended, and she told me the fish tacos were the best she'd ever had. That was good enough for me, along with a Coke. Just one.

"Let me ask you about what happened with Tyler this week," I said.

"The homicide charge."

"Yeah."

Anthony Riddleman shook his head emphatically. "No way in hell. Tyler is a lot of things, some of it good, some of it bad. But that makes no sense. Cold-blooded murder?

Of a politician? Can't imagine it."

"Did Tyler have a temper?"

"We all do, man. Tough to deal with the pressure without blowing a fuse once in a while. Yeah, I've seen Tyler go off on a few people."

"Anyone in particular?" I asked.

He shook his head. "Most of these flare-ups just blow over. Guys learn to let things go."

"Anything else? On a personal level? Hannah asked me to investigate, she doesn't believe Tyler's guilty, so anything you can share with me could be crucial."

Anthony Riddleman sat back and stared up at the ceiling. I couldn't figure out if he was searching his mind for something or simply trying to decide if he should tell me what he knew. I figured it was the latter.

"Look," I continued. "Tyler's facing life imprisonment and possibly the death penalty. Now's not the time to hold back. Even if it's unpleasant. Even if it's something you ordinarily wouldn't tell anyone. Remember I'm not the police, and I'm technically on Tyler's side. Sometimes the smallest detail turns out to be important."

"All right," he finally said. "But you can't share it with Hannah."

"Okay."

"Tyler was cheating on her."

I stared at him. This wasn't big news. "I got that impression," I said slowly, knowing it was more than an impression since Tyler admitted it to me after his tongue got lubricated with the help of a few craft beers at eleven in the morning yesterday.

Riddleman looked down at the table. "I've known them both for a long time, they've had an up-and-down relationship. Thought it might have been righted when they had Madison. But I've seen normal people do crazy stuff. I told Tyler he was nuts for stepping out on her. But some guys do what they're gonna do."

I paused and looked at him, and then something suddenly occurred to me. "You think Hannah might have been cheating on him as well?"

He shrugged. "Who knows, man. But I can't see how that would lead to anyone getting killed. I mean why would it?"

Our food arrived and we ate mostly in silence. I tried to process this, but mostly got nowhere. I changed the conversation to football, always an easier topic for most men. I reminded Anthony I had been a former coach, which led to the usual gossip of who was about to be fired, which coach was likely going where next season, and a bit of talk about how hard it was to move to L.A. My lunch was half the size of Riddleman's and I probably finished it in a quarter the time. I asked about talking with Ray Streams, not because I thought the quarterback would know anything about the murder, but because I was running out of people to talk with. The check arrived and I picked it up, got a receipt in case Hannah asked, which I doubted she would. Anthony thanked me for lunch, said he had a game plan to install for next week's season finale for the Chargers, and departed.

I had logged a full day already and it was only a little after 2:00 pm. I decided to head back to the office and think about whether anything I learned today was logical, useful, or might somehow congeal into a plausible scenario. This only meant that right now I had no decent leads to explore, no one else to speak with, and virtually nothing to go on.

The afternoon drive on the 405 jammed up just past the Marina Freeway, and I exited at Venice and took Sepulveda the rest of the way. I drove past Babe's and wondered if the same cast of characters were getting an early start this afternoon. I drove past Pico and just sneaked through the intersection when the light turned yellow. And that's when it happened, the type of incendiary event that takes you by surprise, the way things tend to go on a lazy afternoon when you least expect it.

It turns out I wasn't the only one who was slipping through the yellow light at Pico, doing so at a speed just a hair beyond what the law allowed. Another car behind me did the same. But then we ran into a wall of stalled traffic and I needed to jam on my brakes in a hurry. The car behind me did the same, only his tires screeched and he needed to swerve to avoid rear-ending me. He hit his horn, which for years had been a very un-L.A. thing to do, but now it was *de rigueur*. Honking one's car horn was becoming more and more socially acceptable as L.A. became more and more like New York: crowded, frustrated, and angry. I glanced at the wildly gesticulating driver in my rear view mirror and looked away. Nothing good comes from making a return gesture, especially the middle-finger salute, another move that's become commonplace, and can signify a reason to declare all-out war.

The other car, a five-year-old black Audi with a scratch along the right door, pulled alongside me, and I could see a couple inside arguing with each other. The man was driving, and he lowered the passenger window and yelled an invective past her and at me. I looked at him, smiled, and waved. Sometimes that diffuses things. Sometimes it does not.

The Audi shot past my Pathfinder, swerved in front of me, and then jerked to a stop. The man got out and started walking toward me in a menacing manner. He had a shaved head and looked stout, the type of stout that came from lots of time at the gym. He wore a black North Face jacket, zipped partway up his chest.

"Hey, what the hell's the matter with you?!" he screamed. "You could've messed up my ride!"

I looked at him and said nothing. There was absolutely no benefit to getting out of my Pathfinder and engaging him. He was standing and I was sitting. He was already in the street and I would need to emerge from my vehicle. He would have the freedom to punch and kick at any angle, and I would have no defense other than my driver's side door, which was not much of a defense. I said nothing and kept a placid expression on my face, which most likely served to embolden him further.

"Come on!" he yelled. "Get out of there, you pussy! I'll kick your ass!"

The man punched my window, not hard enough to shatter it, but enough to heighten my senses. I put my hand on the .357 sitting snugly in my ankle holster, in the event the window did indeed break. But for me, carrying a gun was often a way to diffuse trouble, not ratchet it up. I briefly thought of brandishing my weapon, but when someone is enraged, that might or might not calm them down. It might even exacerbate the situation. For a brief moment, I thought Gail might be proud of the restraint I was showing.

"Fucking faggot!" he screamed, as he finally walked away and climbed back into his Audi. But instead of leaving, he put his car in reverse and backed it into mine. Not hard, but enough to give a jolt. Whatever restraint I had been able to display had now vanished. We both jumped out of our vehicles at the same time and moved toward each other.

"Finally decided to be a man, huh?" he yelled.

"I could be a gorilla like you, but I don't think I could get that stupid," I said, balling my hands into fists, and glancing carefully around to make sure there weren't any cars whizzing by closely.

"Oh, you're gonna get it," he sneered, with the slightest hint of a smile. He took a few steps forward and threw an overhand right, a haymaker designed to be a one-punch knockout. I knew it was coming and side-stepped the punch, but it still grazed the side of my head. I recovered enough to drive my left fist into his solar plexus. He doubled over in pain and I hit him with a hard right to the nose. He yelped in pain and instinctively reached up to his face.

I extended my arms and grabbed his jacket from behind his shoulders. Yanking it forward, I managed to pull half of the jacket over his head. It served to stand him upright, but it also pushed his jacket collar over his head. His arms were effectively immobilized as he desperately tried to throw some more punches, but they were awkward and spastic. I sensed some cars stopping to watch the spectacle as I moved out of his path. If nothing else, I wouldn't get run over.

The big man staggered awkwardly and tried to claw at me. His angry red face was barely peeking out from the jacket, but there was enough of a target there for me to reach. I smashed my fists angrily into his face with a right-left-right combination, and his body slumped. I jerked his collar back down and punched him cleanly one more time, on the side of the temple, hard and loud and vicious. The big man grimaced as he collapsed into the street.

I stood there for a brief moment looking at him. I glanced up at his car and saw the woman in the passenger seat holding her phone up. From the looks of it, she was recording the episode. I briefly thought of confronting her device, but then I realized I wasn't the one who started all of this. I hadn't instigated a car accident, and I hadn't thrown the first punch. A video can show many things, but it would be difficult to obfuscate what had just happened. I looked around and began to relax for a second, and felt pretty good about myself. And then my all-too-brief moment of calm evaporated into thin air when I heard the incredibly loud beep-beep-beep of a police siren. I looked up into the flashing red and blue lights of a motorcycle cop.

The officer wore a black uniform, black jacket and

white helmet. He dismounted his vehicle, spoke something into his lapel microphone, and ordered me to put my hands on top of my head.

"I think you've got things wrong, officer," as I complied with his directive. "I didn't start this."

"Well, I'm finishing it," he said smugly.

"Look," I said, growing a little wary. "It was self-defense. He attacked me."

The officer snapped a pair of handcuffs on me and twisted my arms behind my back as he clicked them together. They were tight and they stung. My wrists already began to hurt. It reminded me of a time, a decade earlier, when I had been arrested on a false charge and ended up spending a few nights in jail. It was the beginning of a hellacious period in my life, and I couldn't believe I might have to deal with something like that again.

"Don't you think you should ask what happened before jumping to conclusions?" I shouted.

He turned slowly and gave me a look. "I don't need to ask anything. I saw the whole thing. You rear-ended that guy, you both got out of the car and then you beat the hell out of him. What's the matter? Didn't your Driver's Ed teacher tell you you're just supposed to exchange information, not punches?"

I shook my head. "How close were you?"

"I was close enough," he responded, and he began to frisk me. He stopped when he got to my holster. "Well, well. What do we have here?"

"I'm licensed to carry that."

"Sure you are. And I'll give you plenty of time to come up with that piece of paper. But we'll do it at the station house. That okay with you, tough guy?"

I tried to think of a way to express my innermost thoughts in a manner that would not create more trouble than I was in already. Taking a trip to the police station, bound with handcuffs, was not how I planned to finish my afternoon. It was not how I planned to finish any afternoon.

Eight

The holding tank at the Purdue Division was noticeably light this afternoon, as it often tends to be. Nighttime was when the men's jail filled to capacity, as drunk drivers, muggers, male prostitutes, and other nocturnal creatures entered, most often after midnight. This afternoon the cell was host to a pair of burglars, a shoplifter, and a high school student who brought a pistol to school, in order to show someone the nasty consequences that came with asking out his girlfriend. What the student didn't know was that today was the day the school imposed a random check on students' backpacks, ostensibly to search for drugs. Discovering a firearm was an unexpected bonus. What was also unexpected was that the student grabbed it back, angrily pointing it at the security guard and earning himself a trip to jail.

I didn't request the one phone call I was entitled to, mostly because I wasn't certain who to call. My wife the attorney would certainly take a dim view of my behavior, even though I had neither instigated nor inflamed the situation. But self-defense was hard to prove, and I had a feeling the woman recording the brawl inside of the black Audi was not going to be on my side.

I thought of calling an attorney friend I had known for a while, but his specialty was slip-and-fall lawsuits, which meant he was more of a financial negotiator than someone well versed in criminal law. Most of the good lawyers in town were very expensive, and I needed to think this through. I even considered calling Cliff Roper, who might be willing to provide me with a referral; in his line of work, football-player clients occasionally wound up on the wrong side of the law. But I suspected he would be more concerned about why I hadn't called him back, and why I hadn't solved his problem. Listening to Cliff Roper give me grief was not something I felt like initiating just yet, especially not from behind bars. After a few hours, I was about to give in and call Gail when the jailor approached the cell and barked out my name.

"I'm Burnside," I said, walking toward him.

He unlocked the cell and motioned me to come out. "Let's go. Your lucky day. No charges filed."

"All right," I said, curious about why I was being sprung, but sensing the answer to that question would be forthcoming soon enough.

"You got some friends with juice," he remarked as he led me down a nondescript corridor and into the police station. It was a path I had journeyed down plenty of times, but almost always as a proud police officer, not as a downtrodden suspect. I didn't like the feeling. And my wrists still ached from the handcuffs.

"Apparently I have a guardian angel," I said.

"Yeah. And he wants to talk with you, too," he said, as he led me through a maze of cubicles and desks, finally arriving at a corner office, and leading me inside.

"He's all yours, Captain."

The beaming face of Juan Saavedra greeted me. He stood up, moved quickly around his desk, and reached out to shake my hand.

"How you doing there, Champ?" he laughed. "Heard you had a little workout on one of my streets."

"Um, yeah, not quite how I planned on spending my afternoon."

"Life throws you curveballs, huh?" he smiled. I looked around for a chair, but there were none. It was not an omission, but rather a clear message Captain Saavedra wanted to send out to his visitors, mostly police officers. He was the one who sat, everyone else would stand. It made for short conversations.

"Well, you're in a good mood," I said. "I suppose I should thank you for releasing me."

"You absolutely should. But first tell me your side of the story."

"Pretty simple. Road rage on the part of one of our good citizens. Looked like he was having an argument with his wife. He couldn't hit her, so I became a convenient target. He forced me off the road, and when I wouldn't engage him, he backed into my car. At that point, I got out, and well, you know. Forced to defend myself."

"Yeah, I saw the video. Nice trick, pulling his jacket over his head. Haven't seen that one since middle school."

I smiled. When someone bigger and angrier than you is coming at you fists first, with cars whizzing by, there isn't a lot of opportunity to maneuver. Putting the assailant in an off-balance position and then trying to neutralize him was the best approach, albeit one that comes fraught with risk. If I hadn't been able to pull the jacket over his head, the outcome of the fight could have been quite different.

"The wife showed you the recording?" I asked.

"Nah, and it wasn't his wife, either. We had cameras stationed at the intersection. The arresting officer only saw part of the altercation. Look, there's no privacy these days. Lucky for you. Not real lucky for Brutus there. He's still over at UCLA Medical. That is until he's released and we can book him."

"Oh? Do I get to press charges for assault?" I smiled.

"In your dreams. There's a warrant out for him. Apparently he forgot to show up to court for a bunch of traffic tickets. Guess it slipped his mind. But it gets better."

"You seem to be enjoying this," I commented.

"Beats most of my other duties today," he laughed. "Turns out this guy's trying to be a UFC fighter. The woman wasn't his wife, she was some TV executive. They were trying to get him some publicity, some good PR for his next match. You know, up-and-coming fighter gets into an altercation with some schmuck who thinks he's tough."

"Dumb idea. Turns out I am tough."

"Yeah, look, be careful about that in the future. I know you can still handle yourself, but you'd be surprised how many guns are out there. Things can go sideways in a hurry. I've seen it."

"Maybe not that surprised. Hey, speaking of guns ... "

"Yeah?"

"You made a pretty quick arrest yesterday. Tyler Briggs."

Juan agreed, looking sheepish. "On orders of the

Deputy Chief. Not my idea, but I didn't have a better one. Assuage the community and all."

"Assuage?" I repeated, raising my eyebrows. "You're sounding like a suit now."

"Always trying to improve myself. You should consider that, too."

"I do try. I just don't always succeed," I answered. "Hey Juan, I heard there was some evidence found at the scene. Article of clothing."

"Right. In the alley behind Glasscock's office."

"A green baseball cap. Letter M on the front," I mused.

"Well," Juan said, sitting back. "You've been doing some bang-up investigating. Yeah, we found Briggs's cap."

"You're sure it's his?" I asked.

"Had his name written on the inside. We also have a weapon found near the scene. Glock 19. Found it sitting right near the cap. Checking DNA on both now, but our guys are optimistic. Normally DNA testing can take a while, but this case is very high-profile, it got moved to the front of the pack. The coroner pulled a couple of 9 millimeter slugs out of the councilman. It all fits neatly. Maybe too much so."

I took this in. A murder weapon found near the scene, an article of clothing easily linked to the suspect. It all made sense, but it really didn't. All the pieces did fit together cleanly, and they all came together right away. It was too neat, too tidy and had all the earmarks of a setup. Police work doesn't get as easy as this, unless someone wants to make it so.

"You don't sound super convinced," I said.

"No, I'm not. Plus, there's another thing that's curious, and that's a motive. Nothing ties Briggs and Glasscock together. Briggs denies everything, but he has no account for where he was this weekend. None. Said he was drinking heavily on Friday night and blacked out. Lost weekend and all. Not the best alibi, but you know, something about all of that tells me he was speaking the truth. Now I suppose it's possible he could have shot Glasscock in a drunken stupor and not remembered."

"Sure," I agreed. "I always forget the people I gunned down when I was drunk. Saves me from feeling bad afterward."

"Uh-huh. Yeah, there's an element here that smells bad. But I don't have the resources to keep looking into this. Mid-year budget cuts took away all my discretionary funds. And I don't feel like going up against the Deputy Chief unless I have something more than a gut feeling."

"I suppose that's where I come in."

"Well, now, it's not like you're in jail or anything."

"I do have you to thank for getting me out. And I'm also being paid to investigate this, so I don't mind being the one to look around some more. Not sure what I'll find, but if we keep poking the bear, eventually we'll get a reaction."

"There you go. Anything I've missed?"

"You know," I said, "There was a rumor that Glasscock was carrying around a handgun."

"Yeah," Juan nodded. "We heard that rumor, too. Didn't find anything on him, his wife didn't know anything about it. Nothing registered under his name. We chalked that up to what it was. A rumor."

"Okay. I take it your guys didn't visit the Snuggle Inn on Washington."

Juan frowned. "That motel? No. Was Briggs there?"

"With some woman other than his wife. Talk to the maid. Name's Teresa. I told her to hold something for you guys, could be evidence. May want to send it to the lab right away."

"All right," Juan said, jotting down a few notes. "You're starting to make me feel good I let you out of your cell."

"You always do the right thing," I smiled.

"Enough with the false flattery. Look, I'll send Detective Brown to see this Teresa. If Orlando gets something, whatever it is, we'll ship it off for testing. But I want you to stay on this and keep me in the loop. Also know that we arraigned Briggs this afternoon and he made bail. Judge set it at three million, but his wife used their house as collateral. Didn't realize how much football coaches make. I'm sure some movie stars are jealous. Can't imagine how much you made at SC."

"Trust me, I was well paid, but I didn't make millions," I said. "Hey, Juan, you know, since I'm here and have your full attention..."

"Oh, crap," Juan groaned. He knew what was coming and so did I. The best time to ask for a favor is right after someone asks you for one.

"I'm wondering if I can ask you about another case."

Juan rolled his eyes. "Just when I give you nine yards, you go and take ten."

"I'm funny that way."

"Okay. I always love hearing detective stories from the

private sector. What is it this time?"

"Domestic disturbance last week," I said, and gave Juan the Hobart Street address where Patrick O'Malley and Fili Snuka lived. Juan typed the address into his computer.

"Yup, attempted burglary," he said as he read the notes. "Interesting, the suspect is also bringing charges. Assault, battery, kidnapping. Said he was tortured. Officers found cigarette burns on his back. Facial injuries, bruises. His wrists had rope burns on them, indicating he was tied up. Sounds like a case of the perp getting his punishment without due process."

"And how is the department responding?"

"Well," Juan said, "it looks like Detective Rob Hatfield is investigating. It's in the Southwest Division, yup, right near your old stomping grounds, USC. Hatfield is about three months away from retirement, which is probably why they assigned it to him. My guess is he'll be investigating this one slowly."

I understood. The slow reaction on the part of the police would send a covert message to the perpetrator that his charges weren't going to be taken seriously. The media had gotten wind of it, but someone at USC managed to quash any follow-up. Not that they needed to push hard, the LAPD had long been known as a department that thrived on patrol work, interceding quickly to restore peace. Investigative work was its Achilles heel, given secondary importance. But that didn't mean the incident would go away forever, especially in some quarters. And I knew the NFL had its own investigative arm, and if Patrick or Fili were going pro next year, this could be looked into more thoroughly.

"Mind telling me his name?" I asked. "I might want to pay him a visit. Just as a public service."

"Geez, Burnside, we should just hand you your badge and gun back. You're doing more police work than some of our guys bother to do."

"I thought of pointing that out before, but, you know. Didn't want to offend."

"Uh-huh," Juan said, and he pulled out a memo pad. "Name's Tristan Lopez. No address listed, but I'm sure that won't stop a snoop like you. And I assume your interest is somehow football-related?"

"Yeah. You probably recognized the names on the report."

"Patrick O'Malley? Hard not to. What's your role here?"

I shrugged. "Keeping the peace mostly. Some of these guys are headed to the NFL, if not this year, then next. Getting harder to do that with a criminal record."

"Okay. Keep me informed on this one, too. And try not to slug anyone else."

"I'll do my best. And I must say you're being awfully supportive here. You normally don't like private investigators running around doing police work."

"I have my reasons," he smiled. "The deputy chief's been a thorn in my side for a while, and I wouldn't mind shoving this Briggs arrest up his ass. Heard he's on the outs with the chief."

"Ah," I said. "And hence, there might be an opening soon downtown at PAB."

"Might be."

"I never thought of you as someone who played office politics."

Juan looked off into the distance. "Firstly, I'm not crazy about the deputy chief, he's a grade-A jerk. Secondly, the wife's been bugging me about money. You know my oldest is applying to college now."

"Wow. Time flies."

"And money flies too. Right out the door. He's applying to a few Ivy League schools. Bright kid. Like to see him do well. But the tuition? Tough to make that nut on a captain's salary."

"He could always apply to a state college. Berkeley's a great school."

"So's UCLA," he said.

"Never heard of that one," I smiled. "But he could always live at home and go to USC."

Juan nodded slowly. "He's applying there."

"Good."

"Yeah," Juan said, a devious twinkle in his eye. "Always helps to have a safety school."

*

After finishing with Juan, I waited another hour for the khaki officer to retrieve my .357. He seemingly needed special approval before he could return it to me. My guess is he was simply taking a long coffee break.

The Purdue Division was only a few blocks from where they towed and impounded my Pathfinder, but fortunately for me, Juan made a call, the fee was waived, and I picked it up without a hassle. I inspected the front end, and there was no noticeable damage from the collision, the worst seemed to be a small scratch on the bumper.

As I drove off, I remembered a community meeting tonight at the Woodland School on Palms. When I arrived at home, the first thing I did was take a shower and toss my clothes into the hamper. Jails are about the least sanitary places, and washing the stink off me felt good in both a practical and spiritual way. My head still hurt from the grazing punch I absorbed, so I took a couple of Advil tablets. I spent an hour with Gail and Marcus, put together a turkey sandwich quickly, and told them I'd be back in a couple of hours.

"Daddy, why do you work at night?" Marcus asked. "I thought most people just work during the day."

I gave Marcus a hug. "I'm not like most people. But I may have a surprise for you."

"Christmas present?" he exclaimed.

"More like New Year's. No promises, I'm working on it."

Marcus gave me a hug, and then Gail gave me a kiss, and I was out the door. I did not bother telling Gail about my brief respite in the Purdue division's jail cell, and she hadn't noticed my swollen knuckles or the red marks on my wrists. Those details could wait for another day.

The Woodland School was a private high school located near Palms and Barrington. It was the type of school you see in the movies, the dreamy ones, the kind where the setting is idyllic, the grounds cared for and the pastel colors of the buildings freshly painted. It was evening, and the few students still on campus had wet hair from showers, most likely having just finished basketball practice. They had the tired look of athletes who had put in a full day's effort. I knew the look well.

The meeting was held in the gym, which had been designed to hold hundreds but tonight only a few dozen souls bothered to show up. A couple of rows of metal folding chairs were arranged, and there was a podium where the leaders hovered. I sat down next to a tanned, handsome man who sported enviable bone structure. He was dressed casually, if casual meant a Lands End shirt, pressed khakis and cordovan topsiders. The handsome man didn't recognize me, but I recognized him. Deputy Mayor Neil Handler was doing his best to be here incognito and succeeding quite well at it.

"Guess they haven't got going yet," I said, wondering how well that ice breaker would work.

The man shrugged. "I don't know," he said. "The meeting, yes. Any real action, I doubt it. They're amateurs going up against pros."

"I guess you know something about all this, tossing your hat in the ring for city council," I said, looking straight ahead for the most part, but glancing at him through my peripheral vision, catching glimpses of his mouth opening as he turned to look at me.

"How do you know that?" he managed.

"Come on," I said. "A good politician's supposed to have a memory for names and faces."

He looked harder at me and I finally saw a wave of recognition. "Oh yeah. From the Charger game the other day. You're Cliff Roper's friend."

"Calling us friends would be a stretch. But yeah, that's where we met. You here tonight checking out who your competition might be on the campaign trail?"

"In a way" he said. "But my daughter also goes to school here. She's in 9th grade. I saw the signs up for a community meeting on local problems."

"Funny they'd have them at a private school."

"Not so much," he said. "Woodland likes to maintain good community relations. They take over the park across the street for tennis and soccer matches. Donating space is their way of giving back."

"I see. Your daughter like the school?"

"Loves it. At $40,000 a year, she better love it."

I shook my head. One more thing to worry about for Marcus, and yet another discussion down the road with Gail. Fortunately for us, high school was way down the road. I was a product of public schools, at least until I got into USC. I knew bright kids would do well in most places. Public schools had enrichment programs in place for advanced students, and remedial programs for ones that were struggling. It was the kids in the middle who sometimes got lost. Marcus was only five, but he struck me as the type of kid who would fit in well anywhere. Convincing Gail of that was another matter.

"You think this place is worth the money?" I asked tepidly.

Handler raised his hands in the 'who knows' posture. "Probably not, I don't think any school is worth that much. But it's a little more engaging than public schools.

The kids here are generally better behaved, and the class sizes are small. But kids are kids, and there's always a bad apple or two in the bunch. One of her classmates had a party last weekend when her parents were away on a ski trip. The liquor cabinet got drained. Ever see a fourteen-year-old girl with a hangover? I'm just hoping it's a lesson for her to learn from."

"How's the optics on that? Deputy mayor of Los Angeles not sending his daughter to a school in L.A. Unified?"

"It just makes me look like every other politician since the dawn of time," he said sarcastically.

I shook my head. "So, what do you hope to learn tonight?"

"Just seeing what I'll be up against in the primary. Helps to have intel on your opposition. But also, the fact that you're the only one who recognizes me says something."

We sat back and watched the spectacle unfold, which was mostly a forum for some muted outrage over the lane closures on Venice, comments about out-of-touch politicians and the need to take back our government. There were a few sensitive remarks of condolence to the Glasscock family, and how no one ever wanted to see things end in such a horrific way. But what was done was done and they needed to move forward with their agenda. A large, bearded man in his early thirties named Roy Woolley declared himself to be a candidate for the Glasscock seat. Dressed in a flannel shirt, and looking more like a lumberjack than a man running an insurgent political movement, he said he was a local business owner, and unlike the past councilman, he would be responsive to the community's needs. The meeting finally broke up with petitions being handed out, and anyone interested in being a volunteer for the Woolley campaign should make their presence know. I turned to Handler.

"You still wondering about your stiff competition?" I asked.

"Nope," he said and turned to leave. "It's about what I thought it would be."

I agreed, although I started to feel this was all a colossal waste of my time. Then I happened to see another familiar face standing off in the corner. He was wearing a rumpled suit, tie loosened, and had that world-weary look that came part and parcel with being an overworked cop. I walked over to him. He looked me up and down as if he expected me to be here.

"Detective Orlando Brown," I declared. "We meet again."

"Figured we would at some point," he said. "You have a funny habit of being nearby a lot."

"Maybe not that funny," I said. "What brings you here?"

"Captain's orders," he replied stoically. "You think I'd be here otherwise? I'd rather be home watching the Laker game and drinking a beer."

This was not what I expected from a homicide detective. Most were dedicated, if not obsessive, about their jobs, and had a natural curiosity that kept them pushing through cases. And they rarely moved into another crime unit; once you work homicide, no other type of police work gives quite the same jolt. But Orlando Brown didn't look obsessed with anything, he just looked weary.

"Interesting," I said. "The captain seems to have some doubts about Tyler Briggs. Do you?"

"Me?" he asked. "I'm here to make collars and clear cases. Got physical evidence near the crime scene, plus an eyewitness who identified Briggs coming into the Glasscock office Friday evening. All I need to know. But I'm a soldier. I do what the brass wants. Unlike you."

"Unlike me?"

"I heard about you. Word gets around. Ex-cop, kicked off the force. Questionable morals, yeah I heard the story. Taking in a teenaged prostitute. Then you turned rogue. Man, you sounded like you were a real piece of work. No wonder you're not on the job any longer."

I felt my insides begin to simmer. It had been a decade since I had been kicked off of the LAPD, wrongly discharged, yet the stories remained. The false narrative, the rumors, the lies that would remain on the internet forever. My legacy, burnished.

"Don't believe everything you hear," I said in a low voice.

"I'll believe what I choose to believe," he declared.

"That's why you're still around after all these years."

"And that's why you're not," he said evenly. "You thought you were a hotshot."

"I was a hotshot."

"Uh-huh. Well, I still got a couple of years to go before retirement, so I'm not rocking the boat. I'll do what the

Captain says. I need to keep my job, so yeah, I'll keep swimming in this cesspool some people call a city. Then I'll move up to Nevada. Far away from all of this crap."

"I'm sure Nevada will be thrilled to hear that," I observed.

Brown glowered at me. "I heard you had a smart mouth. But it's funny how you show up in the oddest places. Like driving Tyler Briggs home. Or like getting Saavedra to have you kicked after you beat up a motorist. Yeah, I wondered what you were doing in the captain's office. Yucking it up. Sounds like you and him go way back."

"We do. Helps to have friends. You should try it sometime."

"Look, Burnside," he said, "I got a job to do. I just can't figure out your role here."

"I was hired by the coach's wife to go and find him. I found him. Now she's hired me to find out who killed Glasscock. Because she doesn't believe her husband did it. My role here is to do some detective work. Someone needs to."

Orlando Brown glared at me. "You think we aren't doing our job?"

"I think you could do it better."

"You smartass SOB," he growled. "If you weren't buddy-buddy with Saavedra, I'd make you pay for that."

"Whew. Lucky for me."

"That's right. And I do things by the book. We have rules to follow. This is why we have a police force," he said, his eyes narrowing. "We don't need private cops messing things up."

"The free market says otherwise. Look, I'd prefer to work with you and not against you. But I'm not here to punch a clock and collect a salary and let things play out the way they will. I'm getting paid to find out what happened. If I'm certain Briggs did it, I'll walk away and tell my client that. And the captain. But until then, I'm here."

"Yeah, you're still here. Like a bad cough that won't go away."

"That's a little rude," I said.

"Oh, did I hurt your feelings? You must be from around here."

"I am. You mean you're not?"

"Louisiana. Came out here when I was ten."

"Why don't you move back?"

He peered at me, not sure how to take that remark. He finally let it slide. "I deal with enough crazy assholes in L.A. I don't need to be adding racist crackers to that equation. At least here I got a badge, so I get some respect."

"Uh-huh," I said, getting another sordid reminder of why some people became cops. Without the badge and the gun and the uniform and the backup, Orlando Brown would just be another ordinary guy.

The detective looked past me and didn't respond. I turned to see what he was looking at, and didn't see anything of interest. I thought back to what I had learned decades ago, that there once was a time when local police forces were not just corrupt, they were underfunded and private detectives were needed. The police couldn't be trusted to do their jobs, and the ones who were honest were often overwhelmed with the caseload. That changed after World War II, when modern police departments were seen as necessary, and resources were allotted to build them. Much of the corruption was weeded out, and the need to seek out private detectives eased. But now that we'd moved into the 21st Century, and people would rather shell out less in taxes, local police departments had far fewer resources, the work started to become overwhelming again, and they had to pick and choose what cases they focused on. Things had come full circle. And with detectives like Orlando Brown, it was no wonder Juan had not objected to my staying on this, notwithstanding the political schemes my old friend was hatching to get himself promoted.

"So, Detective," I said, "can you tell me any more about this eyewitness you have? The one who put Tyler Briggs at the scene of the crime? I've got some doubts about the physical evidence, but this is an element I'm not aware of."

"You want a name? Nice try."

"I know it was one of Glasscock's staffers that saw him."

"Oh yeah?" Detective Brown responded with a scowl, "Then you know what they saw was a man they later identified as Tyler Briggs entering the Glasscock office after most people had left. They didn't see either one come out."

"Didn't this eyewitness think that was strange?" I asked.

“The eyewitness didn’t think anything of it at the time. But you’re right. It was a staffer. That means they’re a city employee. And it was 5:00 pm on Friday. They went home.”

Nine

The next morning reverted back to being dour and dreary, and a fresh layer of fog descended over the region. In most parts of the country, ice and snow were the chilly reminders that Christmas was coming; in L.A., it was fog. I made a mental note to stop at Toys R Us to pick up a few things for Marcus. We had ordered most of his presents online, and while I was still trying to find affordable Rose Bowl tickets, it did not appear that it was going to happen.

I waited until the morning rush hour had subsided, which these days often meant around 10:30 am, and drove to Koreatown. What had once started out as a small ethnic neighborhood near Olympic and Vermont many decades ago, had mushroomed into a vast community with its very own name. It was far bigger than L.A.'s Chinatown, but less of a tourist Mecca. I drove up Normandie, and noticed the usual storefronts with Korean names, the restaurants, dry cleaners, and liquor stores, but now it included accounting firms, law offices, immigration services and medical centers.

The Korean community in L.A. was thriving in a way that other groups were not. It was a community that made a point of helping immigrants assimilate. Businesspeople loaned money to newcomers to open shops, with the pointed understanding that when they became successful, they would pay it forward and do the same for others coming here. It was an effective strategy, although being of Korean heritage was a requirement. Outsiders were not given the same treatment, and the response to any criticism was simply a shrug. L.A.'s Koreans did what other ethnic groups boasted of but did not always back up with action. They took care of their own.

Arthur Woo was someone I had known for a few years, and someone whose family had done extraordinarily well in America in a very short time. His brother Justin had been elected governor a few years ago, and Arthur had offered me a job handling security for him. That I had initially been hired by Justin's opponent, Rex Palmer, was of little concern; they knew what I could do and they respected it. I also knew the family was not very forthcoming, and I would have had problems working for them. Realistically, the only opportunity that could have persuaded me to give up running my own business was a coaching slot with USC. And when I left coaching after three years, I had received another call from Arthur offering me a new job running security, this time for him. Arthur had been running for a city council seat of his own last year, to represent Koreatown, and it did not surprise me that he had won, only that he did not win in a landslide. I considered his offer for roughly two seconds. Arthur was an extremely bright guy, but he would have made a terrible boss.

I parked on Vermont, just north of Wilshire, and walked into Arthur Woo's building. Like Colin Glasscock, Arthur maintained an office in his district, as well as at City Hall. Unlike the Glasscock office this week, Arthur's was humming with activity, vibrant and loud, with serious-looking people moving quickly up and down the hallways. All were Korean.

I entered the reception area, and a young, thin, pretty woman with wire-rimmed glasses looked up at me. She said hello crisply and waited for me to speak.

"I have an appointment with Mr. Woo."

"Ah, you must be Mr. Burnside," she said, rising from her desk and motioning for me to follow her. We walked into a modest office, and she gestured for me to wait until the city councilman was finished speaking into his phone. Arthur Woo talked rapidly, shooting off specific instructions, not waiting for the person on the other end to respond. He ended the call with a quick thank you.

"Mr. Woo, I believe you know Mr. Burnside," she said.

Arthur Woo stood up and smiled as he shook my hand. It was a politician's smile, one that revealed perfect teeth, an agreeable demeanor, and little more. I knew that smile. It could turn into a blistering frown in a moment's notice. His assistant quietly exited the office and closed the door behind her.

"Mr. Burnside. We meet again."

"Under circumstances I would not have imagined. City councilman. Quite a shrewd move. But I guess when your brother's the governor, you don't have a problem with name recognition."

"No," he said. "But I do carry my brother's baggage. When the state budget talks deadlocked last year, it affected my campaign. We powered through it and I won, but it was closer than it should have been."

I nodded. "I assume you like your new job."

"It's fine for now," he said without a hint of any more smiling.

"Oh?" I asked. "Planning bigger and better things?"

"Politics is the family business, Mr. Burnside. We always look at the next rung on the ladder."

I gave a low whistle. "You're running for Mayor Gonsalves's job."

"He's termed out next year. Someone has to be the next mayor. Why not the best?"

"And your brother? He'll be termed out in a few years, too. What happened to your plan for a presidential run for Justin?"

Arthur looked up at the ceiling. "Outside of California there is an anti-immigrant sentiment. We are the victims of prejudice, and the time is not ripe for an amendment to allow him to run. But no matter. Justin will be fine. And I'll be waiting in the wings when he steps down after this second term."

I smiled. Arthur Woo never lacked confidence or bravado. He was an Ivy League educated elitist who made no bones about the fact that he was indeed smarter than most people. That his brother was the governor only meant Arthur likely felt the annoying burden of being born five years afterward. I had learned long ago that it was far better to be on the side of people like the Woos than to be in their path. Not much was going to stop them; an oval office bid only would be derailed by a small matter called the United States Constitution.

"Well, in the meanwhile, how are you enjoying your role as a city councilman?"

"It's a joyous honor," he replied, no hint of joy evident on his placid face, only the suspicion that the mental clock in his brain had begun ticking. "And what brings you here today, Mr. Burnside? Have you reconsidered my offer to handle security?"

"Sorry, no."

"Too bad. I could use someone now. Call me in a year, though. The mayor's office will need a larger detail. Bigger job, bigger paycheck."

"I'll keep that in mind," I said dryly. "But I'm here to talk with you about one of your colleagues. Colin Glasscock."

Arthur Woo looked at me. "Terrible thing," he said. "Colin was a fine man. A pillar of the community."

"Not among the community I've talked with. There seem to be more than a few people who were livid at his actions. Adding bike baths, taking away traffic lanes, approving housing development in dense urban neighborhoods. He was no longer that popular."

"And your interest here is what, Mr. Burnside?"

"I've been hired to look into the homicide charges. The suspect's wife is convinced her husband didn't do it."

"Ah," he said. "The lovely Hannah Briggs."

"You know her?" I asked, eyebrows raised.

"L.A. is a small place, Mr. Burnside. At least in the circles I travel in. Yes, she works in the City Attorney's office. I hear she's competent, nothing more. Quite a beautiful woman, though. Very desirable. More than a few gentlemen have expressed interest in her."

"Oh?" I said stupidly, a casual trick that sometimes

kept the conversation flowing. But the downside with Arthur Woo was that he was a man who told you only things he wanted you to hear.

"A bit of gossip for you," he said. "Of course, I wouldn't know if she took them up on those offers. My sources only go so far. Women who look like that attract many types of men. You of all people should know that."

"How so?" I asked, managing to string two words together instead of one.

"Mr. Burnside, you needn't worry. Your beautiful wife has had offers, too, but she's been faithful. I know for a fact she's turned them all down."

I felt my mouth open and close. I had come here for some information, and I was getting it. The trouble was, the information wasn't necessarily what I had expected, hoped for, or had properly steeled myself against. I knew I had a beautiful wife, and beautiful women were sometimes propositioned by men at all levels. I just chose to not allow myself to go to those dark places, nor consider the possibilities. I trusted Gail unwaveringly. But like all men married to a beautiful wife, I saw the way other men looked at her, and unlike certain smug husbands who took pride in seeing others ogle at their spouses, I didn't like it one bit.

"That's so good of you to share that with me, Arthur," I managed. "But what does Hannah Briggs have to do with Colin Glasscock?"

"Perhaps nothing. But Mr. Glasscock was known to have bedded a number of women outside his marriage. And I heard he was very particular about them. He liked bright, attractive engaging women."

"Don't we all."

Arthur smiled slightly. "Glasscock was said to be having affairs with a few women who worked in city government. One might have been in the mayor's office, one possibly in the city attorney's office. I believe one even worked for the LAPD. There may be more, I'm just giving you the topline on the gossip."

"I don't suppose you have any names, do you Arthur?"

"No, sadly, that I do not. The only commonality they seemed to have was being blonde, so I suppose that rules out your wife. But the rumor around City Hall was that Glasscock had it coming to him. You can only play with fire so long before it finally burns you."

"I see. And have you shared this with the police?"

"They haven't asked me, but if they did I imagine I might. It's of no use to me now."

I took a breath and remembered where I was, in the office of a shrewd politician who had been saving these insidious morsels of gossip, in the event Arthur ever ran against Colin Glasscock in a citywide election. That Glasscock was dead meant the value of the information had diminished to the point where he could hand it out freely. Its currency had died along with the councilman.

"So, you think Tyler Briggs may have indeed committed this murder."

Arthur Woo nodded vigorously. "It all fits together. From what I've been told anyway, by someone at Parker Center who's seen the evidence. This has all the earmarks of a hot-blooded act. I've sometimes heard it referred to as an honor killing. A cuckolded man takes a violent action to defend what's left of his dignity, of which, I understand, Mr. Briggs had very little."

"You don't think this was politically motivated."

Arthur Woo shrugged. "You can't rule it out. But there isn't much for anyone to gain politically. Oh, I've heard a few local activists are going to run for his seat in November, but its moot now. They'll lose. The appointment of his successor will be made shortly."

"Who's replacing Glasscock?" I asked. "That is, if you can speak freely on this subject."

Arthur Woo smiled. "Promise you won't tell the media, but the deputy mayor will be taking Glasscock's council seat. Neil Handler. Professional bureaucrat. He'll be acceptable, won't rock the boat."

"Good to be the mayor's friend," I said.

"Actually the president of the city council makes the selection, but no matter. City Hall is a chummy bunch."

"And you're happy that Handler won't be a candidate for mayor next November."

"I'm not worried in the slightest about Neil Handler. He can handle some local businessmen running in his district. I believe that's your district, too, if you still live in Mar Vista. It's a win-win appointment. Everyone's comfortable with Neil."

I looked at Arthur Woo and marveled at the brimming self-confidence. I knew it wasn't just bravado; he truly believed in himself and his intellect. I wondered where that came from, and guessed, with his brother an even more successful politician, it all started in the home.

Parents who provided direction and structure and goals. We did that for Marcus, but I sensed he would never turn out like Arthur Woo. Marcus was headstrong and had ambition, but he also had two parents who loved him dearly. I wasn't that sure Arthur Woo had been so blessed.

"Well," I said, rising from my seat, "I thank you for the tidbits. You've given me a lot to chew on. And it's also very good to know my wife's been faithful."

"You're a lucky man, Mr. Burnside. To have a wife who's both smart and alluring and has a pleasant personality as well. I've met her at a few functions and have always come away impressed."

"And you're wondering what she's doing with me," I joked.

"I would never say anything like that," he said through a smile. I took pains to not add that he was thinking it.

"I'm indeed fortunate."

"Yes. But of course, everyone has a fatal flaw, we're all humans. Your wife is lovely, but she's not perfect. None of us are."

"What are you implying, Mr. Councilman?" I peered at him.

"Nothing, of course. Just that she's ambitious. And ambition comes with tradeoffs. I've made mine. I don't see my family much, and far too many people know me. Some don't like me. But it's the price one pays for public service. Just so you'll know, Mr. Burnside. In the event your wife chooses to enter politics. Frankly, I think she'd be quite good at it. But like I say. There are tradeoffs, and ambition can rupture a marriage. Your wife has a fatal flaw. And I suspect you do, too. I just haven't quite figured out what that is yet."

*

I left Arthur Woo's office knowing more but understanding less. Nothing he said was shocking, but his remarks were food for thought. And as much as I tried to focus on Tyler Briggs, his marriage and his peculiarities, I found my mind scurrying back to review my own. And I wasn't liking it very much.

I found a Starbuck's nearby, sipped a *grande* Christmas Blend, and wondered at what point they'd stop serving this seasonal roast. Probably the day after Christmas. I thought about Gail and wondered who had approached her. I found my fists clenching involuntarily, and tried to think about something else. I looked around the shop and saw there were about twenty people seated, a few talking, but most were quietly hunched over computers or phones. I was the only non-Asian there, but somehow I didn't feel terribly out of place at all. We were connected in a more important way, we were all Angelenos, and that seemed to trump ethnicity. In L.A. a lot of people came from somewhere else, and even natives like myself, born and raised in Culver City, were forced to mesh. It eventually became a non-issue. You accepted it or you left. There was no other option.

Koreatown was, if nothing else, centrally located. I was close to USC, and given my proximity, I decided to see if I could talk to the perpetrator, or perhaps victim of the burglary incident involving Patrick O'Malley and Fili Snuka. At the very least it would take my mind off of Gail for a little while. I looked up the address Juan gave me, and discovered the man, Tristan Lopez, lived about eight blocks from the intersection of Adams and Hobart. Almost within walking distance. Or running distance.

I drove south on Normandie Avenue, but instead of the growing sense of optimism that greets Koreatown visitors with its shiny new buildings and well-maintained strip malls, the area south of the 10 Freeway was a hodgepodge of urban blight. Shuttered storefronts, graffiti-marred buildings and shops with hand-painted signs littered the landscape. Turning east onto Adams provided little relief; instead of dingy retail outlets, the neighborhood gave way to shoddy apartment buildings. The few private homes I passed were surrounded by white metal fences featuring sharp, pointy sticks, designed to deter potential thieves from jumping over and helping themselves to whatever meager valuables lay inside. This was a few miles away from the historic West Adams district, which featured lovely 1930s gingerbread houses and Craftsmen homes. The only thing that the West Adams neighborhood had in common with the one I was driving through was the name of the street. To say the least, it was depressing.

The address I had for Tristan Lopez brought me to a decrepit, two-story apartment building about a block south of Adams. It was a prefab stucco structure, poorly maintained and painted a shabby-looking mustard-yellow. Iron bars were hammered across all of the windows. A broken bottle lay shattered in the front doorway. Some *ranchera* music wafted out of an open window on the first floor. I climbed the uneven and filthy staircase, and knocked on a door that had a black decal with number 4 glued onto it, the upper-right corner of which had begun to peel off. The door opened, and a slender young man faced me. He had light brown skin, looked to be part Hispanic, part African-American, and he had bruises along the side of his face and a cut on his lower lip. He wore an undershirt and a pair of shorts, and he looked like he had just rolled out of bed.

"Tristan Lopez?" I asked.

"Um, well, yeah," he said haltingly, either because he was surprised a stranger would know his name, or because he was grappling with that elusive question himself. "What's up?"

He looked like he was in his early twenties, about the same age as Patrick O'Malley and Fili, but with a far different future in front of him. Kids who grew up in this neighborhood and wanted out either studied hard or played sports. The majority did not get out, and they wound up sinking into the same decay, parenting another generation of kids who would follow a similar pattern. Poverty was a cycle. People had the potential to break out of its grasp, but most never managed to. Some just didn't know how; others just didn't care.

I flashed my fake badge. "I'd like to talk with you about what happened to you recently."

"What do you mean 'happened'?" he asked warily.

"You know," I said patiently. "At Hobart Street. With the guys you say beat you."

"They did beat me," he said indignantly. "Beat my ass pretty good. Like I told those other fuckers. The ones that took the report."

I pointed to the door. "Mind if I come in?"

He shook his head no. "My grandma's sleeping."

"Okay," I said, figuring not many neighbors in an apartment building like this would be concerned about a resident being questioned by someone with a badge about a crime in the area. This was *de rigueur* in some communities, barely worth noticing.

"You going to arrest those punks?" he asked.

"I don't know," I replied, well aware I did not have the authority to do more than make a citizen's arrest, something that would be a laughable gesture here. "Tell me what happened. And don't lie, I'll know it."

"Hey, look," he began. "I was just doing my job."

"Right," I said, wondering what job might include breaking and entering, and boosting valuables as part of the requirements. "Who do you work for?"

"This magazine company. I was selling subscriptions."

"And you knocked on the door at that house on Hobart."

"Yeah. Well, sort of."

"You sort of did or you sort of didn't?" I asked.

"The door was partway open. Yeah, I knocked, but maybe not loud enough. It swung open, so I walked inside and asked if anyone was home."

"Go on," I said, not mentioning that he had just admitted to breaking the law. Entering a premise uninvited where you didn't know the occupant is called trespassing.

"Yeah, I walk in and ask if anyone's home. Said hello a bunch of times. Heard some noise in the kitchen, I figured I'd check it out. Nothing wrong with that, I figure. Then all of a sudden, this really big dude jumps me and starts pounding on me. Hawaiian guy or something. Damn, but he was big. Then another big dude grabs me and they take me downstairs and tie me up in this chair. Kept asking me what I thought I was doing. One of them burned me with cigarettes."

"This is all because you walked into someone's house."

"Uh-huh."

"You didn't try and steal anything?"

"Nope."

"Didn't try climbing out of window?"

"No. They went and stomped me. They didn't have to act like that. If they didn't want me there, they should have just told me to leave. I would've left. Simple as that."

"You take something? Anything at all?"

"Like I says, man, I was only in there for a minute when they grabbed me."

"They said you took things."

"I says I didn't."

I rubbed the bridge of my nose. These were the worst cases for me. Two sides of the story, each different, each plausible. No other witnesses, no evidence, just two versions of the same story, and you didn't know who was lying. We'd sometimes bring both sides to the station house, put them in separate rooms, and drill them for a while. Make up some nonsense that we found a video proving they were lying. Occasionally that was enough to get a person to come clean and change their story. Sometimes you could physically see it in their eyes that they were lying. When they clung to their version though, it often meant they were telling the truth. Not always, but enough of the time. Unfortunately I didn't have the luxury of having these resources, and I suspected the police didn't have the time or patience to go through this, either. Maybe they just didn't care. Football players at a major university were often given the benefit of the doubt. Celebrity had its share of perks.

"They said you stole some things," I told him. "Money, electronics. Some jewelry."

"No, man, like I told the other five-ohs. I didn't take anything, they just beat me up for nothing."

"Other five-ohs?" I asked, knowing that was ghetto slang for police.

"Yeah, and they didn't do shit. I went to the papers, they put something in the *Times* last week. But then it's like everyone forgets about it. Nothing happens. It's like we don't matter down here."

"Yeah," I agreed, and watched Tristan Lopez carefully, his anger starting to rise.

"Don't worry," he snarled. "I got a few more cards to play."

I didn't like the sound of that. "What are those?" I asked him apprehensively.

"This dude in my hood, his cousin plays for the Raiders. He says if any of those players go to the NFL then he could let them know. They tell me the NFL won't put up with none of that."

"Okay," I said. "Anything else you got up your sleeve?"

"I can call my homies. I know where these punks live. Obviously. You cops never do anything, so maybe we go fix this on our own. This is our hood, not theirs. They need to be taught a lesson. Learn some respect. You just don't pull that bullshit on us and get away with it. It's not like I did anything to them."

I took a breath. This was not an uncommon form of justice in neighborhoods like this, where violence served as a perfectly acceptable substitute for financial litigation. Differences were settled with guns, or the threat of using them. We were eight blocks from Hobart Street, and about a mile and a half from the USC campus. But for all intents and purposes, we were in another country, in another part of the world. The laws were the same, but the rules were not. And the interpretation of justice was immensely different. When I was a patrol officer, I once ran into a woman whose boyfriend had been murdered outside their apartment building a month earlier. I asked if the killer had been caught and she surprisingly said yes. When I asked when the trial would be, she looked at me long and hard, finally saying the matter had been settled privately. She didn't need to say any more. Justice had already been meted out.

"Okay, look," I said, handing him my card. "Don't go taking any action, yet. Don't talk to anyone, don't arrange any meetings or whatever you call them. I've got an idea. Might work out really well for everyone. Especially you. I think I can negotiate something."

"How you going to do that?"

I looked into his hardened eyes. "Can you just give me a few days?"

He stared back at me, and for a brief, fleeting moment, he seemed to soften. He looked down at my card. "Burnside, huh? If you're thinking you can do something for me, well, okay. You got a few days. I just don't know how you're going to fix this."

I thanked him and left, not bothering to tell him that I wasn't quite sure how I would do that, either.

Ten

I drove by the dilapidated Hobart Street house, thought briefly of getting out, but finally decided against it. The residents were most likely out, possibly studying in the library or taking final exams, but there was a better chance they were simply pumping iron at the McKay Center and swilling energy drinks. More importantly though, I had not mapped out any sort of a cohesive plan to get Fili and his teammates out of trouble. I had vague ideas, a few what-if thoughts, but nothing fully formed, and nothing that was worth sharing without being more thoroughly fleshed out and vetted. I decided to turn back to my main case, and also decided, with my grumbling tummy letting me know it was close to empty, that it was time for lunch.

Fortunately, my other client was available and suggested a downtown eatery near where she was finishing a meeting. If nothing else, I was being fuel efficient with my Pathfinder. Lunchtime traffic was starting to build, and I figured I'd wait until the mid-afternoon window allowed me to make the drive back home in a reasonable time. Like many Angelenos, I was cursed with having to rearrange my time due to traffic. Unlike a lot of Angelenos, my schedule had flexibility.

Hannah Briggs was seated at a small table at the back of Bottega Louie. This was not my kind of restaurant, and not just because it didn't focus on burgers, pastrami or

Chinese food. Bottega Louie was a crowded Italian restaurant with an entrance that boasted a gift shop, and it also flaunted brightly colored French macarons in a glass-enclosed pastry case. The dining room was very pretty and very loud. It was painted stark white from floor to ceiling, with white patterned tile on the floor, and white-and-gray-marble tables. Even on a bleak day, the interior was as bright as you could imagine.

I had been to Bottega Louie before, and the food was okay but it was quite possibly the loudest restaurant I had ever eaten in, the acoustics could well have been designed by a rock musician. It was exactly the kind of place we loved taking Marcus to when he was a baby, because any loud infant wailing was quickly drowned out by the din of the chattering restaurant guests. On this day it was more of a roar. The idea of having a talk about a sensitive subject in this environment made me uneasy. But as we sat down, I discovered the brilliance of the place. Not only was it so loud that we'd have some trouble hearing each other, it was so loud that the people sitting at the next table would never pick up a word.

"Hello," I shouted, slipping into a seat across from her. Hannah was dressed in a light blue business suit with a white top. Her platinum blonde hair shined. She fit in well here, a polished professional in a room full of polished professionals. I wasn't that sure about myself, but I tended to not fit in well anywhere.

"Hi," she said. "I'm glad you could make lunch. I was planning to call you today."

"It worked out well. I was in the neighborhood. Sort of."

"Me, too," she said. "Just finished meeting with a defense attorney. Tyler's situation is not looking good. And he's not doing well with it. Anger, shock, fear, depression, all rolled into one. He went out drinking again last night. And again he didn't come home. This time I didn't bother to call you. He's probably sleeping it off in his car."

I was not entirely sure what to say to her. It was a very tough future he was facing, and the thought of a long prison sentence that a guilty verdict could bring would make anyone agitated. And if he were indeed convicted, a long stretch in the pen was actually not the worst scenario. Even though California had not executed anyone in decades, that option still existed for juries.

"I understand the police have some evidence. And an eyewitness placing him at the scene."

Hannah nodded. "I heard. No one in the City Attorney's office will confirm it, but my lawyer found that out, too. They discovered Ty's baseball cap. Oh, I don't know why he insisted on wearing that stupid thing. And his fingerprints on the gun makes no sense."

"Do either of you own a firearm?" I asked.

"No, that's the thing. Tyler's never been interested in guns. It just makes no sense why he would even be at Glasscock's office. They had nothing to do with each other."

I looked at her and pondered how to ask the unaskable question. Whether or not my pretty client was having an affair with the late city councilman. Whether her behavior had elicited a raw emotion in her husband that propelled him to go take care of family business, be it for pride, anger, revenge, or a deluded sense of street justice. In some societies, this type of retribution was acceptable; in more civilized ones, we follow the rule of law, which sometimes means you take your lumps and move on.

The waitress came by at that moment to ask what we'd like. I glanced down at the menu in time to see Hannah order a twenty-dollar salad and an iced tea. I ordered a pasta dish that I could barely pronounce, along with a Coke. The waitress smiled, collected our menus and thanked us.

"Okay, I need to ask you something that's a bit sensitive," I said. "It may be uncomfortable for you."

"You mean was I screwing Colin Glasscock?"

I looked at her. "Well, maybe it won't be that uncomfortable."

Hannah Briggs's mouth tightened. She had on pink lipstick that blended well with her outfit, but not with her demeanor. "The answer to that question is a decided no. And you're not the first to bring that idea up. I'd met Colin and I've talked with him briefly. He insinuated he'd like to get to know me better. I deflected his advances. That's as far as it went."

"Were you screwing anyone else?" I asked, not so sensitively this time.

Her mouth opened briefly and then snapped shut. She glared at me for a long second. "Why would you think that?"

"Because I'm trying to figure all of this out. And there are some big pieces missing."

She looked down. “We don’t have a perfect marriage.”

“No one does,” I said, not liking the answer that was hovering in front of me.

“We’re not even close. And I can assure you, Tyler has done ten times the damage to our marriage than I could ever dream of.”

“So, who are you having an affair with?” I asked politely.

Hannah Briggs’s eyes widened and sparks started to fly out of them. “I don’t like where this is going. I don’t like your questions. Especially since I’m the one who’s paying you. And paying you quite a bit, I should add.”

“And I don’t like wasting my time or your money. I don’t need total transparency, but this has gone well past a simple case of ‘my husband got drunk and didn’t come home last night.’ It’s morphed into the assassination of a public official. So you’ll excuse my manners if they come off as impolite and my questions if they come off as nosy. But you’re holding back something that only implicates you and does nothing to help Tyler. If that’s your goal.”

“My goal?” she exclaimed. “My goal is to get my husband off from a crime I’m convinced he didn’t commit. Tyler’s a lot of things but he’s not a killer.”

I kept my mouth shut for a moment, I thought of what Gail had said, and I agreed with her. Everyone has the capacity to kill if placed into certain situations, and it doesn’t always emanate from self-defense. There are psychological triggers that can be activated with the right words or the right actions. We all have a level of rage inside of us, and I’d seen a few people who came off as the mildest, meekest individuals that ended up committing some of the most heinous crimes when their tolerance levels were surpassed.

"Maybe not," I said softly, trying to lower the heat of the conversation. "But something's going on here that just isn't making sense. You're right. The evidence against Tyler is lacking. Was he even in the alley behind Glasscock's office? If he did it, why would he be that careless as to drop things like a murder weapon with his fingerprints all over it. Granted, people who commit these crimes are often in panic mode. But these items were left near a dumpster where they'd be easily found. They have all the earmarks of being planted."

"I know. But by whom?" she asked, her eyes wide in bewilderment. "And why'd they target him?"

"That's obviously what I'm trying to get to. Do you know who Glasscock was having an affair with?"

She shook her head. "No. I've heard rumors, but I've heard them about other people in city government, too. There's only so much you can believe. In politics, you never know when someone is just spreading lies to trash others. Just to advance their own careers."

"Glad I didn't stick with public service," I commented.

Hannah Briggs buried her face in her hands, although it didn't look like she was crying. I wouldn't blame her if she did, but people who became prosecutors normally have some sort of mechanism to check their emotions. The waitress came over with our drinks and also brought along a basket filled with crusty looking bread. She sat it down with a smile. If she saw Hannah, nothing registered. I smiled back at the waitress and picked up a piece of bread. It was good bread, surprisingly soft in the center even though the crust was exceptionally crispy. I took another bite.

"This whole thing feels like a dream," she said, spreading her fingers a bit so I could see her face. "Or maybe a nightmare. I wish I could just wake up and have everything be the way it used to be."

"I understand," I said between bites. Hannah was far from the first distraught client I had had, and she wouldn't be the last. I started to regret pressing her hard for intimate details about her personal life; people have a way of shutting down when they feel they're being interrogated. And maybe it didn't matter who Hannah Briggs was involved with outside of the shambles she called a marriage. Both her and Tyler were cheating, maybe one did so to get even with the other, but it mattered not. The homicide charges were their real problem now. Marriages can be fixed or ended, but incarcerations were a different story. And being the wife of an accused murderer was bad enough. How she would keep her job as a prosecuting attorney, or worse, explain this whole mess to her daughter one day was a question I couldn't even begin to contemplate.

"Look, I just can't believe someone would kill a local leader over a romantic relationship," she said, finally lowering her hands. "Certainly not Tyler. He just doesn't have that in him."

I shrugged. Tyler Briggs was a football coach, and a football player before that. Even though he played quarterback, a position that is less affected by the violent nature of the sport, physical combat was always nearby.

"Who would have it in for them then? Glasscock's wife maybe?" I asked.

"I've met Colin's wife. Even if she knew about his dalliances, and she probably did, she's not the type of person who would act like this. She might have left Colin. But murder him? No. I can't see it."

"All right. That leaves us with what? Political rivals? Local activists? Clearly, Colin was not popular in his district any longer."

"I don't know," she said. "I thought this was why I hired you."

I sighed. That was indeed why she hired me, but people sometimes have agendas that are not obvious at first glance. And the level of trust I had in Hannah was diminishing by the minute.

"Yes. That's why you hired me. And I'm trying to unravel this. But if it wasn't Tyler, whoever did it was very clever. This strikes me as a setup, a murder someone committed and made it look like Tyler did it. Someone had to have access to certain things. That green baseball cap, for instance. Could someone he knew from the football world have done this and tried to pin it on him? A player, maybe? A coach?"

"Good heavens, you're mad," she snipped, and looked around as if she were going to leave. But something stopped her. "Why would you think that?"

"Because I'm running out of options," I said. "And because that's a stone I haven't turned over yet. Players angry because they got cut, their big salaries suddenly gone. Coaches fired when Tyler was brought in. There's a lot of money at stake in pro football, and the people who work there are very intense people. I'm sure you've met some players, they're not that far removed from street gangs. I'm sure you've met some coaches, some reminded me of the type who go into police work. Maybe ex-military guys. All of them are around a violent culture. So no, I'm not mad. But I am frustrated. Excuse me if I poke at things. It's sometimes the only way to dislodge the truth, whatever that might be."

At that point, our food came. My pasta was good, and I dug in. Hannah picked at her salad as if she were looking for something very particular and not finding it. The din around us grew louder, but the greater the roar, the less I seemed to notice it. We finished our lunch, I paid the bill, and silently decided not to add it to the expenses I would later bill her for. Half of me tried to applaud myself for being a great guy, but the other half wasn't having any part of that.

*

My schedule that afternoon was wide open. I didn't have anything else to do, and I was running out of people to talk to. The ones who spoke with me weren't telling me anything useful. I decided to pay Roy Woolley a visit for that very reason, not because I thought he could tell me much, but because he was now a politician, and politicians were normally chatty. A big plus was he owned a coffee house, and I needed a jolt of energy after my dispiriting lunch with Hannah. There was a Starbucks a couple of blocks away on Venice Boulevard, but I decided it would be bad manners to walk into his establishment drinking a beverage from the competition.

Roy Woolley owned The Roasters, which was as generic a name for a coffee house as one could conjure up. I used to drive by it thinking it was a barbecue joint, until one day when he wisely painted a big cup on the front window, with steam rising from it. There was also a sign that said there was free parking in the back. I had meant to stop in one day, just like I meant to do a lot of things that I never wound up doing. It was the price of having a busy life, but also the result of being a loyal Starbucks customer, which also might mark me as something of a caffeine addict. I had yet to find any other coffee that gave me the same buzz.

It was after 2:00 pm, a time when a lot of people stopped drinking coffee. But there were still a lot of people lounging about The Roasters, a few sipping coffee, and many who were just working feverishly on their laptops. I waited behind a pair of aging hipsters who ordered identical decaf non-fat hazelnut lattes with extra whip and a caramel drizzle on top. Roy Woolley was working the counter and took their order with the nonplussed expression of a counterman who had seen it all, or perhaps one who did not care. Up close, Woolley was an even larger man than I first thought: thick arms, barrel-chested, with a full beard that made him look even bigger than he first appeared.

"You serve black coffee here?" I asked innocently, once the customers before me walked out of earshot.

"We do, indeed," he smiled, "Although it's not our best seller. You have a preference on roast? We have Mocha Java and Italian Roast brewing."

"Whatever's darker, I'll take."

"You betcha," he said, as he began filling a large yellow ceramic cup. "That'll be one dollar."

"Good deal. Better than Starbucks."

"That's the idea. Same coffee for less."

"Sure," I said, wondering if I'd get the same jolt. "Say, is this the place where I volunteer for your city council campaign?"

Woolley looked up at me. "Sure. Happy to get your help. I also have a petition to put my name on the ballot over there by the window. Would love to get a signature," he said, pointing to a well-lit spot in the corner that had various signs and pamphlets laid out.

"Okay," I said, handing him a five-dollar bill and telling him to keep the change. My donation to political insurgency certainly wasn't overwhelming, and it was tied to my hidden agenda of getting a little time with the aspiring candidate. "Mind if we talk for a few minutes?"

Woolley looked at me for a long moment before motioning for one of the counter staff to handle drink orders for the customers behind me in line. He poured a cup of coffee for himself and led me over to the window. We quickly commandeered two chairs that a pair of teenagers had just vacated, ones that the aging hipsters were eyeing but couldn't get to quickly enough. The seats were still warm. The hipsters looked frustrated.

"My name's Burnside," I said and handed him my card. "Nice place you've got here."

"Thanks."

"I noticed a Starbucks a couple blocks away," I said. "That's usually trouble for a small coffee house."

"Normally, yeah," he said, looking at my card. "A private eye, huh?"

"Right. I live in Mar Vista. You can call me a concerned citizen, but I'm here on business. I'm looking into what happened to Colin Glasscock."

Woolley smirked. "No need to look into anything. Seems like old-fashioned karma to me."

"How so?" I asked, eyeing him carefully.

"Glasscock was a selfish bastard. And a coward to boot. You live in Mar Vista? Well then you've seen that mess he's made of our streets," he said, angrily pointing a finger toward the window. "Traffic nightmare. Emergency vehicles can't get through. Fire trucks, police, ambulances stuck in gridlock. Pedestrians getting hit by bicyclists. The preschool down the street complained about a three-year-old almost getting run over."

"That's not good," I said, hoping he'd continue with his rant.

"It gets worse. A bicyclist was hit by a car the other day. The drivers can't see the bicyclists. The bicyclists can't see the pedestrians. Throw in those stupid Bird scooters the kids like to ride now, and it's a nightmare."

"Any of this affect you directly?"

"Affect me?" he asked incredulously. "Aside from my

five-minute drive in the morning taking twenty minutes, no. I get a lot of walk-in business here at the shop, and the regular customers know there's free parking in the back, only for The Roasters, so my place is okay. Got a tech company across the street, this is practically their lounge area in the morning. And I'm diversified. But a number of local stores closed this year because their business was way down. People can't find a place to park, or they get frustrated being stuck in traffic, so they take other routes. This was supposed to be a growing area, they call it Silicon Alley. New businesses, startups moving in. But the city's thrown cold water on that."

"So, a lot of people hated Glasscock."

"Yup. The worst part was he wouldn't meet with his constituents. People here begged him to show up at community meetings and talk to us, but he stopped doing it once they took away the traffic lanes. Never would face people and listen to their concerns. He was a coward."

"I'd guess you're not unhappy with what happened to him," I asked carefully.

"Hey, look. My condolences to his family. But the guy was a prick, and I'm not going to mince words about it. He got what he deserved. He instilled a lot of hate in people, he divided the community and someone got pushed over the brink. Surprised it was that football coach, but there are plenty of angry people around here."

"You thought maybe someone in the business community was involved in this?"

Woolley raised his hands. "Hey, I'm not making accusations. I'm not pointing fingers. But you don't shoot someone at point-blank range without being pretty ticked off about something."

"That's true," I said placidly. "Someone did it."

"Yeah. And something tells me you don't think it was that coach."

"Nope. Too many pieces don't quite fit."

At that point, an elegantly dressed man, who had to have been in his seventies, sporting a carefully trimmed silver goatee approached. He smiled a bright white smile. "Hello there, Roy," he said.

"Carl," Roy said, jumping up and shaking hands. "Good to see you. It's been a few days. I was getting worried."

"Oh, I don't like to get out when it's this cold," he said.

"Good thing you don't live in Chicago," I butted in. "That's a whole different definition of cold."

"You from Chicago?" he asked.

"Nope. Almost moved there, though."

"This is cold enough for me," he said and turned back to Woolley. "Listen Roy, I just dropped another dime in the kitty. I'm looking forward to your campaign. The community's behind you a thousand percent. Don't worry about the money. We'll get a lot of dough rolling in. I'm getting my friends involved."

Roy Woolley gave the man a hug and thanked him profusely. He politely listened to him go on about traffic, before he finally sauntered away. Woolley sat back down.

"Dropped a dime?" I asked.

"Ten grand. He's one of my big donors. I've raised over a hundred thousand so far. I was afraid things would dry up when Glasscock was wiped out. Looks like the cash is still flowing in."

"Then going up against Glasscock was actually good for you," I mused.

"Hate to say it, but yeah. I guess that takes me off the hook as a suspect, huh? Better to run a campaign against a despicable prick than against a ghost."

What he said made sense, but I thought back to an old French expression, *Qui s'excuse, s'accus*, which translates to something along the lines of he who excuses himself, accuses himself. No sense sharing that yet with Woolley, but I really didn't have anything else to go on with him. Instead, I went back to asking him about something else.

"You know, normally a Starbucks down the street is a problem for a shop like yours. But you've managed to survive it."

"Yeah, but I'm the exception. Starbucks is kind of predatory. They look for small coffee houses like mine, then they rent space next door, take away half their clientele, and then wait for them to go under. When the independent goes out of business, they expand and take over their space. Pretty cutthroat."

"How did you avoid it?"

"My family's owned this block for generations. Next block, too. So when Starbucks came calling a few years ago, wanting to move in next door, we told them no."

"And they moved in a few blocks away."

"Yeah, we own that property, too."

I raised my eyebrows. "Why'd you rent to them then?"

Woolley gave a sly smile. "It's in a strip mall. And we also rented to a bagel shop and a dry cleaners and a convenience store. A lot of the parking spaces are taken up by those customers. People drop off their dry cleaning, get breakfast in the morning, pick up a few quick items. Those wanting coffee can't find parking, get frustrated, and they come over here. I figured Starbucks was going to enter this neighborhood anyway, I might as well make it difficult for them."

"Pretty shrewd," I marveled.

"I always think ahead," he smiled.

"Tell me something. You really think you can get elected to the L.A. City Council?" I asked.

Roy Woolley took a long sip of coffee and sank back in the chair, acting as if no one had ever asked him that question. It was a good act. If I weren't a skeptic on human behavior, I might have bought it.

"It'll be tough. Not as tough as running against Glasscock. But I'm optimistic."

"You've heard Neil Handler is getting appointed to fill out Glasscock's term."

"I heard. No big deal, I'm running anyway."

I frowned. "Insurgent campaigns don't usually win, especially if they're going up against an incumbent. Even if the incumbent is unpopular. But how do you think you'd win, an unknown trying to unseat a guy like Neil Handler? Even if he was just appointed, he has the power of the office. And a lot of friends in city government."

"Let's just say that's not a concern of mine," Woolley replied. The sly smile returned to his lips for a moment, involuntarily perhaps, because it passed quickly. But at that moment, it all became clear. He had no intention of winning. He had no intention of running a real campaign. The hundred thousand dollars that was donated to his newly found political career would largely go to other purposes, maybe a new BMW, or remodeling his kitchen. He was not unlike a few politicians you see around today, soliciting donations from anyone who would provide them; they knew taking money made the donor feel good, even though they'd be getting nothing back on their investment. The candidate would pretend to put up a fight, lose by a large margin, and say he did the best he could. It was a scam, a con, a scheme, and a fraud, but it was a legal one, perfectly legitimate in the eyes of the law, albeit bereft of having any moral compass. Woolley's smile was the smile of just another politician. He was indeed running for something, just not what most people thought. He was running to raise money. For himself.

I asked him once more if he could provide any thoughts as to who might have been behind Glasscock's demise, any name at all would help. Woolley just shook his head, smiled yet again, and said he had no idea how to help me. He reminded me to sign the petition that would put his name on the ballot, which I did using a fake name and a fake address, ensuring that it would not be counted once the petition was reviewed by the city clerk. If it even got that far.

As I stood up to leave, I thanked Woolley for his time, more to be polite than because I meant it. I left three-quarters of my coffee in the cup, it wasn't very dark and it wasn't very good, and by now it wasn't even lukewarm. I didn't quite know where I was going next, but as I walked outside into the cool, damp air, I found out. My phone rang, and it was a familiar voice.

"Hello, Captain," I said. "Nice of you to call *me* for a change."

"This isn't a pleasure call," said the grim voice of Juan Saavedra.

"What's wrong?"

"Plenty. Why don't you drop whatever important business you're conducting and swing by. We're on Venice Boulevard, just under the 405."

"Sure. What's going on?"

"Your pal Tyler Briggs. We found his body. Initial reports were that he shot himself in the gut and bled out. Right here under the freeway. But maybe not. Our forensics guy is thinking it's a homicide."

Eleven

When the police have cordoned off an area and labeled it a crime scene, a carnival atmosphere takes shape. The yellow tape, the dozen police cruisers, the forensics team in their dark blue windbreakers all call attention to an event which every driver slows to gawk at. The police also blocked off all but one lane, which guaranteed traffic would be backed up for blocks. As I approached, I noticed a series of lighting cranes erected and boom poles being situated, signifying local news stations were already on the scene. Indeed, a number of crews were setting up for a shoot, and clusters of people were milling about. I didn't know why these shoots needed this many people, but they invariably did.

I drove slowly past the scene and finally found parking about two blocks away; I jogged over quickly. The police and the media had set up operations on the south side of the street, the north side being occupied by a homeless encampment.

Venice Boulevard along this stretch was the dividing line between two communities, Los Angeles and Culver City. The north side had long been used as shelter by about fifty people living in tents, sleeping bags, and in a few cases, cardboard boxes. They congregated under the 405 Freeway because it gave them protection against the sun during summer days, and against the rain on winter nights. But they stayed on the Los Angeles side of the street for the simple reason that the LAPD only rousted them occasionally. The south side was the jurisdiction of Culver City, and any homeless person daring to set up housekeeping there would get a visit from the CCPD within a day and be ordered to remove themselves from the vicinity. The homeless solved that problem by simply moving their belongings across the street. At some point they would have to uproot again, to where was a mystery. These people had no home, so they would simply migrate to the next locale that didn't kick them out right away.

I found Juan Saavedra barking orders to a few uniforms as a number of reporters stood BY patiently, waiting to interview him. A few yards away lay a body covered by a white sheet. Juan noticed me and held up an index finger as he finished his directives. He motioned me to follow him away from the reporters, and we walked toward a Shell station on Sepulveda.

"When did you find the body?" I asked.

"Passerby called it in around noon. Said he was walking to work this morning and saw someone sleeping on the sidewalk. Had a blanket over his torso. Nothing unusual about that these days. But when he was walking home for lunch he saw the same guy and he hadn't moved. Took a closer look and saw a pool of blood."

I glanced back at the underpass. "I didn't notice a whole lot of blood spatter. You indicated this might not be a suicide."

"It's a setup," Juan said. "It was made to look like he took his own life. Make us think Briggs shoved a gun into his stomach and pulled the trigger. Facing life imprisonment, maybe worse, decides to end it all. Another story that fits nicely. But you're right, it's not a suicide. Whoever did this shot him somewhere else and dumped the body. If Briggs had ended it all here, there'd be a lot more of him lining the sidewalk. And there might also be a gun nearby, although someone walking by could have pocketed it."

"How many times was he shot?" I asked.

"That's another issue. Initial indications are that he was shot multiple times. Maybe three or four."

"Not a suicide then," I said. Suicide victims typically fire one shot because once they've pulled the trigger, the injury is severe enough to prevent them from firing again.

"Very unlikely. And whoever did this is an amateur. If they wanted it to be credible, the gun would have been in the mouth or the side of the head."

"There's also the question of why he would do it here," I said. "Guys like Briggs don't live on the street. If he didn't want his family to find him this way, he'd have driven somewhere and done it in his car. Or on a beach. Or gone somewhere other than across the street from a homeless encampment under a freeway."

"Yeah, I don't like this one bit."

"Any sense of when this happened?" I asked.

"Middle of the night," Juan answered. "We interviewed a bunch of those homeless across the street. No one knows anything except he wasn't there last night and he was there this morning."

I shook my head. "No one saw a car stop and someone dragging a dead body onto the sidewalk?"

"We're not dealing with the most upstanding citizenry on this block. We did find one old boy who thought he saw a light blue Mercedes pull up for a minute."

I looked at him. "That's Tyler's car."

"We're checking it out. Look, I need to know a few things. When we brought Briggs in, he lawyered up quick. Yammered a bit in the beginning about how it wasn't him, but clammed up once we began asking some pointed questions."

I thought about this. What Briggs did was actually fairly astute. There was nothing to be gained by cooperating with the police, even if he were innocent. Words could get twisted, evidence misplaced, and the interrogators would convince him that if he had the slightest connection to the homicide, he'd be looking at twenty to life for simply knowing about the crime. The police have forced confessions out of innocent people before, and it took more fortitude than one might imagine to stand one's ground. Detectives were good at wearing people down, and not everyone was able to withstand the pressure. Invoking their right to remain silent and requesting an attorney puts the onus on the police and the prosecutors to prove the charges, something they couldn't always do even if they did have some evidence.

"I take it you didn't get Briggs's side of things when you talked with him."

"Nope. But when Forensics came back and said the fingerprints on the Glock were a match, and the DNA on that baseball cap matched his, the brass didn't think we needed to do more. Like I told you the other day, things didn't exactly fit together and something smelled off. But I wasn't going up against the Deputy Chief with just a hunch."

"By the way, did your guys stop by the Snuggle Inn I told you about?" I asked.

"Yeah, I sent Orlando yesterday. He picked up that syringe you found, got it from the manager. Sounded like the maid's disappeared. We had it tested, matched the blood type to Briggs, but it didn't have his fingerprints on it."

"Your lab guys worked quick."

"This is top priority," Juan said. "Drop everything stuff. When you push people, they can turn things around fast."

"What else was in the syringe?"

"Traces of a drug called Rohypnols," he said.

"The date rape drug," I said.

"One and the same. Odd, huh?"

"Very," I said. Rohypnols was sometimes called Roofies and was primarily a sedative, part of a family of drugs called Benzodiazepines. It was a tranquilizer, about ten times stronger than Valium, and typically men drop it into a woman's drink and then proceed to sexually assault them. It immobilizes the victim, knocks them out, and they normally can't remember what happened or who did what. Occasionally it was deployed by women, who would lure men into a hotel room, slip it into their drink, rob them and leave. A few addicts used roofies for their own high, but that was very unusual.

"Did you know if Briggs had a drug problem?" Juan asked.

"Not that I'm aware of. But to go from alcohol abuse to drug abuse isn't that big a leap."

Juan looked at me. "No, it's not. And it did sound as if Briggs had a bad drinking problem. It's not a stretch to imagine him using drugs, too. And sometimes drug users do strange things to get off. This drug mostly knocks you out. Once in a while we see it used by addicts who also use coke or meth. Wards off depression, supposedly. Who knows."

"That might explain his blackout," I said, thinking Briggs had failed to recall what had happened from Friday night all the way through Monday morning.

"For some guys, getting high is all they want."

"True," I said, not entirely sure that this described Tyler Briggs. I didn't know him well enough to draw conclusions. But what Juan said was not unreasonable.

"Look, I need you to dig here," he said.

"Sure. But what about Orlando?"

He shook his head. "I sent Orlando back to the motel this afternoon to try and find that maid, Teresa, but he said she's disappeared. Didn't show up for work the past couple of days. The manager wouldn't give an address where we could find her."

"And you think I can do better."

Juan smiled. "She may be the key to this and I'd like to find out just how much more she knows. Let's just say Detective Brown is just punching the clock until he retires. He does the basics and not much more. I need someone who isn't going to take no for an answer so easily."

"And you'll be willing to spring me from the brig again.

If need be, of course," I said slowly, not exactly wanting to spend any more time in a cell. I thought of Gail and Marcus and briefly shuddered.

"See if you can keep your activities within the gray area."

"So, you want me to find Teresa and see if she can shed any light on who Tyler Briggs was with last Friday night."

"You think you can do that?" he asked.

I shrugged. "I've been trying to do that for almost a week. Look how far I've gotten."

*

I drove back to the Snuggle Inn, and as I walked into the office, I came upon the same surly manager. He did not look pleased with my arrival, in fact, he looked like rather exasperated. He threw up his hands and let out a big sigh of annoyance. I politely waited for him to finish going through his act.

"You again?" he demanded. "I already told last officer everything."

"Funny, I heard you didn't tell him very much."

"I do not know where that *puta* Teresa is."

"*Puta*?" I asked, knowing it was Spanish for whore. "You sure have a good working knowledge of Spanish."

He shrugged. "This is L.A."

"Tell me what happened with Teresa. You two have a little tiff?"

"What? You are talking shit to me."

"No, I'm talking English to you, and I think you ought

to learn some. And when an officer of the law asks you for the whereabouts of an employee, you tell them."

"Listen," he said, wiping his forehead with a handkerchief, which was odd given that it was barely sixty degrees outside, downright cold for Los Angeles. "Teresa, she no longer works here. She no show up this week. I can't have that. I had to make up the rooms. So I fire her. I hire someone else. That's the way it goes."

"Let me have her home address," I ordered, and placed a fifty dollar bill on the counter.

"I don't have her home address," he responded, eyeing the bill with more than a passing glance. "It's probably a fake anyway."

"So you do have her address."

"Listen. I just have copy of her driver's license. Like I said, it's probably a fake."

"Get it," I said, keeping my fingers on the bill until he returned. It took him a little while, but he came back with a hazy photocopy of a drivers license that looked like it had been copied three or four times. The photo was blurry, but it could have been her. I made out the name and it was indeed Teresa Ortiz, and she lived at an address in South Central.

"Here. This is all I have."

"Looks reasonable. Why don't you think it's real?"

"Most employees are illegals. Most employees lie. No trust them. That's why."

"And how come you didn't give this to the detective earlier?" I asked, pushing the fifty toward him.

The big man shook his head. "He was very rude. I don't

like rude people."

"You don't think I'm rude?"

"You're rude, too," he said, picking up the bill. "But I can deal with your kind of rude."

I folded the copy of the drivers license and put it in my pocket. It was after 5:00 pm and a trip to South Central would take an hour and a half there, and an hour and a half back. And I might or might not find Teresa. I wasn't technically working for Juan Saavedra, but I owed him plenty of favors, and I didn't mind helping him, even though he couldn't reimburse me. With her husband now dead, I was pretty sure I wasn't working for Hannah Briggs any longer, and I was also having doubts as to whether she would pay me, given our last encounter did not go well. My only paying client right now was Cliff Roper and I hadn't returned his last two phone calls. I made a mental note to stop by USC tomorrow after I looked up Teresa.

I drove home, and was disappointed when I walked in the door. The best part of my day was Marcus announcing my arrival in a big, excited voice, smile on his face, running to give me a hug. But he sat on the couch and just looked glum. I walked over and sat down next to him.

"You don't look like a happy camper."

"Mom said I had to have chicken tenders tonight," he said in a sulky voice.

"I thought you liked those."

"I like them from McDonald's. She's using the frozen kind."

"Ah," I said, getting up and taking his hand. "Let's go

talk to Mom and see what's what."

He jumped up and we walked into the kitchen. Chewy, who had been busy scratching at the fleas behind her ears, got up to join us. Gail had the refrigerator door open and was scanning through it carefully. She was still dressed in her business clothes, a gray suit with a red top. Her chestnut brown hair was loose and hung partway down her back. I gave her a quick hug from behind.

"See anything interesting?" I asked.

"Feels like you bought a lot of things at Costco the other day. But it was mostly fruits and vegetables and nuts and candy. And frozen food. Lots of frozen food."

"We're getting prepared for a long winter," I said.

She turned to me and gave a half-smile. I gave her a kiss. Her smile broadened a little. Marcus took that as a sign to jump in.

"Mom, why can't we have McDonald's? I hate those frozen things."

"You don't hate them, Marcus. You may be a little tired of them, though," she said and turned to me. How do you feel about frozen lasagna tonight? Or frozen chicken *parmigiana*?"

"Well, I had Italian food for lunch. Maybe another night?"

"Hmmm. How do chicken tenders sound?"

I thought about this for a very brief moment. "How does going out to dinner sound? My treat."

"Yay!" Marcus yelled.

"Works for me," Gail said. "Where to?"

"McDonald's!" Marcus offered.

"Hmmm," I said, looking at Gail frown. "I think Mom might want something a little nicer, don't you think?"

"What about sushi?" Marcus said. Last year I had taken Marcus to his first sushi bar, and I had assumed he'd be fine with just Miso soup and maybe *Tamago*, which is little more than sweetened scrambled eggs on top of a bed of rice. But when he saw they had eel and octopus on the menu, he insisted on trying them, and to our amazement, and maybe for shock value, he declared they were the best things he had ever eaten. It was a little pricey, but sushi became a part of our meal outings.

I looked at Gail, who was not a sushi eater. "You think you can find something on U-Zen's menu?"

"Sure. As long as it's cooked, I'm fine with that."

Marcus began to celebrate, and I went upstairs to change my clothes and stow my .357 in the safe. Gail didn't like me carrying it when I was going out with the family; the odds of ever needing it were remote, and I always kept a firearm hidden in my Pathfinder, so one was not too far from reach. If we came upon trouble, I'd need to rely upon my razor wit.

U-Zen was located on Santa Monica Boulevard, near Bundy. It was a Japanese restaurant that had been around for decades, long before sushi turned into a phenomenon. Once, sushi was more of a curiosity. But when the trend started, it hit L.A. hard, and soon there were sushi bars everywhere. We liked U-Zen because it was relatively cheap, and they had a full menu so Gail could have teriyaki, tempura or short ribs. And Marcus and I could indulge in raw fish, something in which he was beginning to take delight.

The chefs welcomed us with their usual roar as we walked inside, the traditional greeting to make guests feel welcome. We sat at the sushi bar with Marcus in between Gail and I, and we combed through the menu. I didn't see octopus, but I saw plenty of other things Marcus liked to sample.

"You want eel?" I asked.

"Oh, yeah. I love eel."

"And sweet shrimp?"

"Yup."

"Want to try salmon eggs?" I asked.

He looked at me. "What's that?"

"They're like tiny little orange pellets filled with liquid. They burst open in your mouth."

"Yes!" he exclaimed.

I smiled and ordered the same, along with a few more things for myself. Gail had the short ribs, and in an odd twist, her food, cooked as it were, came out a few minutes before our sushi. I tried to show Marcus how to use chopsticks again, but it was in vain, and I finally told him we'd try again another time. No sense in having him drop a piece of sushi on the floor because he couldn't work the utensils. I told him using his fingers would be fine, but then decided to take him to the men's room so he could wash his hands with soap. When we retuned, our food was waiting for us. Marcus picked up a few salmon eggs ladled over some rice and began eating them one by one.

"Good?" I asked.

"Mmmm," came the happy response.

A middle-aged man sitting next to us watched Marcus with interest. "You look like a very sophisticated sushi eater," he said.

"What's that mean?" Marcus asked, scooping up a few more salmon eggs.

"It means you're adventurous."

"Yup," he answered, more focused on eating than making conversation. I recalled a conversation Gail and I once had with Marcus about being wary of talking to strangers. I wasn't sure if that lesson had resonated deeply, or if he was simply more focused on the dinner in front of him.

I turned to Gail. "How was your day?" I asked, careful to make sure Marcus was engaged with dinner and not listening to us talk shop. In our household, the family business was fighting crime, but that often involved discussing the thornier aspects, ones that were wholly unsuitable for a five-year-old to hear.

"Oh, finishing one case, starting another. The first one was easy. This thief accosted a truck driver in a fast food parking lot. I guess he saw an Apple logo on the truck and figured the driver was carrying a load of expensive cargo. He was. Crates of new iPhones. He thought he hit the jackpot, those devices are worth a small fortune. He didn't realize something, though. Know what it was?"

"Hmmm," I said, picking up a piece of yellowtail with my chopsticks and dipping it into some wasabi-laced soy sauce. "The iPhones had GPS on them?"

"They do. And what shocked the thief was that once the truck driver called it in to his boss – and note that he called his boss before he called the police – the boss turned on one of the iPhones remotely, and activated the tracking."

"And *then* he called the police," I said.

"LAPD simply had to drive over to the garage that the thief pulled into. Imagine how shocked this guy was. He had arrived just five minutes earlier. He was smoking a cigarette, he figured he had some time to unload."

I took another bite of yellowtail. Nice and rich. I looked over at Marcus, still pulling salmon eggs out one by one and rolling them around in his mouth. It reminded me of when I had alphabet soup as a child. I was more concerned with spelling out words, and my mother had to keep reminding me to eat.

"And are they pleading innocent by reason of stupidity?"

"We're doing a plea bargain. Prisons are beyond max capacity, but I think they'll still serve time."

"Good."

"That was an easy one," she continued. "My current case is trickier. Two brothers. They'd go to a Home Depot, load up two carts with expensive product, but both carts were identical. One would pay for his and go put it in his truck. Then he'd go back to the store and hand the brother his receipt. The brother would go to Returns and say his client cancelled on him and he needed his money back. The brothers effectively got the items for free."

"Ingenious," I marveled. "How'd they get caught?"

"They hit up the same Home Depot four times this month. Someone finally caught on."

I smiled. "Imagine if these brothers would only have put their talents toward good and not evil. They'd probably be running Home Depot by now."

"For some it's the thrill of the game," she said. "How are you doing? I heard about Tyler. The whole thing makes no sense. Why would he take his own life?"

"I know. Juan's sure it's not a suicide. Forensics is confirming, but it looks like he's right. I called him a little while ago. No powder burn on Tyler's hand, no gunpowder residue near the wound. It's dressed up to look like a suicide but it's not."

Gail frowned. "I was talking with someone at Arthur Woo's office yesterday. They had heard something about Tyler having left with some blonde at the Alibi room the night Colin Glasscock was killed. I guess that's about the last thing Tyler remembered before he blacked out. And I'm wondering if that blonde had something to do with Tyler ending up on the street this morning. If this was indeed a homicide, whoever did it might have been covering their tracks."

I nodded. "You've got some good detective chops."

"Why thank you sweetie."

"What do you think of Hannah Briggs?" I asked absently, mostly because she was blonde and beautiful.

Gail stopped for a moment. "I don't know," she replied. "She was friendly with the councilman."

"Could she have been having an affair with Glasscock?" I asked.

"Hard to say," she admitted. "Not to be crass, but the rumor mill said Glasscock walked around with an open fly. He was supposedly generous with his affections."

"That's what I'm hearing, too," I said, starting to wonder if there was a single soul in city politics who *wasn't* having an affair with someone. "And when Glasscock was shot, it happened at point blank range, meaning this was probably an act of passion. Maybe revenge, jealousy. If Tyler had done it, it might well have been the work of a cuckolded husband. Pretty sure Hannah was having an affair. Just not sure with whom."

"Oh?"

"Let's just say that when I asked her, she didn't admit it but she didn't deny it, either."

"Interesting," she said. "You've had quite a busy day today."

"It just keeps going. And there's another thing," I said, feeling a bit of trepidation coming through in my voice.

"What's that?" she asked.

"I met with Arthur Woo this morning."

"Ah. The rising star of L.A. politics."

"Yes," I continued. "He's quite a bright guy. Ambitious, too. He said he thinks you have a career in politics. He said he can spot ambition in others."

"I don't know about entering politics. It's an option, but it's a life changer."

"Sure. But Arthur also told me something else. Said that you've gotten some, ah, other types of offers. Of the romantic kind."

Gail turned and gave me an odd look. "Oh? He told you that?"

"Yes."

Gail nodded. "I've gotten offers. A lot of women get them. It's nothing. I turn them all down."

"That's good," I said. "It's a risk that comes with being a beautiful woman."

"That's nice of you to say," she answered. "But it's not about beauty. A lot of women get hit on at the office. Looks aren't always it."

"What is it then?"

"Power. Ego. Some just want to have another notch on their belt. I've heard it said that some men do it because they want to live forever. I never understood that."

I shrugged. "Me neither. But I'm glad you've turned them all down. Arthur told me I had nothing to worry about. But of course, that just made me start to worry."

At that point I felt Marcus tug at my sleeve.

"Daddy?"

"Yes, Marcus?"

"Why would someone walk around with their fly open?"

I looked at Gail and she looked back at me. Neither of us had a good answer ready. And I sensed we both started to silently reconsider having these types of conversations within Marcus's earshot.

Twelve

I awoke just past dawn and, as is my habit, turned toward the bedroom window to get a glimpse of what the day would be like. I didn't need to look past the rectangular panes of glass to see droplets of water sliding down. The weather app said today would be gloomy and gray, and it looked like it was right. I moaned to myself and rolled out of bed quickly. If there was one thing I needed to do to avoid making my morning a full-on disaster, it was to jump on the freeway before everyone else.

There was a drive-through window at a nearby Coffee Bean. Their dark roast was lacking in boldness, but they made up for it with speed and convenience. The 10 Freeway had some minor slowing even before 7:00 am, but the Harbor Freeway was gloriously open as I sailed south, away from the crowded downtown interchange. I exited the Harbor at Century Boulevard and turned toward one of the most infamous neighborhoods in Los Angeles.

The Watts riots in the 1960s put that community on the map forever. Prior to the uprising, the area was known mostly for the Watts Towers, an Italian artist's tribute to garbage, a sky-high series of cylindrical sculptures, decorated with all sorts of throwaways like broken pottery, dented bottle caps, and random shards of glass, items that would most likely be tossed into a recycling bin these days. Watts had morphed into a black neighborhood back after World War II, and while it was still perceived that way, even by many Angelenos, the reality was that the Watts of today was populated mostly by Hispanics.

I drove about twenty blocks until I reached Grape Street and turned right. I came across the address for Teresa's apartment building a few blocks away. It was a standard nondescript, beige two-story building, the kind of building that was ubiquitous in the Southland. The steel security gate was relatively new, painted black, with wire mesh preventing anyone from sticking a hand through and opening it from the outside. Iron bars covered all the windows, even the ones on the second floor. It looked impenetrable from the outside, but access proved easy when a resident exited on their way to work, and simply held the door open for me.

While Teresa's driver's license only gave the street address with no apartment number, this problem was easily solved by scanning the brass-colored mailboxes. Not all were identifiable, but some had scraps of paper with names scrawled in ink. One or two mailboxes did not have locks on them, and were slightly ajar. But I did find the Ortiz name, and it was right above the box marked with a number 7. My lucky day. I walked down the hall, rang the bell that did not work, and then knocked. It opened a few seconds later. Teresa Ortiz was wearing a sweatshirt and jeans, and two small children were seated at the table behind her, eating cereal.

"Hello, Teresa," I said.

Her mouth opened and stayed open. Her eyes darted,

first looking behind me to see who I was with, then behind her at her children, and then back at me. For a fleeting moment I thought she'd slam the door in my face.

"Wait," I said, putting my hand up. "It's not what you think."

"*Señor! Soy inocente*!"she exclaimed.

"Again, I'm not with ICE. This has nothing to do with immigration."

She stared at me. I continued.

"You remember me from last week."

"*Sí*. At ... motel."

"I'm the one who told you to give the syringe to the officers."

"*Sí*. I give to manager, *señor*," she said, her English starting to get surprisingly better. "I no go back there. I am sure he give to the *policia*. My friend told me. She still there."

"I know. But I need to find out more about that woman. The one who was in that room where you found the syringe."

Teresa shook her head. "I never saw woman. I leave at *las seis en punto*. Six o'clock."

"Who would know about that woman. Who worked late last Friday night?"

Teresa shook her head. "Maids leave by *seis*. The manager would know. His name is Vidur. He the only one still there. He always there."

I took a breath. Vidur had been about as helpful as a sixth finger, and there was no reason to assume a return visit would change any of that. I thought of asking him for a list of the guests that night, but I doubted Vidur would give that up without a court order. I decided to try something else.

"So who might know her?"

"*Como*?"

"Might there have been any motel guests who could have seen that woman? Any regulars?"

Teresa thought about this for a moment before replying affirmatively. "*Si*. There is one couple. They come every Friday. They always come at five."

"What do you know about them?"

Teresa looked down. "He is married. She is not."

I smiled. "No, no. I mean, do you know their names, what they look like."

"I no have names. But they are older. Forty, maybe. I hear they have been going there for years. The other maids tell me. Same night each week. Same room. Every week."

"What room do they stay in?"

"*Veintiuno*."

"And what number is that?" I sighed.

She licked her lips. "It is ... twenty-one."

I reached into my wallet and pulled out a twenty dollar bill. She had been more helpful than Vidur, but at this point my expense report was going to go unpaid. Life was not fair.

"*Gracias, señor*," she said gratefully, as she pocketed the bill.

"*De nada*," I said, and watched her carefully. "So, you stopped working at the Snuggle."

"*Si, señor*. I quit."

"Oh. Why'd you do that?"

She bit her lip. "Too many *policia* last week. That no good for me. I feel nervous. I don't feel safe around *policia*. You know."

"What else can you tell me? It's important."

She shook her head and looked back at her kids. "That's all I know, *señor*."

I nodded and realized I wasn't going to get much more from her. Teresa was like a lot of immigrants, here illegally, trying to earn money and trying to stay out of trouble. In some circles, a police presence provided reassurance; for Teresa, the police meant trouble. With two children, she was going to do what she could to avoid authorities, even if it meant quitting her job. But in her world, earning mostly minimum wage, jobs were not hard to find. There was always an employer somewhere who needed cheap help. I thanked her and left.

After checking my traffic app, I saw that cars on the road had already coalesced into full gridlock, helped in part by the light sprinkling of rain coming down. I wasn't terribly far from USC, about twenty minutes, but the drive there would flow evenly as long as I stayed off the Harbor Freeway and took surface streets. I thought this might be an opportune time to catch a few football players before they left their house, and, quite possibly, before they even woke up.

I drove up Broadway, passing not only a wide variety of rundown apartment buildings and dicey retail outlets, but a surprising number of churches as well. It is perhaps not surprising that the worse the economic conditions of a neighborhood, the greater the need to pray for something better. In the five years I worked as a patrol officer in the Broadway Division, I did not see life get any better for residents here. If anything, it had gotten worse.

Hobart Street was quiet, and I parked midway down the block. The house looked in even more disrepair on a murky morning like this, and the sparse patch of dirt that served as a front yard was depressing. The only thing different from my last visit was what appeared to be a gang-related splash of red graffiti on the front wall, a marking that probably meant something to a group of local thugs, but may have gone unnoticed by the residents. I knocked on the door, and as anticipated, after no answer in the first sixty seconds, began banging loudly.

"Okay, okay," came a tired voice as I heard a deadbolt lock being turned. The door opened, and a sleepy looking college student, who barely seemed twenty-one, blinked and tried to focus on me. He was attired in a cardinal t-shirt and white boxers, his torso thick and trunky, although he might have come off as more physically imposing had he been alert.

"Yeah, what is it?" he asked sleepily.

"Let me guess," I said, not guessing at all. "Patrick O'Malley. You've grown quite a bit since high school."

He tried to process what I was saying but could only blink a few more times and answer with a one-word response, along the lines of "Huh?"

"I'm Coach Burnside," I said. "I helped recruit you to SC a few years ago."

A dim sense of recognition began to appear, and the slightest hint of a smile crossed his face. "Oh, yeah. Fili told me you came by the other day."

"Can I come in ?" I asked.

Patrick opened the door without saying anything, and I entered the house. It was as disheveled as it had been the other day.

"You guys should bring in a maid," I said, sweeping some errant clothing off the gray couch and sitting down. "You'll be able to afford it soon."

Patrick sat down. "You want some coffee? I think we might have some."

I waved my hand and decided not to ask what roast. "I'm good."

"I remember you from the Coach Cleary era."

"And I remember you torching my secondary in practice every day. You ran the scout team your first year at SC. Good thing we didn't have to play against anyone like you on Saturdays."

Patrick smiled a shy smile. Maybe it was a sleepy one. He had auburn hair, thick, and wavy. He was a big kid as far as most human beings go, solid, about 6'2" and probably weighed 220 pounds. But as far as most football players go, he was not especially large.

"That was a fun year," he said. "No pressure. I'd go to classes and then at 3:00 pm I'd go play ball. Then I got to sit on the sidelines and watch USC play each week."

"This year had to be fun, though. You're headed to the Rose Bowl against Michigan. You had a great season," I said, vaguely wondering if I should hit Patrick up for a pair of Rose Bowl tickets, before my ethics intervened and I decided against it.

"Thanks. Finals are almost over. After Christmas we go into full practice mode for Pasadena. I've never played in the Rose Bowl game before. Watched it so many times on TV, I'm pinching myself that I'll actually be in it."

"It's an amazing experience, it truly is," I told him. Having played in a couple of Rose Bowls myself, and having coached USC in a few others, I could honestly say there was nothing to quite compare it with. "What are you going to do after that?"

Patrick shook his head. "That's what everyone's asking. I really don't have the answer. Honest, I don't. Agents are telling me I'm leaving millions on the table if I come back to school next year and pass on the NFL for a season."

"You think you're ready for it?"

"Hard to say. I've done well playing college ball. But everybody I've talked to says the NFL is a much different life. Everything's a big deal there. You're under a microscope all the time. Feels like I just started college a couple years ago. I like it here. But I don't know how smart it is to leave all that money on the table."

I looked at him and sympathized. He was a kid in his early 20s, suddenly propelled into the national limelight, and being asked to make a life-altering decision for which he had limited knowledge. People from USC wanted him to stay in school because that would mean another banner season next year. People like Cliff Roper, who stood to profit enormously if Patrick signed with his agency and entered the NFL draft, had their own financial interests at heart. I had no good answer for him. But I at least had a suggestion.

"Have you thought of calling Coach Cleary?" I asked. "He knows the NFL and he knows you. He's still part of the Trojan family, even though he only coached you for one year."

"No," he said, the light bulb practically lighting up above his head. "That's not a bad idea."

"Let me ask you something else. What does your heart tell you? Is the NFL something you really want to pursue right now?"

Patrick shrugged, which gave me part of the answer I was looking for. Going into pro football required a full commitment. It was a grown man's game, and it did not tolerate players who weren't all in.

"Rumor has it," I continued, "that you have an interest in the winter Olympics. True or false?"

"Dang!" Patrick laughed. "Fili was right. You really are a detective."

"I just listen and piece things together. You serious about trying out for the halfpipe?"

"Don't really know. I have fun snowboarding, been doing it my whole life. It's a blast. I've tried some moves and I'm pretty good at them. I don't know about qualifying for the Olympics, that's really big-time. But the feeling I get when I land a trick is unlike anything else. Even throwing a touchdown in front of 90,000 screaming people. And trust me, that is really cool, too."

I processed this and thought about how best to respond to Patrick. That the risks he would be taking with Olympic snowboarding, attempting the dangerous aerial maneuvers that Olympians do, would be enough to scare any football coach half to death. An NFL team would think long and hard about investing a ton of money into a player who could tear up his body trying to land a double-McTwist 1260. Lloyd's of London was reportedly open to insuring almost anything, and they were well known for underwriting college football players against career-ending injuries before turning pro. But I think even they would have some pause about covering the future earnings of an athlete in a sport that was only slightly safer than doing loop-de-loops with a snowmobile.

"Okay," I said. "Can I give you my two cents?"

"Sure. Everyone else has."

"If you want to play football, play football. If you want to be an Olympian, try out for the Olympics. You might be able to do both, but probably not. If you pick football, you won't have time to do what Olympians need to do, which is practice like crazy. If you pick the Olympics, no pro football team will make you a high draft pick. They may not want to touch you at all. So you decide. There's no right or wrong answer. It just comes down to what you really want to do. Money's going to be a part of that decision, you can't ignore it, and you shouldn't ignore it. But it also comes down to what your heart tells you. What you really want to do. And I don't think you can do both."

"Yeah," he said, scratching a two-day-old beard. "I think I get it. That's cool. But even if I pick football, I still have the problem of whether I should leave school. I don't have a lot of time. The NFL says I have to declare in a couple of weeks if I want to go pro next season."

"It's still the same kind of decision. What do you really want to do. Stay in school or leave. That's all it comes down to. I'm not trivializing this, because once you make a decision, you're right, there's a deadline, that's it for next season. But just don't make it too complicated, either."

"Okay. Cool, thanks. But hey, you didn't come down here to talk to me about this. I doubt you were just in the neighborhood."

I smiled and didn't tell him I actually was nearby. "Did Fili tell you about our talk?"

"Yeah. That sounded weird, what happened to that guy who broke in, huh?"

I stared at him. "You weren't a part of it?"

"Nah. I was up at Big Bear for the day, snowboarding. Coaches would have killed me if they found out. They've told me I can't do any of that during the season. But hey, the powder's great right now, I figured I could sneak out once in a while."

"You didn't show up at practice that day?"

"Nah. The guys covered for me with the coaches, said I had the flu. But then this burglary happens here. I guess the thief almost made off with some of our stuff, my high school ring and all. The guys went a little overboard on him. Too bad the whole thing got into the papers. I figured I'd say I was here, because the coaches warned me at the start of the season, that they'd suspend me if I went off snowboarding. I wouldn't get to play in the Rose Bowl."

"And you had to tell a lie about being part of the assault, in order to cover yourself for the first lie of skipping practice to go snowboarding."

"Kind of weird, but yeah."

I shook my head. Leave it to a twenty-one year-old to think that being accused of a felony was the lesser issue when compared to incurring the wrath of his coaches. I didn't tell him that few coaches in their right minds would suspend their star player for the biggest game of the year, just for a rule infraction. A few would, but most would not. I had seen Johnny look the other way once when our star linebacker got into a bar fight in Phoenix and punched out three guys the night before a game against Arizona State. We punished him by making him do extra calisthenics, and by keeping him out of the starting lineup, which meant he missed exactly one play before trotting onto the field.

"Then Fili was covering for you?"

"Pretty much. But someone at SC managed to shut the media report down. We're all good."

I shook my head. "Not exactly."

"What do you mean?" he asked.

"The burglar is ticked."

"So what? It's not like he's going to sue us. Sounds like he got what he deserved."

"I don't disagree. But two things are happening here. One is that this guy is gang-affiliated. Which means he's planning to come back and settle the score. You see that graffiti on your front wall?"

"Yeah, that's weird. But hey, we got four big football players here. Not like we're scared of any street hoodlums."

"I get that. But they play by a different set of rules, and they're smart enough to not come in and start throwing punches. If they come back, they'll be packing something. The other thing is Fili is thinking of going into the NFL this year."

"Yeah, his family needs the money."

"That won't happen if the NFL starts poking around in this. They take a really dim view these days of players getting into trouble with the law."

"Wow. That doesn't sound good."

"No, none of it does."

Patrick sank into his chair. "I feel bad for Fili. Can we do anything?"

I smiled. "Is Fili here?"

"Yeah, he's asleep. You want me to go wake him?"

"Go wake him. I think I can hatch a plan that might work."

*

At one time, the bulk of L.A. traffic converged mostly on downtown, the Mecca that included corporate headquarters for banks, oil companies, and various city agencies. Plenty of traffic still flowed into downtown, but the birth of Silicon Beach, the oddly named and largely despised area of startup tech companies that dotted Venice and Santa Monica, had ensured the traffic logjam would also ensnare those heading to the beach each morning. The drizzle had stopped, but the long slog to the Westside still took the better part of an hour. I stopped at the Starbucks near my office for some personal refueling, went up to my office, and felt better after a few sips of French roast. But I had barely put my feet up on my desk before my phone started buzzing.

"Burnside," came the familiar voice. "You've been up early."

"Johnny," I said. "Been a while. Has the snow been piling up in Chicago?"

"Mild winter so far," he said. "It's fifty-five degrees today. If this is what climate change means, I'm all for it."

"Hold that thought for a few years," I said. "And I think it actually may be colder in L.A. this morning."

"Good thing I moved."

"Good thing I didn't."

Johnny chuckled, and I thought back to when my friend left USC to be the head coach of the Chicago Bears. He wanted me to join him, made me an offer that was more than generous, and Gail and I actually considered it. But it was a life for which you had to have a calling, and I didn't have it. I still didn't see enough of Gail and Marcus, but I saw more of them now than I ever would, had I continued as a football coach.

"I guess you probably know I got a call a little while ago from a couple of the guys," Johnny said.

"Yeah. I'm trying to do some career counseling. Figured maybe you could do some *pro bono* work on that score, too."

"I told them what I knew," he said. "Patrick would be a top three draft pick if he came out this year. But he'd still be a top three if he waited a year."

"Any sense in him waiting then?"

"Maybe. But Fili's the one who really should move on. The funny thing is, Fili's never going to be a first round pick. He doesn't have quick feet, and he can't seem to jump two inches. But he's a block of granite when it comes to trying to move him out of the way. And he's got a good motor, never quits on a play. He's one of those guys that doesn't seem like he'd be that great, but he often manages to be in the right place at the right time. Kind of uncanny. When someone strips a ball carrier, there's Fili right there to pick up the rock. He can't jump, but he manages to know when a QB is about to release the ball and where his passing lane is. Incredibly, he can sometimes get his paws up in time to knock the ball down."

"Fili also has some money issues."

"I know. But money shouldn't be the deciding factor. One factor, certainly. But college guys who come out just because of the money are often disappointed. The NFL's a grind and it's a tough grind. Very different from going to school, and I let Fili know that. He'll probably go in the 3rd or 4th round but he's the type of guy who can end up playing in the league for ten seasons. He'll get paid nicely at first, but the real money will come a few years later. Just have to be patient."

I nodded. "I think I sent them to the right guy. Thanks for stepping in."

"My pleasure. Funny how when you coach a kid well, even if it's just for one season, you're still their coach years later."

"Reminds me of the Bulldog," I said, thinking of our old

head coach, Bulldog Martin, who we played for at USC. "When the Bulldog would call me, I swear I would leap to my feet and shout 'yes sir' into the phone."

"I know. It's different in the pros. Much less of a connection with the players. They come and go. Some are with you for years, but most aren't. It's harder to build that bridge with them."

"Yeah," I said. "And speaking of coaches, you heard about Tyler Briggs?"

"It's been all over the news. Tragic. The arrest was bizarre, I mean, the killing of a city councilman was off-the-charts crazy. But him ending up dying on the streets like this? Truly incredible. I coached against him last year, when we came out to play the Chargers. That was late in the season, and you could tell the stress was eating him up. What do you make of it? News reports said it was initially being ruled a suicide, but they were investigating possible foul play."

"I'm pretty sure he was murdered. The suicide angle doesn't make sense, and the police are pretty sure it was a homicide. They think his body was dumped right at the 405 underpass."

"You involved with this case?" Johnny asked.

"Yup. Tyler's wife called me last Saturday and said he'd gone missing. I found him two days later. Started off drinking, and finished by shooting up. Somewhere along the way he picked up some woman and they ended up in a motel room. Still looking for her, I think she holds the key to all this, but the trail may have gone cold."

Johnny let out a breath. "I met Tyler's wife once.

Coaches' meeting last year. Can't say they were the happiest looking couple, but hey, this profession breeds a lot of divorces."

"From what I can gather, both of them were having affairs. Doesn't explain how Tyler would get arrested or wind up in a body bag."

"If it were last year, I might have suspected Riddleman."

My ears perked up. "The Charger assistant coach? The two of them had been friends for years."

"Hey look, I'm not suggesting anything. And a year's passed, so I would imagine the heat's died down. But Riddleman and Tyler were having personality conflicts. Riddleman was ticked at Tyler's insistence on calling plays during the game, especially plays that weren't working. Felt Tyler was meddling in the QB coaching, and he turned their season into a disaster. I heard they nearly came to blows a few times. But like I said, none of that adds up to murder."

"Nope," I agreed, but filed this away in the back of my mind. "But I must say you hear a lot of interesting gossip. I don't recall that being on ESPN."

"Some people call it gossip, I call it survival," Johnny said. "In the NFL you do whatever you can to win. If you learn something about an opponent, you use it. The other team's QB is having marital problems, well you tell your defensive linemen, and one of them is bound to taunt him at some point."

"You work with some wonderful people," I remarked.

"It's a battle out there. Everything in *The Art of War*

applies to pro football. But I get paid a ridiculous amount of money to do this, and the only way I keep my job is to win. There you have it."

"Not for me anymore."

"Understood," Johnny said. "Hey listen, I'll be out in Pasadena on New Year's Day for the Rose Bowl game. We should get together."

"Sure. Be even better if you can help out with a couple of tickets. I kind of want to take Marcus."

Johnny chuckled again. "Burnside, the family man. Never thought I'd live to see the day. Let me figure something out about the game."

"Appreciate it. Nice to see you fly out here to support Old 'SC."

"Well, it's partly business."

"Oh?" I said.

"I want to take a good look at Patrick. Up close during game conditions. See how he performs in a high profile contest. Doesn't get much bigger than the Rose Bowl, national title games notwithstanding."

I shook my head. "Johnny, the Bears don't have a top three pick this year, you guys are having a decent season. And the only way you're going to get a top three pick next year is if you tank. The worst teams pick first, and if the Bears are one of those teams, you may get fired. How are you ever going to get a shot at Patrick?"

"We have the Browns' first round pick for next season," Johnny told me. "Traded for it a couple of years ago."

"Ah," I said, and things became clear. The Browns were normally terrible, and they were likely to be one of the first teams to select players in the draft. And if Patrick didn't declare for the NFL this year, he likely would next year. And Johnny Cleary and the Bears would be waiting for him.

"You understand now," Johnny said.

"Oh yeah," I said slowly. "Your advice to Patrick was to stay in school another year. So you'd be able to grab him when he became available. Very clever."

"And I have you to thank for it."

"Indeed," I said, feeling a slight twinge of guilt about sending Patrick to speak with Johnny, although sensing I'd get it over soon. "And those Rose Bowl seats better be really good."

"I'll arrange for the best seats in the house."

"I'm glad you're doing well, Johnny," I said, and thought of an old saying that seemed applicable here. If you can't be rich, it's good to have rich friends.

Thirteen

Since Room 21 at the Snuggle Inn was not visible from the street, I pulled into the motel's parking lot at 4:00 pm on a Friday afternoon that was growing colder by the hour. And I sat in my Pathfinder and waited. This was the untold reality of being a private investigator, the burst of action and the scintillating conversations being far offset by the long, empty stretches of time where we do little but watch and wait. I wiled away the time thinking about how I would tell Cliff Roper that the QB he wanted to sign would not be signing with him this year. I thought of whether I would approach Hannah Briggs again, be it to express condolences or to request payment for my services, even though the only results that emanated from my efforts were a homicide arrest, and then a few days later, a trip to the morgue. I wondered whether Johnny Cleary would get us fifty yard line seats. But I mostly sat and stared at the white door of Room 21 for a little over an hour, waiting for something interesting to happen. Finally it did.

The woman who approached the room had just climbed out of a late-model silver Lexus, shiny and pristine from what was most likely a very recent visit to the car wash. The woman herself looked to be in her early forties; dark hair, attractive, and slender. She was dressed in dark slacks, a teal sweater, a thin gold necklace, and a black leather waist coat. She gave off the casual feel of old wealth, confident and relaxed, walking toward a tryst, an event which was most likely no different than going to get her nails done. I exited my car and walked toward her.

"Excuse me," I said. "Do you have a moment?"

The woman looked me up and down, the bemused look turning into a smile. "I suppose," she said, in a surprisingly deep voice that struck me as professionally trained. "What can I do for you?"

I flashed my fake badge. She looked at it and her bemusement seemed to turn to boredom. "Did I forget to pay a parking ticket?"

"No," I responded. "And this actually doesn't have much to do with you at all."

"What a relief."

I pulled out a photo of Tyler Briggs and showed it to her. "Have you seen this man before? Maybe here at the motel?"

The woman inspected the photo for a few seconds. "I've seen him. He was here last week. Saw him at the ice machine. He was wearing a baseball cap, but it was the same guy. He looked familiar, but I couldn't place him. I think I might have seen him on TV once, but who knows. Half of L.A. has been on TV at some point."

"Okay," I said carefully. "Did you see a woman with him?"

"I did. She was helping him get ice. He looked kind of unsteady, like he had had one too many drinks at happy hour. Maybe a few too many."

"Did it look as if there were any problem between them? Any animosity?"

"No, not at all. In fact, they looked like they were having great fun. Giggling about getting the right pieces of ice, that sort of thing."

"What did the woman look like?" I said.

"She was blonde, a little petite I guess. Very pretty, though. Maybe in her thirties."

I considered this and thought about how to present the next question. "We have reason to believe this woman may have been involved in a capital crime," I said slowly. "If we were to have you sit down with a police sketch artist, do you think you'd be able to describe her?"

"I'm not sitting down with anyone from the police," she told me.

I stared at her. "May I ask why?" I inquired politely, thinking I might need to have Juan send over a few officers to coerce her back to the Purdue Division.

"The person I'm meeting tonight is a public figure. I don't want to have to explain anything about my business or his. Or why we're here. Or let the world know, especially his family, about what's been going on with us. You do understand, I hope."

I did understand indeed, the understanding that her personal comfort was more important than catching a criminal who was intimately involved in one, or perhaps two homicides. And that this woman's own moral elasticity would allow her to have a regularly scheduled sexual rendezvous with a married man, but not cooperate with law enforcement to catch a cold blooded killer.

"I recognize your concern," I said as sympathetically as I could. "And you'll understand why it is of the utmost importance that we find this woman. I need to see your driver's license. Now. Or you'll be placed under arrest, and you may be charged with aiding and abetting a murderer."

"Oh please," she responded. "If you're trying to scare me, you'll need to work harder at that. I didn't do anything wrong, and your charges will be laughed out of court."

"Do you have the time or inclination to go to court and find out?" I asked pointedly. "And does the man you're meeting want to be dragged into this as well?"

She stopped and stared at me without verbalizing her answer. I continued.

"You're withholding information from the police," I said, knowing full well I wasn't the police, and there was no crime in failing to provide a pushy private investigator with a description of another motel guest. But she did finally begin rifling through her purse and eventually handed me her driver's license. The photo matched, and I wrote down her information. Peggy Merman, lived in Pacific Palisades, age 52. She looked good for her age.

"This has to do with the Glasscock murder," she said suddenly.

"That's right," I answered, eyeing her carefully. "And just so you know, we can keep your identity private. Same with whoever you're meeting here."

"And just so *you* know," she said, "you really don't need a sketch artist. I can point you to exactly who that woman was. I don't have a name, but I know where she worked."

I stared at her. "Go on."

"On Sunday afternoon, I turned on the news, it was

right after one of those football games ended."

"Was it the Chargers game?" I asked.

"Might have been. I'm really not much of a football fan. But I tuned in just as the game was ending, and they cut away to the local news."

"What channel?"

"Probably channel 2, that's what I normally watch. Anyway, they had reporters on the scene where Colin Glasscock was killed, and they were interviewing staffers from Glasscock's office. That pretty little blonde was one of them. I thought it was odd that I had just seen her here Friday night. I didn't make much of it at the time, everyone has a private life. Do you think she was involved somehow in Glasscock's murder?"

I did indeed. Whoever was with Tyler Briggs at the Snuggle Inn last Friday night was the one who knocked him out with a date-rape drug, and the one who got Tyler's fingerprints on the murder weapon. They were the one who dropped his baseball cap in the alley behind Glasscock's office. All to make it look like Tyler Briggs had done the shooting.

*

I didn't bother to call Juan Saavedra just yet, because if Peggy Merman was correct, we indeed wouldn't need the services of a sketch artist. I drove home quickly and gave Gail and Marcus hugs before rushing into the den and turning on the TV. I checked the Recorded Programs on my DVR, and was relieved the Chargers game had not been deleted. Marcus had forgotten all about watching a replay of the game, as five-year-olds are prone to do. I fast forwarded past the game and onto the local news, and there she was. Short, blonde, pretty, and curvaceous. Just like in person. She was talking about how much Colin Glasscock had meant to the community and how much he meant to the staff. Her eyes glistened with tears. It was quite an act.

I put in a call to Juan, but all I got was his voice mail. I left a message asking him to call me right away, saying it was urgent. I thought of calling Orlando Brown, but I knew there was a Laker game on, and also that bringing him into this might cause more harm than good. In the end, my natural curiosity won out and I knew I would approach her myself. And since I didn't know much about this Peggy Merman, and whether or not she actually knew the curvy blonde – and might inform her that I was on her trail – I decided to move quickly. Thanks to the internet, I could find out where Emma Wick lived, and she lived remarkably close to us. I thought of telling Gail where I was going, but my job worried her enough. And I knew she would try and convince me to let the police handle this.

Emma Wick resided in a townhouse on Marcasel Avenue in Mar Vista, an unusually wide, sweeping street that was quiet and lined with palm trees. Only a few cars were parked on the street, most were in driveways, and the air was still and silent. There was a half-moon out, enough to give the neighborhood sufficient light. It was about a week past being full, well beyond the type of moon that always seems to bring the craziest people out of the shadows.

I found Unit 4, the entrance tucked into the side of the building, about fifty feet removed from the street. I rang the doorbell, and it was answered quickly. Emma Wick was dressed in faded jeans and a scoop-neck red sweater that revealed generous cleavage. She gave me a puzzled look.

"Hi," she said tentatively. "Your Gail's husband, aren't you?"

"Yes. May I come in?"

She opened the door curiously and allowed me to enter. She didn't offer me anything to drink or to sit down. She looked past me at something across the room. I turned and looked too but I didn't see anything.

"What is this about?" she asked.

"It's mostly about the murders of Colin Glasscock and Tyler Briggs. I think I know how you did them. What's missing from the picture is why you did them."

She stared at me for a second and started to move across the room. I grabbed her tightly by the arm, and she lunged, but she only succeeded in tripping and falling to the floor.

"No!" she screamed.

I yanked her arms behind her, when I realized I had forgotten my plastic cuffs in the Pathfinder. There was no way to go get these, so I improvised, ripping an electric cord from a computer printer, to bind her hands behind her back. It wasn't perfect, but nothing about this case was perfect. I looked across the room again. I walked over and opened the drawer of a maple end table and looked inside. It had a stack of magazines and a few knick-knacks. There was also a Glock 19. I took out a handkerchief and pulled it out.

"I think I've hit the lottery."

"There's no law against having a gun," she protested, squirming to try and free her hands.

"There are plenty of laws against shooting people."

"You can't prove anything. You don't know a thing."

"I'll tell you what," I said. "I'll paint you a picture. There's some pieces missing. Feel free to fill them in. Don't worry. I won't tell anyone."

She stared at me and said nothing.

"You and the councilman were having an affair. You were far from his only conquest, but you thought you were special. You were his assistant. You were the one closest to him. You knew everything about him, his schedule, his private life, his rocky marriage. He was successful, and he was a likeable, good-looking guy, so you did what a thousand women do every day. You fell in love with a married man."

She nodded ever so vaguely, in a way that struck me as almost involuntary. I continued, not exactly knowing what I was talking about, piecing it together as I went, but nevertheless detailing a textbook case that just seemed to repeat itself. I might not be right on everything, but I was sure I was getting warm.

"And he told you he'd leave his wife. And he told you the affairs with other women meant nothing to him. That he couldn't control himself, that they were the aggressors.

And he always came back to you. But after a while you finally figured out he wasn't going to leave his wife and he wasn't going to stop screwing other women. The difference here was that most women in this position would hurl a few insults, a veiled threat, or maybe even a lamp. In your case, it escalated."

She shook her head. "Again. You have no proof. You have no evidence. No one will believe you. Your word against mine. And I'm a respected civil servant."

I laughed. "Not so civil apparently. But there's going to be proof. Lots of it. The gun in the alley to start off."

"Try finding fingerprints," she sniffed.

"Maybe we'll look at whose fingerprints were on the bullets left in the magazine. And the steering wheel on Tyler's car after you dumped his body. Not to mention the eyewitnesses who saw a light blue Mercedes pull up to that underpass in the middle of the night. Oh, there's proof. Bunches of it."

She stared at me. I still thought I saw her arms wiggle. I continued.

"Back to your motive. Maybe your breaking point came when you finally confronted him and he turned you away, maybe he disrespected you somehow, maybe he set you off in one of the hundreds of ways that men can set off women. Whatever he said or did outraged you, and made shooting him in the head a lot more appealing than simply walking out the door and never seeing him again."

"A fool," she muttered blankly.

"Excuse me?"

"I did confront him. I demanded he leave his wife."

"I take it the answer to that was no."

"It wasn't just no. He said a man in his position couldn't afford a scandal. He told me I should have known that. He was a public official, a community leader. People looked up to him. He asked me how I could be so foolish. He thought I was a fool for thinking he'd end his marriage for me. He said that would end his career. He ... he laughed at me," she said, her voice quivering, her eyes giving off the appearance that she could have been in a dreamlike state.

"Okay," I said.

"I could handle rejection. I could not handle the scorn."

"I understand that. Yeah. I get it. But here's what I don't get. No one was in the office. It was after 5:00 pm on a Friday. I know what it's like to work for the city. No one else was there. All you had to do was leave. You climbed out a window and into an alley behind the office. It was dark, and no one would see you there. If you walked out the front door, someone might. That was smart. What wasn't smart is what you did next."

"I was scared."

"Of course you were scared. It's scary to kill someone. But you could have gotten away with it. And even if you'd been caught, something like this, a crime of passion, even taking down a city leader, maybe you would have spent a few years in prison and then you'd walk. And with a good defense attorney, you might even have had a slim chance of getting off. But you had to cover your tracks. My question is why Tyler Briggs? Why did you pick him?"

She rolled her eyes. "I met him at a holiday party a few

weeks ago. He came onto me. His wife was ten feet away and he's hitting on me. Are all men pigs? Do any of them have a shred of decency?"

I didn't respond immediately, and I couldn't help thinking that this was coming from a woman who had been sexually involved with a married man. It's funny how life can look very different when you're seeing it through a different lens.

"There are probably a few," I said, careful not to get into a back-and-forth on ethics and morals with a double murderer. "So you called Tyler. Probably from a pay phone so it wouldn't be traced. That is, if there are any pay phones left these days"

"There's one at the 7-Eleven. On Sepulveda."

"Yeah," I said, wondering vaguely if she knew of that tidbit in advance, but decided it was more trivia than relevant. "And you asked Tyler to meet you for a drink. Somehow The Alibi Room is where you had your rendezvous. I imagine you made your intentions known to Tyler right away. The bartender said you didn't spend a lot of time flirting over drinks."

"No," she said quietly. "No need."

"You ended up at the Snuggle Inn. You dropped some roofies, that date-rape drug, into Tyler's drink at some point, and that knocked him out. Before he passed out, you had sex with him at the motel; Tyler seemed to remember that part, anyway. He said you were hot."

A brief flash of interest crossed Emma's face, but it quickly went away.

"Where'd you get the drug, by the way? The roofies?" I

asked.

"They're not hard to find. If you know where to look."

"And the syringe?"

She shrugged. "It's part of a needle exchange program the city's involved in. I slipped one in my purse."

"Sounds like you've been planning something for a while," I commented.

"My situation with Colin was going nowhere. I needed to do something. I just didn't quite know what. "

"Okay," I said, starting to wonder how much of this murderous rampage had been pre-meditated and how much had been thought up on the fly. My guess was it might have been a combination, the furious thoughts turning to possibilities over time, but once she pulled the trigger and killed Colin Glasscock, some of the next steps had to have been improvised. It was part of the scenario. When a person shoots someone they love, much of their thought pattern goes haywire, at least for a little while.

"Then after Tyler passed out, you got his fingerprints all over the gun. And you also took his baseball cap. The green one with the M on it. You know that was his Miami Hurricanes cap, right?"

"I didn't know that exactly."

"I thought it was funny that his name was printed inside the cap. Grown men don't normally do that. But the police will check the handwriting, as well as the prints on the syringe. I'm surprised you left that at the hotel. Maybe you weren't thinking straight."

"Uh-huh," she said blankly.

"Then you went and shot him up with roofies so he'd

have a good, long sleep. You returned to the alley, planted the gun and the baseball cap, and waited for the police to put two and two together and end up with three. Of course it helped that you were the one who told them about Tyler supposedly entering the office at 5:00 on Friday. Right before you went home. You were the last one in the office. No one else could have known who came to see him."

"How do you know that?" she asked weakly.

"Because the arresting detective told me. He just didn't say who the eyewitness was. Turned out to be you. The police go and arrest Tyler and you figure your problems are solved. They match the prints on the gun that had just been fired, see the baseball cap with Tyler's name on it, and it's game, set and match. Sure, he'd tell the cops about this sexy blonde he picked up, and maybe they might even check it out with the bar or the motel, but you're still the mystery woman. No one knew you at either place. And again, even if you did get fingered, it was still Tyler's prints on the gun. Which leads me to a question. Whose gun was it?"

Emma gave an odd little smile. "Colin's. He had a few of them."

"All were Glock 19s?" I asked.

"I don't know what you call them. But yeah they were all the same. Colin had received death threats. He was scared. He carried one and kept another in his desk."

"And you lifted both of them."

She shrugged and smiled again.

"You used one to kill Colin and the other to kill Tyler. That leads us to the next bit of the puzzle. Which is why did you bother to shoot Tyler? The police had him, they had him but good, and it looked like an open-and-shut case. You were in the clear."

"Was I?"

I looked at her, and it dawned on me. "Okay. You realized Tyler could implicate you, and that was a risk. You got lucky when he kept quiet after his arrest and lawyered up. Didn't say a word to the police. But that might have changed over time. So, you arranged another rendezvous, maybe to talk things over, maybe you said you had an idea about who really killed Glasscock. But I'll bet you also promised to give Tyler the ride of his life."

Emma brought out her smile. It was something she seemed to dial up at will. "Something like that."

"And you did. His last ride. At some point you pulled the gun on him and shot him in the abdomen. Tried to make it look like a suicide. Only problem was you shot him multiple times. People who commit suicide are only able to pull the trigger once. Were you really trying to make it look like a suicide when you dumped the body? No blood spatter, nothing that fit the profile. You didn't even leave the gun."

Emma looked down. "I wasn't thinking clearly. I had to get him out of the car. I couldn't drive around like that in his Mercedes, him dead in the next seat."

I shook my head. "I imagine you were thinking a few thoughts very clearly. You killed Glasscock out of hot-blooded rage, but you went and killed Briggs in a way that was cold-blooded and dispassionate."

"You believe I'm some kind of monster, don't you," she

said in a low voice.

"I think you got yourself into a bad situation, and then you made it a hundred times worse. It was a stupidly hatched plan, but you're hardly a criminal mastermind. You just knew you needed to get rid of Tyler Briggs. He was the only connection that led back to you. With Tyler out of the way you could rest easy. He started out as the fall guy and then you realized he had become a much bigger problem. One you had to flick away."

She stared at me, and for a brief, fleeting second, I saw an innocence, a vulnerability in her eyes. I had struck something, I just didn't know what. But as quickly as that came, it left just as fast. And at that point, she jerked her hands free and scrambled to her feet.

I grabbed at her and she put one hand on my face as she dug her nails in. I yanked her fingers away, but she lunged again for the Glock and she almost got to it. I dived on top of her and wrestled her arms behind her back again. I rolled her partway over on her side and drew my .357 and pointed it at her. She continued to wriggle against my body, but she couldn't squirm free. I yanked her up by the hair and pressed the gun flush against her nose where she could not help but see it. She stopped wriggling. Her eyes widened in fear and her breath came in spurts.

I reached over and smacked the Glock with my free hand and it skittered off the end table and behind the couch, well out of reach. I let go of her hair and ordered her to crawl to the other side of the room, and to lay face down with her hands over her head. Surprisingly, she did what I told her. I went over to the other side of the room and gingerly picked up the murder weapon with a tissue. At that point my phone rang. The number was blocked, but I answered it anyway.

"Yeah."

"It's Juan. What's happening?"

I told him and gave him the Marcasel Street address. He had already reached his home in Orange County but he would turn around and head back here. He said he'd send uniforms over right away and hung up. Two minutes later the uniforms were on the scene. It took Juan over two hours to arrive, but not surprisingly, the news vans arrived shortly after Juan did. His interview played on every local news show.

Fourteen

Emma Wick was booked for two homicides. Detective Orlando Brown was conveniently away for the weekend, so another homicide detective interrogated her. I had gotten most of the story correct, and given that I had found the murder weapon in her end table, Emma did not put up much of a fight. After a lengthy discussion, she finally told the whole story to the detective, wrote it down, and signed. Tyler's blood-soaked Mercedes was found in a Taco Bell parking lot down the street from the Roasters, and Emma's prints were all over the steering wheel. They were also matched to the syringe Teresa Ortiz found in the motel room of the Snuggle Inn. Why she left it there was still a mystery, although there is a school of thought that suggests deep down, some people just want to get caught.

I used to wonder why criminals confessed to crimes; sometimes they did so without much evidence against them. In the end, I finally concluded much of it came down to guilt, that overbearing, existential weight that was too heavy a load for most people to carry. Only the most hardened criminal or borderline sociopath could move forward with their life and be unaffected by the cross they bore, the taking of a human life for reasons that were indefensible and craven. Confessing relieved most people of that burden. It was, in a way, cleansing.

I visited Hannah Briggs, not to hand her an invoice but to express my condolences. Regardless of the broken state of her marriage and the mutual infidelities, she did lose her husband in a horrific way, one that first painted him as a murderer himself. That Tyler Briggs was subsequently killed by a woman he was having an extramarital liaison with did little to improve his public reputation, and it also made it highly unlikely Hannah Briggs would be able to continue in the City Attorney's office. A prosecutor who was tarred with a very public humiliation, even through association with her husband, would be problematic. But her life would go on, albeit in only a slightly different direction. When I went to visit Hannah in her Silver Strand home, I ran into Anthony Riddleman, the Chargers QB coach. It looked as if he and Hannah were more than just friends.

Juan Saavedra came up smelling like a rose, as the arrest of Emma Wick indeed made the deputy chief look bad for targeting Tyler Briggs. There was no official announcement, but Juan indicated changes would be brewing at Parker Center. Neil Handler was sworn in to replace Colin Glasscock, and the first thing he did was move the district headquarters to a building a few blocks away. It was still not in Mar Vista; I guess he felt the traffic problems would be too much to endure.

I received a surprise phone call from a producer at Fox Sports. She told me she was the one who had been in the car with the pugilist, the one who attacked me after ramming his car into mine. After recording our brief match in the middle of Sepulveda Boulevard, she had graciously uploaded the video onto YouTube and it had already received hundreds of thousands of hits. It was titled, "UFC Guy Gets Beat Up By Everyday Joe." She wanted to schedule a rematch, to be broadcast as a Pay-Per-View special, and said there would be some good money in it. I told her to go soak her head, and pull the video down. My guess is she did neither.

Marcus received a number of board games for Christmas, including Monopoly, which Gail thought might be too advanced for him. I told her he'd grow into it. I also gave him my old iPad, wiped clean and de-fragged to remove any remnants of searches for firearms and criminal behavior; the last thing I wanted was a five-year-old exposed to the difference between a Glock 19 and a Sig P320. The old iPad brought a new kind of joy to him. It did for me as well, as I went out the day after Christmas and bought a new one for myself. That my iPad was a few years old did not prove to be a problem for Marcus, he was thrilled to have it. I also let him know we'd be taking him to the Rose Parade, followed by the Rose Bowl game afterward. He was thrilled.

After buying my new iPad, I took it back to the office to set it up. After a few hours of the frustration that comes with being a technophobe, I decided to go to lunch and call the help desk afterward. As I was trying to figure out if I should have a burger or a burrito, my door opened and a familiar, but not unexpected figure strolled in. He looked around and shook his head in disbelief.

"How do people live this way?" Cliff Roper asked.

"I don't live here."

"You spend a lot of time in this office. The least you can do is put up some artwork. Or maybe buy a decent chair for your clients to sit in," he said, as he pulled a utilitarian office chair over, making a point of brushing a few specks of dust off of the seat.

"So nice to see you, too," I said. "Thanks for asking how I am."

"Does it bother you that I don't care?"

"No, and it doesn't surprise me, either."

"Real nice," he said. "You ought to be more supportive, considering I fixed that problem you created."

"A problem I created?! I didn't create any problems. And I didn't even have any problems. That is until you walked back into my life."

"Hey, hey, hey," he said, pointing a finger at me. "Watch your mouth. I'm the one paying your fee, which means I'm paying for this dump."

I sat back and looked at the small, slender, volcanic man in front of me, whose body fit snugly into his two thousand dollar suit. Cliff Roper never failed to instill a certain level of awe. A wildly successful agent, capable of either cajoling or dominating anyone in his path. He was the star of every room he entered, and I knew there was little point in putting up a fight. The only option was to indulge him until he chose to leave.

"Okay," I said. "I'll bite. Tell me how you bailed me out of *my* problem."

"Fili Snuka. One of your SC boys. Was about to get smoked by some local gangbangers down in the hood. I asked you to help dislodge Patrick O'Malley from this, uh, situation. Not his whole crew."

"It was a package deal."

"Yeah, and it cost me ten large to pay off that punk, Tristan Lopez. For another ten, I could have had him whacked. He was lucky I was in a good mood that day, and was willing to hand over a large pile of green."

"I'll let him know that if I ever see him again," I said. "You paid Tristan personally?"

"Are you joking? Of course not. I don't get involved in the messy stuff anymore. I run a respectable agency. One of my runners took care of the payment."

"Ah," I said. "Respectable. I forgot who I was talking to. I also forgot about the time you yourself were brought up on manslaughter charges."

"Totally bogus, and I was never found guilty of anything," he declared angrily. "Don't bring up the past. You of all people should know that."

"Okay," I said. He had a fair point. "But I think it's going to work out okay for you financially. Long-term wise."

"We'll see," Roper said. "Yeah, I signed Fili to my agency, that was good. But he's looking like a fourth-round pick. Big difference between him and Patrick, who'll go number one whenever he declares for the draft. The difference is millions. Lots of them."

"You take what you can get in this world. You know that."

"Yeah, and I gave a lot to get Fili, just to maybe get a shot at Patrick next year."

"What does a fourth-round pick earn?"

"If he makes the team, and that's a big if with a fourth-rounder, he's looking at getting maybe $600,000 a year.

Only half that is guaranteed, and again, he only gets salary if he makes the team. I'm looking at just fifteen percent of that. Do the math. It may not be that much."

"That's still more than the ten grand you paid Tristan Lopez," I pointed out.

"Hey, I'm not in the business to break even," he declared. "And I've got expenses, too. I got to get this kid's head together and get him ready for the Combine and then teach him how to do an interview. And how to behave when he talks to coaches. What to say, what not to say. How to comport himself."

"Comport?"

"Yeah, comport. Do I have to teach you everything?" he asked.

"Stick with the basics and I'll be fine."

"Well, the basics are I have to get him to a gym and have him build up his strength. He weighs half a ton, but he's got to be able to lift more weight. And he can't jump worth crap. Which means I've got to get him some training. That costs, and these kids never have any money. I'm paying for it."

"It's an investment. If he makes it in the league, there's a big payoff down the road. You know that."

"Yeah, and I also have to invest in paying off the kid's uncle, some paralegal schmuck that signed him to a sweetheart contract. The uncle didn't like it, but I told him I'd report him to the NFL for signing a kid without being registered with the league. Threatened to blackball him for life. Got his attention, and he voided the contract, but I still had to hand him some coin. Damn families, most of them are leeches. They just see dollar signs."

"Unlike you, of course," I pointed out.

"Hey, I'm a businessman, but I'm also a father-figure. Fili's dad's sick, and guess who's going to be holding his hand when the time comes. There's a lot I do that people don't know about."

"And some of that's stuff you don't want people to know about," I mused.

"I swim in the same pool as everyone else," he protested. "I'm just better at it than most people."

I did not deny that. I also didn't feel a shred of sympathy for Cliff Roper, who was a millionaire many times over and could afford investing in a few kids who might not make it into the NFL. He could also afford to pay off a sketchy gang member who was weighing retaliation for a beating at the hands of a few football players, the morality of all that notwithstanding. My suggestion that he make the Tristan Lopez situation go away in exchange for Fili signing with Roper's agency worked out for all concerned, except perhaps for the uncle, who would receive less money than if Fili had remained under contract with him. I reconciled that with the fact that had Fili stayed with the uncle, there was a better than average chance he would have dropped in the draft. And there was an even bigger likelihood Fili would have been cut from the team and washed out of the league before the end of the preseason. Sometimes things work out for everyone.

"Say, how did those young coaches do on their job interviews with that school across town?" I asked. "The ones we went to the Charger game with. I think their names were Devon and Alshawn."

Roper shook his head. "They didn't get offers. Had too much champagne the day before and showed up hung over. Look, being an agent is a crapshoot. If the guys work out, I stand to make money. If they don't, I get zilch. Nada. Nothing. In fact, I lose money. Things aren't what they seem to outsiders."

I agreed with that. "Did you get a chance to speak with Patrick?"

"Of course I did. You think I'm going to miss out on talking to a kid that'll sign a thirty million dollar contract one day? Guys like Patrick, they're what I live for. I'm just glad you didn't totally mess that up."

"I'm glad to hear that I didn't. I'm not sure how I could have, though."

"Oh, you could have," Roper sneered. "Believe me. You almost did. What are you doing, telling the kid he ought to do what he wants to do. What's wrong with you?"

"What's wrong with me?" I exclaimed. "To tell a kid to listen to his heart and choose the path he really wants to go down? What's wrong with me? What's wrong with you?"

"Nothing's wrong with me. What's wrong with you is you don't respect money. This kid is money. You don't walk away from tens of millions of dollars because you prefer doing slopestyle tricks on rock-hard snow that might break your back and earn you pennies for your trouble. This is the big leagues we're playing in. What his heart wants doesn't matter."

"I don't think you understand," I said. "If his heart isn't into playing pro football, he shouldn't do it."

"What do you know about heart?"

I gave him a long look. "At least I know mine works."

"Hey, hey, hey," Roper sneered, pointing his finger at me once more. "I'm not going to tell you to watch your mouth again."

I laughed. "You going to sic your runner on me? I can handle myself."

"I was going to give you twenty grand for helping me sign Patrick," Roper said. "I still might if he signs with me next year. That is, if you can watch your mouth and be pleasant for a little while."

I processed this. "Then Patrick's not signing with you this year."

"You finally get it. Yeah, he's going to spend another year at USC and then reevaluate. I did get a leg up on other agents, though. If he picks the NFL, all I got to do is remind him how I made the Tristan Lopez problem disappear."

"Maybe it'll all work out," I said.

Roper stood up and pulled out an envelope from his suit pocket. He tossed it on my desk. "There's the payment for your services. I always believe in making sure no one walks away feeling bitter. Everyone gets compensated for their time, and you're getting more than you deserve. But I will tell you I'm holding something back. I was going to give you four Rose Bowl tickets. Out of the goodness of my heart, which does exist, whether or not you believe it. But I'm tired of your insults. So I'm giving the tickets to someone else."

I didn't say anything about the tickets, but I did thank Cliff Roper for the money, a gesture he noted with a quick nod before he turned and left without saying anything more. I opened the envelope and counted out five thousand dollars in crisp hundred-dollar bills, which might have come straight from a bank, or maybe from his safe. It was an odd realization, that his payment for my work was exactly one-half of what he handed to a gangbanger for the simple act of being quiet and going away. I didn't bother to tell him I was going to the Rose Bowl with Johnny Cleary, and that there was a fair chance our seats would be better than his. Then again, they might not be.

*

It goes without saying in L.A., that despite whatever inclement weather has descended upon the region over Christmas, no matter if it rains on the last day of the year, or the second day of January, New Year's Day always manages to be sunny, warm, and full of promise. The world tunes in to Southern California on January 1st to watch Pasadena's Rose Parade, to ogle at the beautiful people waving to the crowd from ornately designed floats under a canopy of blue skies. It is our signature moment, and the region rarely ever disappoints. It is as if to show the rest of the world how to throw a party. This year would be no exception. It would be a beautiful day, with lots of sunshine, and a brilliant blue sky, perfectly choreographed, as if the climate itself had been delivered straight from central casting.

Marcus's birthday brought him another bounty of toys, some more old-school board games, safe toys like a few stuffed animals and a nerf football, and a slew of clothes. We began his birthday celebration the night before, on New Year's Eve, because our final series of gifts would be on New Year's Day, and we had some special plans for him.

New Year's Day in Pasadena is a day unlike any other. I had been to the Rose Parade half a dozen times, in various ways. When I was young, my mother once took me up to Pasadena the night before and we camped out in sleeping bags on the sidewalk, securing a spot along the parade route. Another time I went to an all-night New Year's Eve party a block north of Colorado Boulevard, and we walked down to watch the parade as it grew near. One time I was given tickets to sit in the bleachers, which was the most civilized way to watch the parade, but insanely expensive if you had to pay for it. This year, our friends, the Alperns, taught us a new method.

The Rose Parade begins at 8:00 am, but that's just when the TV viewing kicks off. The parade itself lasts almost two hours, which means by the time the first float nears the end of the parade route, it's almost 10:00 am. We roused a grumpy Marcus, gave him some Cheerios in the car, and drove over to pick up the Alperns at 8:30 am. Ben, his wife, Malia, and their son, Jake, climbed into the Pathfinder after we loaded the back with the necessary hardware. The drive to Pasadena took all of 25 minutes, as most of L.A. was either sleeping, watching the Rose Parade on TV, or had already gotten to Pasadena many hours ago. We found parking a few blocks away from where the parade route turned onto Sierra Madre Boulevard.

Ben and I each carried a seven-foot metal ladder and an eight-foot-long plywood shelf. When we reached Sierra Madre, we moved up against a storefront away from the street and set up the ladders six feet apart. We slid the two plywood shelves between the ladders and *voila*, we had seating for a pair of five-year-olds. We lifted our sons up onto the makeshift plywood benches. All of a sudden, a pair of kids who were barely three feet tall could look over the heads of all the adults and have a clear view of the parade. Our wives squeezed in with the crowds to get a closer view, but the dads stayed in the back, right next to the high benches, in the event the plywood did not hold and the kids came tumbling down. But the plywood held firm, and the kids were delighted. Periodically we would hand them juice boxes or string cheese sticks, and everyone was happy. The parade swung by a few minutes later, and we spent the next two hours watching the glorious floats glide by with their vivid colors and stunning designs, interspersed with some amazing marching bands. However beautiful a sight the parade is to watch on TV, it is even better in person.

Like Gail, the Alperns neither knew much nor cared much about football. So, after the parade, we drove over as close as we could get to the Arroyo Seco, a dry creek that cradled one of the world's most famous stadiums in its basin. Marcus and I got out, and I handed the Pathfinder keys to Gail.

"You're sure you'll be able to get home easily?" she asked.

I shrugged. "We can always go by train. Take the Gold line into downtown and catch the Expo home. If we need to, we'll call you from the Bundy station."

Gail kissed us both goodbye, warned us not to eat too many hot dogs at the game, and said she'd make something special for dinner. I took Marcus by the hand, and we walked down the long hill leading from the parade grounds near Orange Grove Boulevard, toward the Rose Bowl Stadium at the bottom of the basin.

The walk took about half an hour, and because it was downhill, and because Marcus was thrilled to be going to the Rose Bowl game, there were no complaints about it. I began to dread the thought of leading him back up the hill at the end of the game, with darkness descending early. My guess was I would be carrying him back up the hill. We arrived at the Will Call window and found two tickets waiting for us. Once inside, we went ahead and procured hot dogs and Cokes and found our seats, with Johnny Cleary and his wife waiting for us. The seats were indeed right on the 50 yard line, about thirty rows up. They could not have been more perfect. I looked around and saw Cliff Roper about ten rows above us. He nodded at me, his face briefly revealing a quizzical expression, but soon enough he noticed Johnny and understood immediately why I had better seats than he did.

"Nice day," Johnny said, as we took our seats. "The

weather always behaves here on January 1st."

"Yup. And everyone watching back East in zero-degree weather suddenly wants to move here."

"It's a nice life. We're staying over at Shutters in Santa Monica."

"Ah," I said. "Nothing quite like the warmth of standing in a rich man's sun."

Johnny nodded. "I never thought I'd be in this position. When I played in the NFL everyone made a good income, but it was nothing like it is today. It's like Monopoly money."

"I can only imagine. Say, Johnny, I wonder if you might drop us off at home on your way back to Santa Monica? Gail took the Pathfinder."

"No problem," he said.

"I look forward to riding in the Jaguar, or whatever luxury car you rented."

"I didn't exactly rent a car," Johnny smiled, "but I'll ask the limo driver to take a detour into Mar Vista."

I smiled back. "Your generosity is appreciated."

"What's the point of having money if I can't spoil my friends? And if we get to draft Patrick next year, you'll be part of the reason why."

"Works for me."

The 1st half of the game was a tepid affair, something akin to a boxing match where both teams were feeling each other out, but neither willing to go all in with any bold plays. Marcus did not act bored at all. In fact, he managed to absorb himself fully in the spectacle, with the marching band, the colors, and the pageantry. USC ended the 1st half being down 6-3, with both schools only scoring on field goals. The teams continued this conservative play until the middle of the 3rd quarter when Michigan tried to pull a reverse, but only managed to fumble the ball. USC recovered at midfield. And then the Trojan offense came onto the field and pulled a surprise of their own.

The flea flicker is a play that works, not just because of deception, but because it takes a lot of skill and timing for a team to pull it off correctly. Every football play requires teammates to work in unison, but this is especially true with the flea flicker. Not every quarterback can do it well. Patrick O'Malley was one who could.

The play began as an ordinary run up the middle, with Patrick handing the ball off to the tailback who looked as if he were going to plow straight ahead into the heart of the defense. The receivers feigned as if they were going to halfheartedly throw a block, instead quietly slipping downfield. Patrick took a few steps back and watched. As expected, the defense converged on the tailback, and the safeties inched toward the line. But all of a sudden, the tailback stopped and pitched the football back to Patrick. In that brief moment, the defense froze, stopping to process just what was happening.

Running a proper flea flicker requires the quarterback to catch the ball from the tailback, a toss which may or may not be accurate. And unlike taking a snap from center, when the ball is placed squarely in the quarterback's hands with the laces facing up, the grip will often be wrong. The quarterback needed to adjust the football in his hand, to position it where his fingers were directly on the laces. Next, he then had to find one of his receivers racing downfield behind the secondary. He would set his feet correctly and fling the ball a good fifty yards, where the receiver could catch it without breaking stride. And the QB has about two to three seconds to do all of this, and do it properly.

With deception being a big part of the flea flicker, USC's offensive line pretended to be run-blocking, pushing the defense back so the tailback could gain yards. But when the tailback stopped to pitch the ball back to Patrick, a number of defensive linemen had no blockers in front of them, and they had a clear path to Patrick. So in addition to executing the play, Patrick also had to take note of a few 300-pound defensive tackles who were roaring toward him.

Patrick grabbed the football as he backpedaled. He spun the laces, set his body and scanned the field for an open receiver. He found one and heaved the football toward him, and indeed, Patrick got knocked down just as he released the pass. Downfield, the receiver had raced ten yards behind his coverage, the safeties, who were desperately sprinting to catch up. But Patrick put enough mustard on the pass so the receiver caught the football just as he was crossing the goal line for a touchdown. The crowd on the USC side of the Rose Bowl leaped up in unison and roared. The band began to play "Fight On" and everyone on the Trojan sideline began jumping up and down. On the other side of the field, a dispirited Michigan team walked slowly and dejectedly to the bench.

The Trojans scored two more touchdowns in the second

half and held Michigan scoreless the rest of the way, winning the Rose Bowl game 24-6. As the clock ran out, Johnny rose and motioned for us to follow him. We walked down the steps and onto the field. A security guard in a bright yellow windbreaker ran over to stop us, but he was soon standing in the shadow of a 350 pound lineman, who placed a giant hand on his shoulder and told him we were okay. Fili Snuka said we were family.

The End

About The Author

David Chill is a USA Today bestselling author. He was born and raised in New York City and educated in the public schools. After receiving his undergraduate degree from SUNY-Oswego, he moved to Los Angeles where he earned a Masters degree from the University of Southern California. David Chill is the author of ten mystery novels: *Post Pattern, Fade Route, Bubble Screen, Safety Valve, Corner Blitz, Nickel Package, Double Pass, Tampa Two, Flea Flicker*, and *Swim Move*, all featuring Burnside, a private investigator and former LAPD officer and college football star. David Chill is also the author of *Curse Of The Afflicted*, a political suspense novel which chronicles the journey of a political pollster diagnosed with cancer.

Post Pattern was awarded a prize in the St. Martin's Press contest for New Mystery Writers. The Burnside series has received much critical acclaim, and all of the novels in this series have spent time on the Amazon.com best seller lists. David Chill currently lives in Los Angeles. If you would like to contact David Chill directly, please email him at the following: davidchill3214@gmail.com

If you enjoyed Flea Flicker, then be sure to read the next book in the Burnside Mystery Series....

Swim Move

Here is a sample chapter of this terrific mystery...

SWIM MOVE PREVIEW

Chapter 1

It is an unfortunate truth that children often pay the price for the sins of their fathers. In the case of Amanda Zeal, however, she seemed to have lived a dreamy life for the better part of her twenty-four years. But looks are deceiving, and Amanda had committed a few costly sins of her own during that stretch.

I had played football with Amanda's father back in high school, and we had not bothered to stay in touch. That was fine by me. Her father, Phil Zellis, was a tenacious guy who never shied away from a fight. In fact, he would instigate many of these, often taking curious steps to provoke physical altercations. It didn't matter if the other kid was bigger or smaller than he was. What mattered was Phil being able to prove he could dominate anyone in his path. He called it getting respect. The school psychologist called it something else.

It had been a few decades since I had last seen Phil, and like most of us who landed in middle age, he looked quite different as an adult than he did in high school. But Phil's changes were largely cosmetic. When he entered my office, he was wearing a black leather waistcoat over a navy blue cashmere sweater, and had on tailored gray slacks. He sported a shiny gold Rolex, and his tan loafers had tassels on them. Even the haircut seemed expensive. From a distance, he probably appeared dapper and elegant and handsome. Up close, however, he looked like none of those things. His physique was sturdy and tough, and he didn't come across as someone to be taken lightly. His face conveyed a hoodlum-like quality, albeit a hood who had managed to acquire an awful lot of money.

Amanda walked into my office behind him. She had an athlete's physique, square shoulders and long arms, and she was as attractive as he was repulsive. Her demeanor was confident and poised. She had long blonde hair and a pretty face, accented with soft-violet eye shadow and deep-red lipstick. She was dressed in a tight black top and tight black pants. They looked nice on her. Everything looked nice on her. I started to wonder if the two of them were actually related.

"Burnside," he said, reaching out to shake my hand. "It's been a while. You look good."

"I know."

The slightest hint of an ugly smile appeared quickly in the

corner of his mouth. It disappeared just as fast. Amanda just gave me a bored look and didn't say anything. They sat down.

"You were probably surprised by my call this morning," he said.

"Not much surprises me these days," I said slowly. "But I don't expect much, either."

Phil took this in. "I should have kept in touch. But you know, life gets in the way."

"I'd say life's been good to you," I observed.

"Good and bad," he said. "Like everyone else, I guess."

For Phil, it was probably more good than bad. "So, what have you been doing the last twenty-five years?" I asked.

"I'll give you the short version. Got married early. Suzy was my college sweetheart. We were married junior year."

"Let me guess. She was pregnant."

Amanda stopped looking bored and Phil shot me a suspicious glance. "How did you know?"

"Deductive reasoning," I smiled, wondering if he would understand I was lying. But Phil's story was not all that unusual. I had a few teammates at USC whose girlfriends ended up pregnant. Some players went and married them, but most of these couples ended up divorcing within a few years and moved on. Except for the kids, though, whose lives were forever shaken by their parents' split. When it came to girls, I made sure I took precautions, the careful approach of someone who had lost both of his parents before his eighteenth birthday. When life throws you curveballs, you become tentative about what else the world has in store for you.

"You're right," he admitted. "We got married, we had Amanda. Our next kid, Aaron, we waited five years for him. At least I had a paycheck by then. Working in Suzy's family business."

"Good job security," I remarked.

"Best kind there is."

"And now you're divorced."

The look Phil shot me this time was less suspicious and more annoyed. "You figured that out, too?"

I smiled and shook my head. Before Phil came over, I took some time and combed through the internet. Even though Phil and I both grew up in Culver City, his journey was far different from mine. We had played football together, but while I managed to secure a scholarship to USC, Phil went to Vassar College in upstate New York, a pricey school that had no football team, and to my knowledge, did not give scholarships to C+ students. Phil was the type of kid who was bright but never applied himself. There was something inside of him that was troubled. His parents, mostly his father, managed to lift him out of whatever adverse situation he got himself into. I had no idea if Phil ever worked through his demons. Most people did not.

"No," I said. "After you called, I got curious, so I did a background check on you. Some things are matters of public record."

"Like marriages and divorces."

"Right," I said, not bothering to add property values were also readily accessible. The son of a policeman, Phil had come a long way from Culver City to Beverly Hills, from a modest house off of Jefferson Boulevard to a twelve-million-dollar mansion north of Sunset. I didn't enter those subtle details into our conversation. Some things did not need to be said. At least not right away.

"You married?" Phil asked.

"Yes."

"Kids?"

"One. We're looking at schools now for the fall."

"Colleges?"

"Kindergarten. He just turned five."

"Wow," Phil said, leaning back. "You started late. My daughter's almost twenty-five. My son's nineteen, he just entered USC last year."

"Good school," I said approvingly and turned to Amanda. "By the way, I've seen you on TV a lot the past few months. College football games. I guess you shortened your name to Amanda Zeal. Was Zellis too hard for the play-by-play guys to pronounce?"

That finally got Amanda to look slightly amused. "No. But it's not uncommon for people in the media to change their names. Have one that's catchy. Seems to be working for me. I'm trying to move up to NFL games soon."

It didn't hurt that she was very attractive, I thought, although being pretty was only part of the job of a sideline reporter. On air, Amanda came off as savvy and confident, and she seemed enthused to be doing what she was doing. In person, it was another story.

"You used to be a football coach at SC," she said. "Too bad you left before I started. I could have interviewed you at halftime."

I looked past her at the blank wall on the other side of my

office. I really should hang some pictures. I thought about what she said. In my brief tenure as a football coach, I avoided the media like the plague and let our head coach, Johnny Cleary, talk with them. I was blessed with the innate ability to make an inflammatory comment at just the wrong time. The last thing I wanted was a camera documenting that.

"Interviews are for head coaches," I said. "That's one of the things they do well. Talk without really saying anything. But I'm sure a lot of them are happy to speak with a pretty girl, even if she's in front of a TV camera."

"Yeah, pretty," Phil muttered. "That may be part of her problem."

"Dad ... "

"Look, Amanda, that's part of your problem. That's always been part of your problem."

She glared at him and turned away. I turned back to Phil.

"Is that the reason you're here?" I asked curiously, wondering if a psychotherapist might have been a better choice for them.

Phil nodded. "Amanda's been a magnet for guys since she was twelve years old. Remember the Moose? I had Moose go and have some conversations with a few of them," he said, rubbing his knuckles and giving me a knowing nod. Moose was an unsavory character from our high school days. Even though Phil Zellis had become a Beverly Hills denizen, it was clear he obviously hadn't left his working-class roots behind.

"Good Lord, are we going into this now?" Amanda sighed, exasperated.

"Old habits die hard," I pointed out.

"Well," said Phil, "I admit I got into my share of scrapes as a kid."

"Probably more than your share," I clarified.

He nodded again. "My dad taught me how to fight. And to never back down from a fight."

"If I recall, you provoked an awful lot of them."

He shook his head. "No. It was always someone else. Kid cutting in front of me in line. Someone not looking where they were going and banging into me. Not apologizing. Not showing respect. I didn't start any of those fights. But I sure finished most of them."

I remembered that well. "That's why your dad had you go out for football. Good place to get your aggressions out."

Phil looked me square in the eye. "You psychoanalyzing me?"

"Sort of," I said. Football was one of the few places where a guy could physically manhandle someone, lift them up and slam them to the ground, without any fear of criminal charges being brought. In fact, when done at a propitious moment, they would often get showered with applause. In any other setting, they would be looking at jail time. On the football field, they'd be more likely to get a trophy. It was a game that attracted all sorts, some who were well-adjusted, others who were borderline psychopaths.

"And if I recall, you got into a few brawls yourself, Burnside."

I didn't disagree. Instead, I decided to redirect the conversation. "Tell me more about your daughter's situation."

Phil Zellis paused for a moment. "So, Amanda's had

plenty of boyfriends. Maybe too many. I don't like the latest one."

"You don't like any of them," she snarled.

"He's your dad," I said. "He's not supposed to like your boyfriends."

Phil glared at me. "Maybe you should lay off the wisecracks."

"Sure," I said.

"Take a good look at my daughter. She's got a shiner. Covers it up well with makeup, but you can see it if you look hard enough. Her boyfriend, Wyatt, he had some bruises on his face."

I looked hard. I didn't see much. "This Wyatt have a last name?"

"Angstrom," he replied with a sneer.

I turned to Amanda. "So, what happened?"

"I fell down."

I turned back to Phil. "You think this Wyatt hit her?"

"I don't know. She said they were attacked on the street. And she fought back," he responded, a measure of pride forming in his voice. "Probably better than he did."

I looked over at Amanda. She was gazing out the window. I turned back to Phil.

"Tell me more," I said.

Phil gave a small smile. "I had given her some pepper spray for protection. That ended whatever dispute those punks had. Amanda and her boyfriend were able to make it back to her apartment okay. Well, not exactly okay. But she took care of the situation. Her boyfriend supposedly owns a gun, but she told me he didn't have it on him last night.

Might have saved him from getting beaten up."

"Interesting. You teach your daughter how to fight?" I asked, noticing Amanda had balled her right hand into a fist and the knuckles were starting to turn white.

"Sure, I taught her to defend herself. But she usually didn't need to. I got her into sports early on. Swimming, soccer, basketball, karate. Girls who play sports are just more confident. That's what makes this episode so unusual. She said these guys pulled up in a van and attacked them. No idea why."

"This true?" I asked her.

"If he says so."

Phil's eyes narrowed and he studied her for a moment. "Baby, would you mind waiting outside? It'll just be a couple minutes."

"With pleasure," she said, pulling out her phone as she walked out. She closed the door hard enough for us to notice, but not so much that it slammed.

"Amanda doesn't seem to want to be here," I noted. "Or want any help from me. If she was attacked, it might have been random and it might not have. Probably not, is my guess. But if she's not willing to cooperate, it'll make any investigation I do more difficult."

"She doesn't want the publicity," Phil said. "Thinks it'll affect her job. I'm more concerned with her safety. I told her I was pulling rank. I need some answers. I don't want this to happen again."

"Okay. Let me ask you something personal. And I'm not trying to psychoanalyze your family. Just trying to learn more. Your daughter have any problems growing up?"

I waited for Phil to shoot me another look, but it didn't happen. Instead, he considered this for a moment. "She was a little rebellious as a teenager. Tested limits. I guess we all did. Maybe she more than most. The divorce and all. Probably harder on her than us. I don't think she ever really forgave me or Suzy."

"Okay," I said. "What would you like me to do here? Find out what happened?"

"Uh-huh."

"Did Amanda and Wyatt file a police report?"

"They did. For what it's worth."

"Where did they say it happened?"

"Beverly Hills. On their way home, walking back from dinner."

"She still live with you?"

"Nah. I told her she could, but you know. Wants her independence. She has an apartment a few blocks south of Wilshire. Just off Beverly Drive."

"Where were they going to dinner?"

"Some sushi bar," Phil peered at me. "Why does that matter?"

I peered back. "Sometimes it matters, sometimes it doesn't. The more I know, the more I can help you."

"Oh, like in *Jerry McGuire*. Help me to help you."

I nodded and didn't say anything. The quote originally came from an old cop movie called *Prince Of The City*. But there was nothing to gain by correcting a wealthy client over a trivial matter.

"Look," he said, "I should also tell you that I hired the Moose again to look after her. Provide some security and all.

Amanda wasn't crazy about that, what with her going out with this Wyatt guy and all. But I told her, baby, the President of the United States has a team shadowing him. You're in the limelight now. Get used to it."

I thought back to high school. The Moose was Anthony Machado, a teammate on the football team, a 6'6" monster who could intimidate people with just an angry glare. The assets Moose brought were clearly brawn over brains. His grades were so bad that he barely graduated from high school. He didn't get any scholarship offers, and his parents did not have the financial wherewithal to pay for college. While he did receive financial aid to play at a junior college in Oklahoma, he flunked out after one year. Even the most accommodating of colleges still had a few academic standards, with reading and writing a basic requirement for matriculation.

"You kept in touch with Moose after all these years," I remarked.

"I've hired him here and there. He can be useful. Moose isn't the sharpest tool in the shed, but he has some, well, presence. And he could use the money. He's had a rough life."

I frowned. "Just what kind of business were you running, that you'd need someone like Moose for?"

"Nothing illegal, I can assure you, but sometimes it helps to have a big guy around. I had to deal with some union guys. But no, our business was office products. Plastic desk accessories. You know, those stackable letter trays, the little gizmos that hold paper clips, pen-and-pencil cups. That kind of thing."

I glanced down at my desk. There was a phone, a laptop, a yellow legal pad, a few pens scattered haphazardly nearby, and a *grande* cup of Starbucks that had grown lukewarm. No desk accessories. I probably had some paper clips somewhere, but they were most likely in my top drawer. I didn't bother to look.

"Okay."

"My ex's family started the business. Suzy's grandfather actually. He was an engineer, he began by making plastic containers for cosmetics companies. After a while, the cosmetics companies found it cheaper to buy their containers overseas. The Orientals can do everything cheaper."

"I believe they prefer to be called Asians now," I gently pointed out.

Phil Zellis shrugged. "Who cares what they want. They were going to put Suzy's family out of business. My father-in-law noticed that most of the desk accessories back in the day were made out of metal. He figured, why not come out with a line made of plastic. More colorful, nicer design. They already had the injection-molding machines, they could make plastic look like anything. Worked out. The business took off."

"And then he brought you in."

"Yeah, after Suzy and I graduated, I needed a job, and I needed to support a family. She didn't have a head for business, she majored in art history, can you believe that? Her father took me in and taught me the ropes. Then he had a heart attack at age forty-five. Her grandfather had retired by then, and I think he was also developing Alzheimer's. She didn't have any brothers or sisters, and her cousins were a bunch of entitled idiots who didn't want to work for a living. So it fell on me. All of a sudden, at age twenty-five, I'm running a multimillion-dollar business."

"You fell into something good."

"Yeah. Went well for quite a while. But you know, nothing lasts forever in this world."

I decided not to probe any further on Phil's family business for now. I also decided to look further into Moose.

"Okay," I said. "If your daughter filed a police report, there's at least something to work with. But I'll need a few things."

"Like what?"

"Mostly contact info for your daughter, the boyfriend, your ex-wife. You have a current wife?"

Phil looked at me. "Yeah. But I don't call her that."

"I wouldn't either. Plus, how to contact Moose. And maybe your father, too, you can never tell what other family members know. Your dad still live in Culver City?" I asked.

"Yeah, but not in the same place. He's retired. Lives up on Culver Crest now."

I nodded. Culver Crest was the ritzy part of Culver City, up on a hill, with a view. It was nothing compared to Beverly Hills or a lot of other tony Westside neighborhoods, but as far as Culver City went, this was pricey real estate.

"Your dad must have done well. For a public servant."

"You'd be surprised at how well cops do in retirement these days. He got a big payout when he retired from Largo Beach. Something to do with disability. Nice pension takes care of expenses. And his trips to Vegas."

I thought about this. When we were growing up, there was

always something unseemly about Phil's father. Police officers were paid well compared to other civil servants, but they were hardly at the level of investment bankers. Yet Phil's father always seemed to be driving a new car, while my mom struggled to make payments on a fifteen-year-old Honda Civic. And Phil's family often went to Cabo or Cancun for vacations; we drove down to San Diego if we went anywhere at all. And there was the issue of attending Vassar College, where tuition was close to what my mother made in a year. Things didn't add up.

"All right. I'll poke around and see what I find. You know about my fee?"

Phil smiled slyly. "You mean, you're not going to do a solid for an old high school teammate?"

"No."

The smile disappeared. "How much?"

"A thousand dollars a day. And I require a two-day retainer. We'll see what I come up with. You'll get your money's worth. Most people do."

He reluctantly reached into his pocket, pulled out a checkbook, and began scribbling. "You know, ever since we sold the business a few years ago, I've been a little more aware of money. Got a big pile of it, but no more coming in. It's all just going out."

I decided not to sympathize. Phil Zellis could surely make do with his big pile.

"Here you go," he said, then stood up to leave. "I assume I'll be hearing from you in a couple of days."

"You will."

"Look, I know it's been years since we've gotten together,

but I've always thought of you as a friend. I hope now that I'm employing you and paying you good money, well, I hope it doesn't affect our friendship."

"Why do you bring that up?" I frowned.

"I've had a few friendships that went south after we established a business relationship. The people thought my paying them somehow diminished them in my eyes. I hope you don't feel that way."

"Not at all," I said, as I peeked at the check before folding it in half and putting it in my pocket. "In fact, I think our relationship just got a whole lot better."

www.ingramcontent.com/pod-product-compliance
Lightning Source LLC
Chambersburg PA
CBHW020608260626
47157CB00003B/918
9780990416791